William Garmonsway Wrightson

Memorials of the Family of Wrightson

Part First

William Garmonsway Wrightson

Memorials of the Family of Wrightson
Part First

ISBN/EAN: 9783337122850

Printed in Europe, USA, Canada, Australia, Japan

Cover: Foto ©Raphael Reischuk / pixelio.de

More available books at **www.hansebooks.com**

MEMORIALS OF THE FAMILY OF WRIGHTSON.

W. G. Wrightson

MEMORIALS

OF THE

'amily of Wrightson

"To raise up the name of the Dead upon his inheritance,
that the name of the Dead be not cut off from among his
Brethren."—*Ruth* iv. 10.

PART FIRST

WILLIAM GARMONSWAY WRIGHTSON

M.A. CANTAB.

LONDON

PRINTED AT THE CHISWICK PRESS

FOR PRIVATE PRESENTATION ONLY

1894

PREFACE.

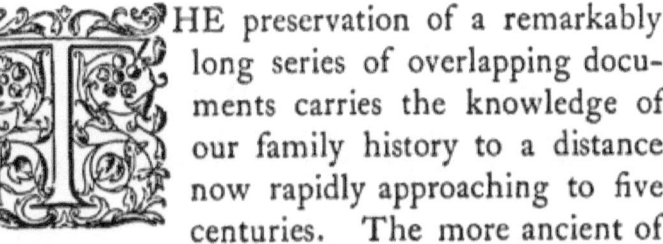HE preservation of a remarkably
long series of overlapping docu-
ments carries the knowledge of
our family history to a distance
now rapidly approaching to five
centuries. The more ancient of
these documents, although indicating that our
earliest mentioned ancestors belonged to that substantial class known in Mediæval times as Frankelyns, are chiefly occupied with the disastrous results of our participation in the Catholic rebellion
of 1569, known as the Rising of the North.
Those, who died or were born in the time of
Charles the First and Cromwell, passed through
a period of considerable depression ; but, from
that time to the present, the family has continued
to rise with tolerable steadiness. Our pedigree
includes no less than thirteen generations ; and
the chief interests, which gather round it, are all
more or less connected with that land-ownership,

which is indeed essential to the maintenance and proof of any pedigree of such a length. In its main line, at all events, our Family has been represented by an absolutely unbroken series of independent Tees-side landowners with amounts of property ranging from two or three hundred to two or three thousand acres.

The mere existence of such a prolonged pedigree is enough to waken interest among those whose names appear, or may appear, upon it. For as Gibbon, the historian, somewhere says, " Experience has proved that there is scarcely any man of tolerable family, who does not wish to know as much as he can about it ; nor is such an ambition either foolish in itself or hurtful to society." I myself have always considered that a sympathetic interest in an honourable past is one of the best guarantees for an honourable future, inasmuch as it fosters that beneficial self-respect, which must be largely based on the knowledge of antecedents worthy of respect. Indeed the late Lord Macaulay goes so far, as to make the national possession of this sort of sentiment the test of continued national pre-eminence ; for, says he, " A people, which takes no pride in the noble achievements of remote ancestors, will never achieve anything worthy to be remembered with pride by remote descendants."

If the simple story of our Family had not contained much to encourage, not pride, but wholesome self-respect, it could scarcely have inspired sufficient interest to carry me through the prolonged labour of producing a work designed exclusively for the domestic circle. It has been indeed a work of love ; and, while slowly collecting, arranging, and casting into a literary form, my multifarious materials, I have often felt as though I were a sculptor chiselling a marble monument to the loved ones who have passed away. No one could have had better opportunities for accumulating information, and no one could have had more tender and reverent feelings than I have had in seeking to perpetuate the memory of those, who, in a comparatively private sphere of life, have gradually created and at last bequeathed to their descendants a tradition of well-nigh spotless honour, uprightness, and integrity.

It is certain that among our remoter descendants there will be those who will value my picture of simple north-country English life, as much as I should have valued one transmitted from past centuries. What must be lost in personal, will be gained in social interest. Hence, so far as consists with more accurate information, it is my earnest request that, in all future editions of the First Part of these Memorials (ending with the death of my dear parents), the main text may be preserved substantially intact.

That First Part, filled with the records of many ancestors, I now dedicate and entrust to the various branches of our Family, to be guarded and preserved as *the most precious of all their heir-looms*, until, perchance a century hence, some other loving Chronicler may add a Second Part, crowded I trust with names of wider influence and fame, though scarcely of more honest worth than these.

W. G. Wrightson.

The Old Hall, Hurworth-on-Tees,
24th *June* 1894.

AUTHORITIES.

N.B. Except in one case (viz. IV.), the whole of the extracted portions of the English Authorities are given *verbatim*, but not *literatim*: and for the punctuation and capitals I alone am responsible. The Latin Authorities are here given as translated by legal experts. Insertions of my own are placed within square brackets.

I. FAMILY OF MARKENFIELD derived from following sources,—

  a. Pedigrees in *Harleian Soc. Publications*, vol. xvi.
  b. *Testamenta Eboracensia* pub. by Surtees Soc. vol. iv.
  c. *Hist. of Yorkshire*, vol. 1 by G. Plantagenet Harrison.
  d. *Lartington Court Roll* (see App. C).
  e. *Yorkshire Pedigrees* by Joseph Foster.
  f. *Book of Knights* by Metcalfe.

The Markenfields were one of the oldest of the great York-shire families. Their chief residence was at Markenfield Hall near Ripon, which was built in the time of Edward II. by John de Markenfield, Chancellor of the Exchequer. The following is the main line of male descent for the last six generations of their known pedigree.

SIR JOHN MARKENFIELD. His will (b), dated 1431, and proved 1448, mentions his manors of Merkyngfeld and Eryom,

B

and lands in Richmond etc. He is the first Markenfield whom, in 1428, I have as yet found connected with Eryholme. He was not knighted at the date of his will.

|

JOHN M. mentioned in his father's will; and in 1457 as a free tenant of the manor of Mickleton (d), which makes him the first Markenfield whom I have as yet found connected with the parish of Romaldkirk.

|

SIR THOMAS M. His will (b), dated 8 Apr. 1497, and proved 20 June, 1497, mentions his lordship of Markynfeld, his manors of Erthom and Asmonderby, and lands etc. in Richmond, Newsom, and Unthank [in parish of Romaldkirk], within the liberty of Richmond. He died 4 May 1497.

|

SIR NINIAN M. born 1473; knighted after the victory of Flodden-field 1513 (f). His will, dated 1 Oct. 1527, and proved at York 5 July 1528, mentions his manors of Markynfeld, Aymonderby, Romondby, Scrutton, Ereholme, Ereby, Newsome, and Unthank, in co. York.

|

THOMAS M. mentioned as under age in father's will; mar. Margaret, dau. of John Norton, and sister of the famous Richard Norton of Norton-Conyers "the patriarch of the Earls' Rebellion" (e), *i.e.* the Rising of the North.

|

1. THOMAS M., engaged in the rebellion commonly known as the Rising of the North in 1569-70, and was in consequence attainted of High Treason [see Authority VIII].

2. JOHN M., engaged in the above rebellion, and appears as a prisoner in Durham gaol in 1569-70 [see Authority IV].   He

also was attainted of High Treason, though, according to Froude's *Hist. of Eng.*, he was under age at the time of the rebellion.

According to the above Harrison's *Hist. of Yorkshire*, p. 23, " Sir Thomas Merkynfelt, knt., was . . . . . also seised of 8 messuages and 8 carucates of land with the appurtenances in Eryon in the said county, which he held of the king in capite as of the honor of Richmond, as the half of one knight's fee of the yearly value of £19 7*s.* . . . . . He died 4 May, 12 Hen. VII, and Ninian Merkynfeld, his son and heir, was then aged 24 years and upwards."

> Obs.:—The carucate is a somewhat variable extent of tillage land. According to the manorial records it is generally 120 acres, but this is an area for assessment, not representing the true area any more than our rateable value does the rent. Vinogradoff tells us that old agricultural treatises say the hide or carucate contained 160 or 180 acres according to whether the land was cropped on the two or three course system. The tillage land therefore held by Sir Thomas Markenfield was probably from 1280 to 1440 acres. The pasture, wastes, and woods, which pass under the name " appurtenances," would increase this area to such an extent, that I have no doubt his " 8 carucates of land with the appurtenances " represent the whole of Eryholme,—a township of 2199 acres, which township is I believe identical with the manor.

II. PLEA OF DEBT on the De Banco roll for Easter term 37 Hen. VI [1459], membrane No. 232. At Pub. Rec. Office.

"William Huddeswell of Richmond by his Attorney surrenders himself on the 4th day [of the Term] against Robert Playce, late of Halneby in the county [of York] aforesaid, esquire,—*Richard Wrightson late of Eryom* in the county aforesaid, yeoman,— Robert Perkynson late of Jolby in the co. afsd., yeoman,—John

Symson of Morehouse of Sketon in the co. afsd., yeoman,—
John Dent of Thorp upon Teyse in the co. afsd., yeoman, of a
plea that each of them should render to him 10 marks, which
they owed and unjustly detained from him etc. And they did
not come. And it was commanded the Sheriff that he should
summon them etc. And the Sheriff now says that the afsd.
Robert Playce was summoned etc.

Judgment:—Let him [*i.e.* Mr. Playce] be attached that he
be here in the quindena [*i.e.* the 15th day from the feast] of
Holy Trinity etc. And concerning all the afsd. other defendants
the Sheriff says that they have nothing etc. Therefore . . . . . ."

> Obs. :—The date of this document is the year before the
> approximate date of the birth of John Wrightson of
> Eryholme (a man of property) who stands at the head
> of our proved pedigree : and its value lies in the proof
> it affords of the presence of our family at Eryholme
> well before 1459. The above Richard was doubtless
> a junior relative of the then holder of our family
> property. Too much must not however be made of
> the Sheriff's statement that four out of the five
> defendants had "nothing"; as it no doubt facili-
> tated his work to ignore the smaller men, and to fix
> on the one important county gentleman. From the
> pedigree of Place of Dinsdale and Halnaby in Surtees'
> *Hist. Dur.* vol. iii, p. 236, it would appear that Wm.
> Huddeswell was a son-in-law of Mr. Place.

III. FEET OF FINES, co. York, Michaelmas Term,
3 and 4 Eliz. [1560-2]. In Pub. Rec. Office, London.

"No. 43. Between Anthony Vsburn, plaintiff, and *John
Wrightson and Agnes his wife*, deforciants, of one messuage, two
cottages, one toft, one garden, one orchard, sixty acres land, ten
acres meadow, twenty acres pasture, forty acres moor, and forty
acres furze and heath, with appurtenances, in North Cowton.
John and Agnes admit it to be the right of Anthony ; and for
themselves and their heirs remit and quit-claim to him and to

his heirs ; *and warrant to him and his heirs against the heirs of the said John.* John and Agnes receive forty pounds for the concession."

> Obs. 1 :—From this ancient record of a sale of land under the fiction of a disputed ownership, we see that this 170 acres was exclusively Wrightson property, for the "warrant" is only against the heirs of John. The wife took part simply for the sake of "barring dower."
>
> Obs. 2 :—I have searched the North Cowton Registers (baptisms commencing in 1568, burials in 1572, and marriages in 1601) up to 1700, and the name of Wrightson does not occur. The parish of North Cowton is only separated from the Westfield of Eryholme by about a mile and a half. Hence there can be no doubt that the above are the "John" and "Agnes, widow," buried afterwards at Eryholme.
>
> Obs. 3 :—From Denton's *England in the 15th Century* (pp. 144-153) I gather that by the middle of the 15th century the arable land of England was almost exhausted. Its average yield of wheat was only about 8 bushels an acre from 2 bushels of seed; and it might be rented at from 2*d.* to 4*d.* an acre. An acre of hill side with a sprinkling of gorse or furze for fuel was worth two, and an acre of meadow was worth eight, acres of arable land. By 1560 things were rising in value, so that here, as also in Auth. VII, the £40 is probably only a nominal sum.

IV. THE BOWES MSS. vol. xiii. At Streatlam Castle. [1569-70.]

(1) "The information of the costables [*i.e.* constables] of Richmond and Richmondshire geven to S^r george bowes knyght provest M^r shall [*i.e.* Marshal] in the northe p^{ts} of all suche as did Joyne theymselffes wth the rebells at any tyme during the Rebellyon wth in [*i.e.* within] theyr seu^r all Costablerycs [*i.e.* several Constableries]."

. . . .

Eriholme:—James frear const.
Willm blakye
thomas wrightson
george blakye
mathew sadler
Richard wetherelt
John wynspere."

(2)   " The fyrste of Jenuarye 1569[-70].
Prysoners Remaninge in the Jayle at Durham in the custodye of Sr George Bowes knyghte marshall under the righte honorable thearle of Sussex Lorde Leteveñt in the northe.

. . . .
John Sayer of Worsall Junior
Robert conyears younger brother to John conyers esquire
Richard conyears of horden esquire
John markenfeyld brother to thomas markenfeyld esquire
Richard mennell of Kilvington gent
Robert thompson s^r vaute [*i.e.* servant] to Robert conyears
John Blaykey of eryholme
george Blaykey of eryholme
henry Branson of eryholme
John wryghtson of eryholme"
        etc. etc.

(3) " S^r george bowes
        I have sett the nōmbes [*i.e.* numbers] to be executed in euery towne [*i.e.* township] under the names of euery towne as I did the other book wch draweth unto ij^c [*i.e.* 200] whereof *you may use your dyscretyon* in taking more or less in euery towne *as you shall see fyt* cause for their offences and fetnes for example so as in the hole you pass not of . . . . syd [*i.e.* side] of such the number of ij^c among whom ye may not execute any that hathe frehold or noted wealthye for so is the qes mat^s plesir [*i.e.* the Queen's Majesty's pleasure]
                                January."

Obs. :—The writer of the above letter is of course the Earl of Sussex, and the year must be 1569-70. Richmondshire consisted of the five wapentakes of Gilling-east, Gilling-west, Hangeast, Hangwest, and Halykeld. The numbers of Rebels whose names appear in these lists are as follows:—In Richmondshire 1,241 ; in Cleveland 215 ; in Birdfurth and Ridale 145 ; in Thirsk 76 ; in Darlington ward 481. Total 2,158. The number appointed to be executed in Richmondshire was 231. Those Rebels, whose names I have noted in the Eryholme registers at later dates, were of course among those who escaped execution.

V. HOMBERSTON SURVEY, vol. ii, p. 145, at Pub. Rec. Office.

This official survey of the manor of Eryholme was made 4 May 1570. It describes the holdings and rents of the free-holders, leaseholders, and copyholders. The lord's demesne was evidently leased, for Wermley holds the "site of the Manor" with closes etc. containing 80 acres, which at his rent would equal 2*s*. 3*d*. per acre. The rents are as follows. *Freeholders*, Richard Wrightson 3*s*. 4*d*., Thomas Wynsper 6*d*., Ralph Johnson 9*d*. Total 4*s*. 7*d*. *Leaseholders*, William Wermley £9, Geo. Blakye 15*s*., Eliz. Burnett 35*s*., Thomas Nesom 30*s*., John Bussye £4, Wm. Blakye 30*s*., James Freere 60*s*., Wm. Nesom 30*s*., Unianus Breere 15*s*., Edward Pulham £6 1 8, Eliz. Burnett, widow, £6 1 8. Total £35 18 4. *Copyholders*, Richard Wrightson 35*s*., Tho. Wynsper 35*s*., Wm. Wermley 35*s*. Total £5 5 0. The first and last of these three lists commence as follows. "Rents of the Free Tenants of the Manor aforesaid. *Richard Wrightson* holds one tenement built with divers lands, meadows, and pastures, all and singular which premises the said Richard holds freely by charter in free socage by the service of —— part of one knight's fee, and renders therefor by the year at the feast of Martin only three shillings and fourpence." "Rents of the Tenants at Will [*i.e.* Copyholders] of the Manor aforesaid. *Richard Wryckson* [*sic*] holds one tenement built with all necessary houses and with *a fourth part of all those lands called Westfield,* all and singular which premises the said Richard holds at the will of the lord, and renders therefor by the year at the feasts aforesaid equally thirty-five shillings."

Obs. 1 :—Judging from their quit-rent the Wrightsons held eight-elevenths of the area of the three freeholds of the manor : and from a consideration of this survey I am led to conjecture that these three freeholds may very likely have amounted to about 700 acres. If this conjecture be correct, the Wrightson freehold would amount to about 500 acres. As to the Wrightson copyhold, I assume it at 100 acres, not only because that is about a quarter of the present Westfield, but also because, if leased a couple of generations later at the same rate as Wermley's superior land, it would amount to about the £12 mentioned in Authority XII.

Obs. 2 :—The English Manor is an exceedingly complex historical growth, which acquired both its name and its highest development under the Franco-Norman feudal system.

The most prominent feature of the old feudal system was the tenure of land by military service ; so that those of the laity or clergy who held land, whether directly under the king (described as tenants *in capite*) or indirectly under a mesne (or intermediate) lord, were bound to render personally or by deputy a certain definite amount of military service to their feudal superior. An estate yielding twenty pounds a year was in those times well able to bear the tax of furnishing and maintaining a fully armed horseman or knight for forty days in any year that the king might chance to require his services. Such a landed property was called a knight's fee, and the tenure by which it was held was called that of knight-service or tenure in chivalry ; and thus we often find a manor, and indeed much smaller portions of land, described as forming some fractional part of a knight's fee. According to Spelman there were in England no less than 67,000 knights' fees ; but the impossibility of carrying on foreign wars with those, who were only bound to serve for forty days, very soon led to the institution of Scutage (or Shield money), which was a pecuniary commutation of such military services, usually amounting to twenty shillings on each knight's fee. This scutage, and other occasional taxes, enabled a king to hire mercenary soldiers.

A fully developed manor included the lord of the manor,—the free tenants, who held of him by regular feudal tenures and owed suit to his court,—and the villeins or customary tenants, who held their land according to the custom of the manor in villenage or base tenure. Looked at territorially we may say that, leaving out of account the waste and grass land used in common by the lord and all his tenants, the land of each manor was divided into three parts, viz., the Demesne, retained by the lord for his own use; next, the portion held by the free tenants or freeholders, who at first held their lands on condition of following the banner of their lord to lawful war; and lastly the part (assumed to have originally belonged to the demesne) now occupied by the customary tenants, whose lands were for long held on condition of performing on their lord's actual demesne a certain amount of agricultural work, most carefully recorded in the manor court-roll kept for that purpose. When the military obligations of a lord were commuted into a money payment, the freeholders assisted him by the payment of small quit-rents, which served also to relieve them of the old military service : and similarly, between the lord and his customary tenants there came gradually into being arrangements, by which the so-called "base" services were so fully commuted into fixed money payments, that freeholders, even of noble birth and large independent possessions, were able without loss of dignity to hold customary estates, although in legal proceedings they continued to be described as "tenants at the will of the lord" for ages after both lord and tenant had become bound to act simply "according to the custom of the manor" and not otherwise. The evidence of title to a customary estate was a copy of the part concerning it in the manor court-roll; and it is from this circumstance that customary tenants have acquired the name of copyholders.

A copyholder's interest does not extinguish the lord's estate in fee simple. Hence, if a copyholder leaves no one to claim admittance, or if he destroys his customary interest, the land he has held will revert (escheat) to the lord. This must frequently have happened amidst the loss of life wrought by Scotch invasions, civil wars, and pestilences like the Black Death. And, when we remember that the custom of the manor is the sole basis on which stands the whole fabric of the copyholder's estate, we see how he might forfeit his property by disregarding that custom. He might also do so by allowing himself to acquire a common law interest in the land. Thus, if the lord of a manor demises the freehold of a copyhold tenement for a term of years, and the lessee assigns the term to the copyholder, the customary interest of the copyholder will be extinguished, for a common law interest and a customary interest cannot coexist in the same person at once, and consequently one of them must be determined, namely the customary. In other words, when the custom of the realm (*i.e.* the common law) and the merely local custom of the manor come together, the custom of the realm prevails. When a copyhold reverted to the lord, he might at any time regrant it as a copyhold, provided he had created no common law interest in the land higher than a tenancy at will. He might, in a grant of this kind, alienate the tenement by parcels and apportion the rents and services; but he was not allowed to alter them in any other way. He could neither add to nor diminish the ancient rent, nor make the minutest variation in other respects, for he was not permitted to create what would in effect be a new copyhold. In arranging for such a voluntary grant, the lord could however name the amount of the admittance fine; and by this means secure for himself any increased value in the land.

Pollock tells us that 'personal justice was as

essential to feudal tenure as military service. The lord was bound to do justice to his tenants, and the tenants were bound to attend his court that he might be able to do justice.' Of the manor courts there were at most three, viz., the Baron, the Customary, and the Leet. In the court Baron (*i.e.* the court of the baron or lord of the manor), which was held for all questions touching the freeholders, the free socage tenants sat as judges, while the lord's steward acted merely as their registrar. In the Customary court, for all questions touching copyholders, the copyholders acted merely as jurors, while the lord's steward sat as judge. The court Leet was not necessarily incident to a manor, but was a criminal jurisdiction existing in those manors whose lords had under the Anglo-Saxon laws possessed "sac and soc" (words expressive of jurisdiction), or who since the Conquest had received grants in which these terms were used. In this court the steward sat on behalf of his lord as the king's representative.

VI. PATENT ROLL, 16 Eliz. [1574] Part 6; granting Eastfield and Westfield to Rowland Spence. At Pub. Rec. Office.

". . . . . and also all that tenement called the *Westfield* now divided into divers closes with appurtenances, situated, lying, and being in Eryholme aforesaid, now or late in the several tenures or occupations of William Wormley, *Thomas Wrightson*, John Winspere, and Elizabeth Burnett, or their assigns or any of them, late parcel of the lands and possessions, *which John Markyngfield of high treason attainted lately had and held for the term of his life.* . . . . ."

> Obs. :—This authority doubtless indicates the line of private misrepresentation adopted by interested private persons, and is of no real weight as against the official Homberston survey.

VII. FEET OF FINES, co. York, Michaelmas Term, 17 and 18 Eliz. [1575] Part 2. In Pub. Rec. Office, London.

" This is the final agreement made in the Court of the Lady the Queen at Westminster within one month of Michaelmas in the seventeenth year of the reign of Elizabeth.......... Before James Dyer, Richard Harpur, Roger Manwood, and Robert Mounson, justices, and other faithful subjects of the Lady the Queen then there present. Between John Myles plaintiff and *Edmund Wrightsone and Isabella his wife* deforciants of three messuages forty acres of land, ten acres of meadow, sixty acres of pasture, and one acre of wood, with appurtenances in North Cowton, whereof a plea of covenant was summoned between them in the same court to wit that the aforesaid Edmund and Isabella acknowledge the aforesaid tenements with appurtenances to be the right of the same John as those which the same John has of the gift of the aforesaid Edmund and Isabella, and those they remised and quit-claimed of themselves the same Edmund and Isabella and *the heirs of the same Edmund* to the aforesaid John and his heirs for ever. And moreover the same Edmund and Isabella have granted for themselves *and the heirs of the same Edmund that they will warrant to the aforesaid John and his heirs the aforesaid tenements with appurtenances against all men for ever.* And for this acknowledgment, remission, quit-claim, warrant, fine and agreement, the same John gave to the aforesaid Edmund and Isabella forty pounds sterling.

York."

VIII. "EXCHEQUER BILLS[1] AND ANSWERS, Eliz. York, No. 385." At Pub. Rec. Office. [1589-90.]

" The joint and several Answers " of Rowland Spence and Agnes Wrightson, widow, defendants to the Bill of Complaint of Edmund Wrightson complainant.

The said defendants [severally say] that the said Bill of Complaint is very uncertain, untrue, and insufficient in the law to

---

[1] The actual Bill of Complaint is missing; but its nature and contents may be gathered from these Answers to it, and from Authorities IX and X.

be answered unto for divers very manifest and apparent matters
and causes therein contained as the said Defendants by their
Counsel be informed, the advantage of the insufficiency whereof
unto these Defendants at all times hereafter saved, for answer
thereunto these Defendants say and first—

The said Rowland Spence, one of these Defendants, for himself severally saith that *the Queen's Majesty, that now is, was
lawfully seized in her Highnesses demesne as a fee, in right of her
Highnesses Crown of England, by the attainder of John Markenfield and Thomas Markenfield of high treason, of, in, and upon, the
said tenement called the Westfield* with appurtenances in the Bill
mentioned; and her Majesty so being thereof seized did,—by
her Highnesses letters patent,[1] under the great seal of England
bearing date at Westminster upon or about the twentieth day
of February in the sixteenth year of her Majesty's reign for a
certain sum of money to her Majesty's use by this Defendant
Rowland Spence paid,—demise, grant, and to farm let, unto
this Defendant Rowland Spence, among other things the said
tenement called the Westfield, then divided into divers closes
with the appurtenances, to have and to hold the same unto this
Defendant his executors and assigns from the feast of St.
Michael the Archangel then last past before the date of the
same letters patent unto the full end and term of one and
twenty years then next following and fully to be complete and
ended [*i.e.*, from 29 Sep. 1573 to 29 Sep. 1594] yielding therefor yearly to her Majesty her heirs and successors among other
things the yearly rent or farm of seven pounds of lawful English
money at the feast of the Annunciation of the Blessed Virgin
Mary and St. Michael the Archangel by even portions or to the
like effect as by the same letters patent ready to be shewed more
at large may appear. By virtue whereof *this Defendant entered
into the said Westfield* with the appurtenances and was thereof
lawfully possessed accordingly, which lease in truth for the lands
in variance was *for the benefit of Sir George Bowes Knight* [who
died Aug. 1580], *then this Defendant's master*, which reserved a

---

[1] Authority VI.

sum of money of the tenants being in possession to suffer them to enjoy the same. Whereupon *this Defendant, so being thereof possessed, in trust for the benefit of the said Sir George Bowes, by direction of the said Sir George Bowes this Defendant's said master, did permit and suffer the said Agnes Wrightson the other of these Defendants, who among others had paid money to Sir George Bowes for the same, to hold, occupy, and enjoy, a fourth part of the said Westfield* during the interest of this Defendant in the same, answering a certain yearly rent for the same according to the rate of the entire rent reserved to her Highness upon the said lease, as lawfully this Defendant thinketh he might do, which hath been accordingly occupied by the space of fifteen years, and in which original lease there is not full six years to expire.

And the said Agnes Wrightson, the other of these Defendants, for herself severally saith as the said Rowland Spence hath said, and further that the said Rowland Spence so being of the said Westfield by force of the said letters patent to him by her Majesty made as aforesaid possessed did and yet doth permit and suffer this Defendant to occupy and enjoy a fourth part of the said Westfield answering a certain yearly rent for the same as aforesaid as lawfully this Defendant thinketh he might and may do. And these defendants further say that, after the said lease made, the Queen's Majesty being seized of the reversion of the same in fee by the attainder of high treason of the said *John Markenfield, who at the time of his attainder was tenant for life of the said Westfield,*[1] and of the said *Thomas Markenfield who had the inheritance thereof in him and his heirs* at the time of his said attainder, *did grant her Highnesses said reversion thereof unto Thomas Calverley esquire in fee,* wherefore the Plaintiff is not, as this Defendant thinketh, to be relieved in this Court, and in very truth the ancestors of the said John and Thomas Markenfield were always time out of mind until the said attainder lawfully and solely seized in fee of the said entire Westfield wholly with the appurtenances. And the said Plain-

[1] Authority VI.

tiff or any his ancestors never had any estate or interest in the same other than by lease at will or sufferance of some of the Markenfields, if they had any such at all as these Defendants verily think they had not. And these Defendants further say that, if either the said Complainant, his ancestors, or other freeholders of the said lordship of Eryholme had any freehold at any time in the said Westfield, yet they passed the inheritance of the same away to some of the said Markenfields, lords of the same Manor, in satisfaction or recompense of lands of as good value to them assured for the same in other places of the said Manor of Eryholme. And these Defendants further say that all the persons that during memory have occupied and enjoyed the said Westfield, before the said letters patent of lease so made to this Defendant Rowland Spence as aforesaid, did occupy and enjoy the same but at the will or sufferance of the lords of the said manor of Eryholme being owners of the freehold of the same and under some of the said Markenfields answering a yearly rent for the same and the said Plaintiff or any his ancestors never had any estate or interest in the said Westfield by exchange or otherwise in such sort as he now pretendeth unless at will or by lease long since expired or determined ; and these Defendants further say that the said Thomas Markenfield before his said attainder and his ancestors from time to time did displace the tenants of the said Westfield and place new tenants in their rooms at their wills and pleasures as these defendants [are prepared] to prove and the said Thomas Markenfield himself did displace one William Johnson who occupied a parcel of the said Westfield and did place one Robert Burnett in his room who paid him a fine and gressome [1] and a yearly rent for the same until the time of his said attainder and all the tenants and occupiers of the said Westfield did always before the said attainder from time to time answer and pay their several rents for the said Westfield to the said Markenfields only and not to any other person or persons whatsoever and answering the fines and gressomes [1] for the said whole Westfield until the

[1] *Gersuma,* is an exaction or demand.

time of his said attainder wherefore these Defendants verily think and well hope that in equity there is no cause that the said Plaintiff should be any further received in this honourable Court the same suit against these Defendants to maintain without that that [*sic*] by the said agreement in writing purporting an *Exchange of certain lands and tenements therein contained in the Bill mentioned, made between the said persons in the Bill named the time therein alleged the said Nynyan Markenfield in the Bill named did* in consideration of other grounds therein mentioned, which the said freeholders in the Bill named granted by the same Deed to him and his heirs in exchange, *give and grant among other things unto the said freeholders the said West-field* to have and to hold to them and their heirs in such manner and form as in the said Bill of Complaint is pretended. Or that by force thereof the said freeholders entered accordingly. Or that afterwards a fourth part of the said Westfield was allotted to the said John Wrightson which he and his heirs had ever since enjoyed, paying a certain yearly rent to the said Markenfield and his heirs, and died so seized as in the said Bill of Complaint is pretended. Or that after his death the same descended to Richard his son who also died seized. Or that the same then descended to *John, son and heir to Richard,* who also died seized, whereby the same descended *to the Plaintiff* who was thereof seized accordingly, as in the said Bill of Complaint is surmised and without that that [*sic*] this Defendant, Rowland Spence, hath wrongfully entered into the Plaintiff's said fourth part of the said Westfield and conveyed and granted his interest therein unto the said Thomas Wrightson in the Bill named. Or that the said Agnes Wrightson the one of these Defendants now wrongfully occupieth and possesseth the same to the utter overthrow and impoverishment of the said Plaintiff and clean contrary to all right, equity, and good conscience, as in the said Bill of Complaint is pretended. Or that the said Plaintiff and his ancestors ever since the said pretended Agreement have occupied and enjoyed the said Westfield. Or that there is any cause that the same should be rather demised to the Plaintiff the ancient tenant thereof than unto and herein before not sufficiently confessed and avoided traversed or denied is true. All which matters these Defendants are ready to aver and prove as this honourable Court shall award, and pray to be dismissed out of the same with their reasonable costs and charges by them wrongfully sustained concerning this suit.

Pre . . . in curia tertio die Februarii Anno 32 Reginæ E.

J. SAVILE

"The Replication [1] of Edmund Wrightson, Complainant, to the joint and several Answers of Rowland Spence and Agnes Wrightson Defendants. The said Complainant replieth, avereth, and maintaineth, his said Bill and all and every the matters and things therein contained to be certain, true, and sufficient in the law to be answered unto, and saith that the same Answers and the matters and things therein alleged are uncertain, untrue, and insufficient in the law, to be replied unto for divers and sundry matters and things therein apparent, the advantage of the exception to the insufficiencies and uncertainty thereof to this Repliant at all times hereafter saved. He further replies and saith in all and every matter and thing as in the said Bill he hath before said this that he will aver and prove, *by force and virtue of the said Exchange in the said Bill mentioned, the fourth part of the said Westfield in the said Bill likewise mentioned was allotted to John Wrightson great-grandfather of the Repliant* in severalty and ever sythens [*i.e.* since] hath been by the said John and his heirs, or his or their assign or assigns, so occupied and enjoyed accordingly, and that also he died seized thereof in his demesne as of fee, and that By and *after the death of the said John the said fourth part of the said Westfield descended and came to Richard his son,* who also was seized in his demesne as of fee and died so seized, By and *after whose death the same descended to this Repliant's father, and after his death unto this Repliant,* as in the said Bill is alleged. And with this also that he will

---

[1] Dated "Termino Paschæ anno xxxii regni reginæ Elizabethæ" [*i.e.* from 6 May to 1 June 1590].

C

aver and prove that the said *Richard Wrightson, grandfather to this Repliant, being of the premises seized as aforesaid, demised the same and All other his Freehold lands in Eryholme unto Thomas his younger son, uncle unto this Repliant, and late husband to the said Agnes, one of the defendants, for the term of twenty years, which expired about six years sythens* [*i.e.* about May 1584], by force whereof the said Thomas was thereof possessed and occupied and enjoyed the same accordingly, *the reversion thereof then and now being in and of right belonging unto this Repliant,* and that the same hath been occupied, enjoyed, set, and let, as *parcel of the inheritance of the Repliant's said great-grandfather, grandfather, and father, and* [*was*] *never claimed, used, or occupied, sythens the said Exchange as any parcel of the said Markenfield's inheritance . . . . .*"

[The rest of this Replication amounts to nothing more than a long series of denials to statements which have already appeared in the Answers to the Bill.]

IX. EXCHEQUER DEPOSITIONS, Miscellaneous. 32 Eliz. Mich. No. 1946, Durham. At Pub. Rec. Office. [1 Sep. 1590.]

" Depositions taken at Darlington in the county of Durham the first day of September in the two and thirtieth year of . . . our Sovereign Lady Elizabeth . . . . ., before John Conyers esquire [? and] George Pudsaye gentlemen by virtue of her Majesty's [? commission].

Thomas Wyndspyer of Eryholme in the county of York, yeoman, of the age of four score years or thereabouts [born about 1510], sworn and examined on the part and behalf of Edmund Wrightson plaintiff against Rowland Spence and Agnes Wrightson defendants saith as follows,—

. . . . . that he knoweth the parties, plaintiff and defendants, and the said parcel of ground called the Westfield now in variance.

. . . . . that he hath heard it credibly reported that *there was Agreement made in writing between Nynyan Markenfeild, then lord of the Manor*, and the freeholders of the same *purport-ing an Exchange of certain lands* and tenements therein mentioned. And this he knoweth of his own knowledge for that he himself occupied some part thereof for the space of forty years . . . .

. . . . . that, *after the death of the said John Wrightson*, the premises in variance did descend and come unto *Richard Wright-son the son*, and that the said Richard did enter and died possessed thereof by possession or reversion for that *he thinketh that Thomas Wrightson had a lease of some part thereof.*

. . . . . that the said *John Wrightson was son and heir unto Richard Wrightson.* And that the premises in variance descended and came unto the said John Wrightson.

. . . . . that *the complainant was son and heir of the said John Wrightson.*"

X. EXCHEQUER DECREES AND ORDERS, Eliz. Series I. No. 17, folio 211. At Pub. Rec. Office. [8 Feb. 1590-1.]

Decree dated 8 February, Hilary Term, 33 Eliz.

" Ebor :—In the matter in variance in this Court, between Edmund Wrightson plaintiff and Agnes Wrightson defendant, touching the entry, title, and right, in and to one messuage tenement and a parcel of ground called Westfield in Eryholme within the county of York *claimed by the plaintiff to be parcel of his own inheritance* in Eryholme, and *claimed by the defendant to have [been] parcel of the possessions of Markenfeild of high treason attainted* and by her Majesty to have been demised to one Rowland Spence [who died in April 1590] for years yet enduring [*i.e.* to 29 Sep. 1594], and that *her Majesty hath sithence granted the inheritance thereof to Thomas Calverley and his heirs in fee farm*, and that therefore there is no cause wherefore the plaintiff should be relieved in *this* Court, if the allegations in his Bill were true, but rather to be remitted to *try the said title by the course of the Common Law.* . . . . . . It is therefore Ordered that the plaintiff shall delay against the said defendant in an Action of Trespass in the office of Common pleas : And that the defendant by her attorney shall appear gratis and plead the general issue triable at the next Assizes— to be holden within that county. . . . . ."

> Obs. :—In the Court of Chancery the proceedings were by a petition to the Lord Chancellor, called a " Bill of Complaint,"—an " Answer " by the defendant,— followed by a " Reply ": evidence was given by means of " Depositions " filed ; and the suit was concluded by the " Judgment," or " Decree." The proceedings in the old equity side of the Court of Exchequer were clearly of a similar kind.

· XI. WILL OF EDMUND WRIGHTSON OF ERY-HOLME, dated 13 Feb. 1629-30, proved at Richmond 28 Sep. 1630.

". . . . . . I Edmund Wrightson of Eryholme . . . . yeoman . . ."

". . . . . . *my wife Isabell*, in consideration and respect of the thirds of *my lands situate and lying within the territories of Eryholme*, shall have and enjoy after my decease, if she outlive me, one Close of land called the Fatting Field, another Close of land called the Gosling Ings, and one garth called the High Garth, during her life natural: and for house room, if she cannot quietly have and enjoy the house wherein I now dwell, then to have the parlour in *my son John* his house. . . ."

". . . . . . to *my daughter Isabell Nesome*. . ."

". . . . . . to *Ann Wrightson, John Wrightson's daughter*. . ."

". . . . . . to *my son Thomas Wrightson's children,* viz. *Thomas and Edmund.* . . ."

". . . . . . desire my wife Isabel to give . . . . to *Thomas Neesome's* children, if God send her [*i.e.* Isabell Nesome] any. . . ."

". . . . . . my mind and will is that my wife Isabel and *my daughter Dorothy Wrightson,* seeing that *already I have given well of my goods* [*and*] *means to all the rest of my children and that they have had their Portions,* shall have all my goods and household stuff after my decease equally to be divided betwixt them and live together, if they can agree. And for that my daughter Dorothy hath done for [*i.e.* hath attended on] me in my old age, I would have my wife Isabel to deal well with her at her decease and to give her what she is able towards her preferment."

". . . . . my wife Isabell executrix. . ."

> Obs. 1 :—The aged Testator was near death ; and his short will was both written and attested by Mr. John Idson, the Vicar of Eryholme.
>
> Obs. 2 :—A very aged inhabitant of Eryholme informed me in 1888 that he remembered the name " Gosling Ings " belonging to land in the hollow between Westfield House and the scar opposite to Newbus Grange.

XII. EXCHEQUER BILLS AND ANSWERS, York.

7 Charles I. [1632], No. 235.   Pub. Rec. Office.

" To the right honourable Richard Lord Weston, Lord high Treasurer of England, Sir Francis Cottington knt., Chancellor of the right honourable Court of Exchequer, ... and to the rest of the Barons there—

Complaining Sheweth unto your Lordships your Orator [= Petitioner], Sir John Calverley of Littleburne in the County Palatine of Durham knt., That whereas your Orator holdeth in fee farm of his Majesty the Manor and Lordship of Eriholme with the appurtenance in the County of York by a great yearly rent and is indebted unto his Majesty, And whereas your Orator is and hath been for many years past seised to him and his heirs in fee farm as aforesaid among other the demeanes [*sic*] of the said Manor of and in one Messuage or tenement with appurtenance and a fourth part of all the land and ground called the Westfield parcel of his said fee farm lying and being in Eriholme aforesaid, And whereas one *John Wrightson of Eriholme aforesaid yeoman hath for divers years last past held the said Messuage or tenement with the appurtenance and the said fourth part of the said land and ground called the Westfield afore-*

said at the Will of your Orator under the yearly rent of twelve pounds . . . ., and whereas there was behind and unpaid unto your Orator the sum of thirty pound for two years' rent . . . . . . your Orator . . . . having a purpose to displace and remove the said John Wrightson out of the said Messuage and lands . . . . ., being of far greater yearly value than the said rent, thereupon the said *John Wrightson together with his brother Thomas Wrightson of Eriholme aforesaid, yeoman,* about Christmas then next ensuing, which was in the said year of our Lord God *one thousand six hundred twenty and nine* came unto your Orator's house at Littleburn aforesaid and intreated . . . . that the said John Wrightson might continue tenant . . . ., In consideration whereof, as well the said John Wrightson as also the said Thomas Wrightson then and there faithfully promised . . . . both to pay . . . . the said thirty pound arrear . . . . . and continue the payment of the said yearly rent . . . . for so long time as the said John Wrightson should or might continue the possession or occupation of the said Messuage and premises . . . . . ., whereunto your Orator agreed and accepted of the said promise. . . . . But now so it is . . . . that the said John Wrightson and Thomas Wrightson have as yet paid . . . only fifteen pound of the said thirty pound . . . nor any part of the said twelve pound arrear. . . And your Orator further sheweth that he . . . ., by his servant [*i.e.* agent] . . . . made an entry into the said Messuages and premises . . . . and *required the said John Wrightson to remove and depart from the same and to leave the possession thereof unto your Orator, which the said John Wrightson by the Animation of the said Thomas Wrightson utterly refuseth to do* . . . . ., which said doings . . . are contrary to all equity and good conscience and to your Orator's damage of one hundred pound. Therefore and for that your Orator as a fee farmer and a debtor to his Majesty as aforesaid and by the said doings of the said John Wrightson and Thomas Wrightson is like to be disabled to pay his fee farm rent and debt unto his Majesty. And for that *the said promises and agreement aforesaid were had and made and done secretly and in private* between your Orator and the said John Wrightson and Thomas Wrightson and that your Orator wanteth such proof of the same as by the strict rules of the Common law is required so as your Orator is without . . . . . remedy thereupon unless your Lordships in equity vouchsafe unto him relief therein." . . . .

XIII. ADMINISTRATION OF WILLIAM WRIGHTSON of Richmond, dated 3 Nov. 1714.

The administration is granted at Richmond to " *Thomas Wrightson of Springe House* in the County of Durham, yeoman ; and *Thomas Heslopp of Richmond* in the County of York." Wrightson administers, and Heslopp is his surety to the Bond of administration.

XIV. WILL OF THOMAS WRIGHTSON of Richmond, dated 3 Jan. 1715-6, proved at Richmond 9 Sep. 1717.

" I Thomas Wrightson of Richmond in the County of York, yeoman. . . . ."

" . . . . to *my brother John Wrightson* all that my free Burgage or Tenement with the Garth and Appurtenances thereunto belonging, to him his heirs and assigns for ever."

" . . . . to *my brother-in-law Thomas Heslope of Richmond* aforesaid his heirs and assigns for ever all that my Moyetie or half part and all my right and title to those two acres of land in the Westfield of Richmond aforesaid and those two Closes adjoining the Westfield of Richmond commonly called Easton Closes."

" . . . . to *Richard* Wrightson, *son of my brother Richard Wrightson.* . . ."

" . . . . to the poor of Richmond aforesaid the sum of four pounds. . ."

" . . . . all the rest . . . . . I give and bequeath to my said brother Thomas Heslope, and do make him sole Executor. . . ."

XV. MARRIAGE SETTLEMENT, dated 28 March 1711.

". . . . . . John Wrightson, the Elder, of Hardstones [now Spring House, see p. 98 note] in the parish of Long Newton in the County of Durham, yeoman. . ."

". . . . . . John Wrightson, the Younger, *son and heir* of the said John Wrightson the Elder. . ."

". . . . . . John Wrightson the elder and *Ann his now wife.* . ."

". . . . . . Thomas Robinson of Middleton one Row in the same county . . . . and Margaret Robinson daughter of the said Thomas Robinson. . . ."

". . . . . . a marriage . . . . . between the said John Wrightson, the younger, and Margaret Robinson. . ."

> Obs.:—In the phrase " Ann his now wife " the word
> " now " is lost at the damaged end of a line in the
> original deed; but it is recovered from an old office
> copy of the same deed.

XVI. INDENTURE, dated 12 July 1740.

". . . . William Wrightson of Spring-house in the parish of Long Newton . . . . gentleman. . . ."

". . . . the said Richard Garmonsway by indentures of Lease and Release . . . . the Release bearing date on or about the fifteenth day of July . . . . 1720 . . . . did . . . . sell . . . . unto John Wrightson deceased, *the Father of the said William Wrightson, by the name of John Wrightson of Middleton Erow alias one Row* . . . . all that Messuage . . . . . and all those . . . . thirty-two acres . . . . situate within the town and township of Sadberge . . . . bounded . . . . on the lands then of *John Wrightson, the elder*, on the west. . . . ."

XVII. INDENTURE, dated 18 May 1722.

". . . . . . John Wrightson of Spring House, parish of Long Newton."

XVIII. MARRIAGE SETTLEMENT, dated 31 Oct. 1754.

" . . . . Thomas Wrightson, the elder, of White House in the parish of Middleton St. George in the county of Durham, Gentleman, and Elizabeth his wife. . . . ."

" . . . . *Thomas Wrightson,* the younger, of the same place, gentleman, *younger son of the said Thomas Wrightson the elder.* . . . ."

" . . . . Margaret Garmonsway of Great Burdon in the county of Durham. . . .'

" . . . . a marriage is agreed upon . . . . between the said Thomas Wrightson the younger and Margaret Garmonsway. . . . ."

" . . . . William Wrightson of Cockerton in the said county, gentleman. . . ."

XIX. RECONVEYANCE OF WHITE HOUSE ESTATE, dated 12 June 1828.

" . . . . Thomas Wrightson of Neasham Hall in the same county, Gent., of the 13th part. . . . ."

" . . . . called and known by the name of West-Hartburn otherwise White House, situate and being within the township of Middleton St. George . . . . formerly in the occupation of John Arrowsmith . . . . . . afterwards of John Elgie, afterwards of *Thomas Wrightson, great-grandfather of the said Thomas Wrightson party hereto.*"

XX. ESTATE MAP, dated 1756.

At Dinsdale Rectory, and referred to in the following letter to me.

Manor House, Dinsdale on Tees, Darlington, Aug. 18th 1885.

DEAR SIR, You are quite right about the old map. It is dated 1756, "Mr. John Wrightson's ground"—the road "to Girsby" runs through it. It is not *this* Dinsdale, but "Over-Dinsdale" in Yorkshire, the other side of the Tees.

Yours truly,

SCOTT F. SURTEES.

XXI. WILL OF WILLIAM WRIGHTSON OF SEDGEFIELD, dated 5 Jan. 1808, proved at Durham 23 May 1810.

" . . . . the last will and testament of me William Wrightson of Sedgefield in the county of Durham, Gent."

" . . . . to *my nephew John Wrightson, eldest son of my late brother John Wrightson* deceased, the sum of £1,000, and to *my nephew Thomas Wrightson, younger son of my said brother,* the sum of £1,000."

" . . . . to *my nephew William Wrightson, son of my late brother Thomas Wrightson* deceased, the sum of £200."

" . . . . to my god-daughter, the daughter of my said nephew William Wrightson . . . ."

" . . . . to *my niece Ann Price,* the wife of Liscombe Price of the City of London, Attorney-at-Law, for her life . . . . the child or children of my said niece Ann Price . . . ."

" . . . . my late wife . . ."

" . . . . and appoint the said John Chilton and my said nephew William Wrightson, Exörs. . . ."

XXII. A DECLARATION, dated 23 April 1808.

"April 23 1808, I *William Wrightson of Sedgefield* . . . . do publish and declare that I have made a present and free Gift of one hundred pounds to *my nephew Mr. Wrightson of Neasham,* as a mark of my friendship and regard, and as a small requital for any trouble he may have had at any time in assisting me in the management of my affairs, and I declare it to be over and above anything that may be *named for him in my last will.*—William Wrightson."

XXIII. WILL OF MRS. NANNY GARTH OF COCKERTON HALL, dated 7 July, 1827, proved at Durham 12 Dec. 1829.

" . . . . the last will and testament of me Nanny Garth of Cockerton in the parish of Darlington . . . widow . . ."

" . . . . to the use of *my relative Richard Wrightson*, son of John Wrightson late of Thirsk . . . deceased. . . ."

" . . . . to the use of *Thomas Wrightson of Neasham Hall. . . .*"

" . . . . unto Dorothy Beckett of Northallerton . . . . the niece of my late dear mother. . . ."

" I request that my remains may be deposited near to my late dear husband John Garth esqr., deceased, in the Parish Church of Darlington . . . . but in case that cannot be allowed then . . . . . to Long Newton church yard . . . . as near as may be to *my late dear father and mother William Wrightson and Ann Wrightson.* . . . ."

XXIV. CHANCERY SUIT.

Part 1, contains the report of the case of Topham and wife *v.* McGregor and wife, as tried at the Durham Spring Assizes, March 1844.   Part 2, contains the case of McGregor and wife on Appeal before the House of Lords, where judgment was delivered against them by Lord Brougham, 23 July 1850. Pub. by E. Billing, Parliamentary Printer.

" Mr. Richard Wrightson, late of Cockerton House, in the township of Cockerton, in the parish of Darlington . . . . Mrs. Nanny Garth, the last preceding owner thereof, who died on the 1st Decr. 1829 . . . . . the said Richard died on the 29th Nov. 1830 without issue . . . . . leaving the appellant, Cordelia McGregor, ... his only sister . . . ." (Pt. 2, p. 1.)

' Cordelia was married to Patrick McGregor in June 1828 at Guisbrough, co. York.' (Pt. 1, p. 4.)

' *Cordelia's and Richard's mother was a Hardcastle.*' (Pt. 1, p. 26.)

' *Richard's father was Mr. Wrightson of Thirsk,* a solicitor.' (Pt. 1, p. 68.)

' Richard was twice married; the second time in 1827 to Eliza Henrietta, dau. of the Rev. Henson, Rector of Kilvington, near Thirsk.' (Pt. 1, see pp. 1, 3, 4.)

'Richard had *no nephews or nieces*, but a great many cousins, among whom was *Thomas Wrightson of Neasham, a second cousin.*' (Pt. 1, p. 3.)

'Richard had been an officer in the North York Militia from the summer of 1812 until the regiment was disbanded in 1816.' (Pt. 1, see pp. 4, 56, 68.)

'Mrs. Garth so devised her property in Sadberge, Long Newton, and Middleton St. George, that it came in reversion to Thomas Wrightson of Neasham.' (Pt. 1, p. 7.)

XXV. RELEASE, dated 1 Sep. 1849.

" . . . . . Eliza Henrietta Topham, formerly Eliza Henrietta Wrightson, widow of *Richard Wrightson late of Cockerton Hall* . . . ."

" . . . . . *Thomas Wrightson, late of Neasham Hall, but now of Haughton le Skerne* . . . ."

" . . . . *Nanny Garth late of Cockerton Hall* . . . ."

" . . . . Richard Wrightson, son of John Wrightson late of Thirsk . . . ."

XXVI. WILL OF WILLIAM WRIGHTSON OF NEASHAM HALL, dated 21 Jan. 1803, with codicils dated 4 Nov. 1803 and 8 Feb. 1814, sworn to at Durham 11 Feb. 1828.

" . . . . the last will and testament with two codicils annexed of William Wrightson formerly of Morton Palmes in the Parish of Haughton le Skerne . . ., but late of Nesham Hall in the Parish of Hurworth . . . ." (*Probate.*)

" . . . . . my *eldest son Thomas Wrightson* . . . . . my second son John Wrightson . . . . . my third son William Wrightson . . . . . my fourth son Robert White Wrightson." (2nd codicil.)

" . . . . . my freehold messuage farm and lands called *White house farm* situate in the township of Sadberge . . . ." (2nd codicil.)

" . . . . . my wife Mary Wrightson." (1st codicil.)

" . . . . my late Father-in-law Robert White." (1st codicil.)

" . . . . *my cousin John Wrightson of Thirsk* in the county of York, gentleman."

" . . . . Mrs. Ann Price, the wife of Liscombe Price of the city of London, gentleman."

" . . . . . Elizabeth Wrightson, spinster."

" . . . . . Thomas Wrightson of Easingwold in the county of York, gentleman."

XXVII. WILL OF THOMAS WRIGHTSON, dated 25 Nov. 1859, with codicils dated 3 April 1860 and 10 Sep. 1861, proved at Durham 14 May 1872.

" . . . . the last will and testament of me Thomas Wrightson, *formerly of Neasham Hall* . . . ."

" . . . . My freehold," etc., etc., "in the parishes of Haughton le Skerne, Long Newton, Middleton St. George, and Hurworth upon Tees . . . ."

" . . . . . my brother John . . . . . my brother William . . . . . my sister Isabella . . . . . my sister Margaret . . . . . my sister Eleanor . . . . . my sister Elizabeth . . ."

" . . . . . my dear wife Rebecca Gilchrist Wrightson and *my son William Garmonsway Wrightson* . . ."

" . . . . . my daughter Rebecca Ingram Wrightson . . . . . ."

" . . . . my daughter Mary Wrightson . . ."

" . . . . *my second son Thomas Wrightson* . . ." (1st codicil.)

" . . . . . *my third son John Wrightson* . . . ." (2nd codicil.)

> Obs. :—The properties above referred to are Spring House (often described as in Long Newton), Middleton-one-Row, a moiety of Haughton Grange, and the remains of his father's property at Neasham.

XXVIII. OUR "R. B. G." PEDIGREE of 1770.

First Generation

John Wrightson of Naryholme [*sic*] in the North Riding co: York

Second Generation

CHILDREN OF JOHN

John Wrightson of Spring House in com Durham = Margaret daur and coheir of Thomas Robinson
   William Wrightson merchant; died at Newcastle unmarrd.

Thomas Wrightson of Aryholm [*sic*] aforesaid = Elizabeth daur and coheir of Thomas Robinson and sister of John's wife

Third Generation

CHILDREN OF JOHN

William Wrightson of Cockerton in com Durham = Ann daur of Thomas Becket Rector of Kirby Whisk in com Ebor.
   Thomas Wrightson died unmarried

CHILD OF THOMAS

John Wrightson of Dinsdale com Ebor 1770 = Ann daur of John Cornforth of Cockhew com Durham

Fourth Generation

CHILD OF WILLIAM

Nanny Wrightson

CHILDREN OF JOHN

Ann, daur of John Wrightson
Elizabeth, daur of John Wrightson
John Wrightson born at Dinsdale
Thomas Wrightson

Obs.:—The above pedigree is contained in one of the MSS. of the late Sir Ralph Bigland, Garter-King-of-Arms, at the Heralds' College in London, under reference "R. B. G. vol. iv, pp. 38, 39." The only date is appended to John of Dinsdale; and as it is neither that of his baptism, marriage, or burial, it is clearly the date in his life at which the pedigree was made.

XXIX. OUR No. 1 DOMESTIC PEDIGREE, dated 1800.

" The Pedigree of the Family of the Wrightsons of Spring House in the parish of Long Newton. 1800—

Tradition goes no further back than about the year 1620 or 30, when Two Brothers were living at Ariholm in Yorkshire. The elder lost a pretty Estate there by contending with the Lord of the Manor: married and left two sons, John owner of Spring House and Richard the younger who dyed young at sea—The younger Brother went as Captain in King William's expedition to Ireland: married there, from whom sprang Alderman Wrightson of Dublin's Family—so far tradition only.

The above John. Born about the year 1635. Married one Ann Heslop who dyed about the year 1680 by whom he left Three sons, John, Thomas, and William, all born at Maltby in Yorkshire, and dyed at Spring House about the year 1720.

John, born about the year 1786 [*sic*], married Margaret the eldest coheiress of Thomas Robinson . . . .

Thomas of Dinsdale, born about the year 1691, married Eliz. the youngest daughter of Thos Robinson aforesaid . . . . .

William, born about 1793 [*sic*] dyed unmarried at Newcastle about the year 1720." [And so on; mentioning the names, and showing correctly the relationships of Nos. 20, 24 ; 27 to 29; 31 to 35; 37 to 44 inclusive; and then a portion torn off.]

> Obs. :—The above is written on a sheet of paper with the water-mark " 1794." The hand-writing is that of a very old man, being both tremulous and careful. There were only three old men in the family in 1800, viz., Nos. 32, 35, and 33. The first could not have been the writer, for the dates of his own and daughter's births and of his wife's death are only approximated. Nor could the second, for his wife is simply referred to as " *a* Mary White, who died *about* 1790." The third, viz., John W. of Dinsdale, is clearly the writer ;

for, whilst of the 7 dates belonging to himself and his children not one is approximated, of the 23 others belonging to his own or the previous generation only three are unaccompanied by an "about": again, whilst the information concerning himself is so full that he even tells where his late wife's sisters are buried, he only troubles to carry on the family descents through his own children: again, his own death has been inserted by a later hand: and lastly, the pedigree belongs to his descendants through Mrs. Ann Price, having been lent to me by one of them, viz., Mr. James Dallas of the Exeter Museum, who before knowing me had unfortunately made it the basis of a very defective account of our family published in *The Genealogist.*

Obs. 2 :—The aged writer blunders among dates ; *e.g.* he makes his "Ann Heslop" die before the birth of her children,—places the birth of No. 27 a century wrong,— the birth of No. 29 after his death,—and puts a "3" for a '5' in "1635," see Authority **XXXI.**

XXX. OUR No. 2 DOMESTIC PEDIGREE, dated 1800.

"The Pedigree of the Family of the Wrightsons of Spring house in the Parish of Long Newton in the County of Durham in the Year 1800.

Tradition goes no further back than about the Year 1620, when two Brothers lived at Aryholme in the County of York, the eldest of whom lost a pretty Estate there by contending with the Lord of the Manor, was in the Army, married and left two Sons, John the owner of Spring house as above, and Richard who died young at Sea.—The Younger Brother went as Captn in King William's Expedition to Ireland, married there, from whom the present family of Alderman Wrightson's of Dublin came—so far Tradition only—

John Wrightson born about the Year 1635 married one Ann Heslop from about Richmond who died about the Year 1680, by whom he had three Sons, John, Thomas, and William, all of whom were born at Maltby in the said County of York, and died at Spring house aforesaid about the Year 1720.

John Wrightson of Spring house, born about the Year 1686. . . .

Thomas Wrightson of Dinsdale in the County of York, born about the Year 1691.

William Wrightson, born about the Year 1693, died at Newcastle unmarried about the Year 1721." [And so on; mentioning all the Wrightsons contained in Authority XXIX, and in addition Nos. 45 to 50 inclusive, as well as the children of Mrs. Ann Price ending with Sarah, " born in the Year 1785." These additions may well have all existed in the torn-off portion of the previous pedigree.]

> Obs. :—The above appears to be a revised copy of Authority XXIX. It is written on an old sheet of paper in a fine free hand, and contains no date later than 1800. It was lent to me by Mr. James Dallas ; and seems to have belonged to Sarah, the youngest daughter of Mrs. Ann Price.

XXXI. OUR No. 3 DOMESTIC PEDIGREE, about 1815.

"The Pedigree of the Family of the Wrightsons of Spring House in the Parish of Longnewton in the County of Durham.

Tradition goes no further back than about the year 1620, when two Brothers lived at Ariholm in the County of York, the older of which lost a pretty Estate by contending with the Lord of the Manor, they both belonged the Army, the older married and left three sons, John the owner of Spring House as above, the next name not known, who went as Captain in King William's expedition to Ireland, married there from whom sprung the present Alderman Wrightson of Dublin's Family, and Richard the youngest died young at sea.

The above John, Born about the year 1655, Married one Ann Heslop from about Richmond who dyed about 1715 by whom he had three sons, John, Thomas, and William, all born at ——— in Yorkshire, he died at Spring House about the year 1723.

John, born about the year 1686. . . . .

Thos of Dinsdale in Yorkshire, born about the year 1691. . . . . .

William born about the year 1693, died unmarried at Newcastle about the year 1721." [And so on; mentioning all those contained in Authority **XXIX**, and in addition Nos. 45 and 47 to 59 inclusive.]

> Obs. :—The original portion of this pedigree is in my father's school-boy hand. The last date this portion contains is the birth of his youngest sister in 1809, and the first circumstance added in his matured hand is the death of his kind relative John of Thirsk in 1817. Hence I date this pedigree about 1815. Although in writing this original portion my father has brought it within the present century by inserting his own and the birthdays of all his brothers and sisters, yet otherwise it is clear he was simply copying an edition of Authority **XXIX**, in which, while 10 dates have been altered for the better, 5 have been altered for the worse. He most likely made this copy while staying at Thirsk, for he had had no assistance from my grandfather in respect of the much more exact dates he had previously collected in Authority **XXXII**.

XXXII. LIST OF DATES of 1809 or 10 in the handwriting of William Wrightson (42) of Neasham Hall.

" Thos. son of John Wrightson of Spring House was baptized the 25th day of March 1712.

Wm. son of John Wrightson baptized the 6th day of Feb. 1714.

Margt. Robinson.   Bapt. March the 8th 1688.   Died 1766.

Hannah Robinson.   Bapt. June the 28th 1690.   Died 1755.

Elizabeth Robinson.   Bapt. March the 29 1696.   Died April the 10th 1774.

Thos. Wrightson.   Bapt. March the 15th 1691.   Died Nov. 5th 1768.

John Wrightson. Bapt. March the 23d 1717. Died Nov. 12th 1803.

Thos. Wrightson. Bapt. Nov. [*sic*] the 23d 1719. Died Nov. 4 1767.

Wm. Wrightson. Bapt. June the 25th 1723.

Margt. Wrightson. Bapt. Sept. the 19th [*sic*] 1719. Died Jan. 21st 1797.

Wm. Wrightson. Bapt. October the 4th 1755.

Margt. Wrightson. Bapt. Sept. the 9th [*sic*] 1758. Died March the 23d 1797.

Mary Wrightson. Born [*sic*] Feb. the 8th 1768.

Isabella Wrightson. Born July the 22d 1796.

Margt. Wrightson. Born October the 1st 1797.

Thos. Wrightson. Born July the 16 1799.

Eleanor Wrightson. Born Jan. the 2d 1801.

Mary Wrightson. Born August the 27th 1802. Died Feb. the 23d 1807.

John Wrightson. Born June the 25th 1804.

Wm. Wrightson. Born March the 10th 1806.

Robt. White Wrightson. Born December the 2d 1807.

Mary Elizabeth Wrightson. Born October the 10th 1809."

Obs. :—This list, on paper with the water-mark " 1806," must have been made by my grandfather before the unmentioned death of his uncle William in Apr. 1810, but after the last date in Oct. 1809. I have discovered all the parishes where the Wrightson baptisms and burials above indicated took place, with the *one exception* of his grandfather's baptism on " March 15th 1691."

XXXIII. ERYHOLME REGISTERS.[1]

" Certified Copies of 32 Entries in the Parochial Registers of

---

[1] I have not deemed it necessary to print the whole of the certified or non-certified extracts taken from the numerous Parochial Registers referred to in the construction of our Pedigree. But I can assure the reader that wherever the name of the Parish (connected with the Baptism, Marriage, or Burial) is given, the entry has either been certified by the Incumbent or verified by myself.—W. G. W.

Eryholme, co. York, with remarks on the same in brackets, extracted and made by the Rev. Walter Edward Stewart.

(N.B. With the accidental exception of 1576, the whole of the years mentioned below commenced on the 25 March. Hence, for example, 19 Feb. 1585 = 19 Feb. 1586 New Style.)

BURIALS.

1578. The 22 of July was Richard Wrightsone buryed.

1579. The 22 of July was Thomas Wrightsone buryed.

1585. The 19 day of Febru. was John Wrightsone buried.

1587. The 27 day of November was Agnes Wrightsone buried.

1587. The 5 of January was Agnes Wrightsone widow buryed.

1603. The 25 day of August was An Wrightsone buryed.

1618. The 20 day of Aprill was Elizabeth Wrightsonn wife to John Wrightsonn buried.

1623. August 3 was Margaret the wife of John Wrightson of Eriholme buryed.

1630. April the 10 was Edmund Wrightson of Eriholme buryed.—*who ought ye Frehold now Listers and Rickabys and was Cheated out of it after Qr. They have a Bad Title :*

(N.B. The above addition to the much older entry has been made by the same hand which entered a few registers about 1690.)

1631. March 7 was Barbarie Wrightson the wife of John Wrightson buryed.

1642. Isabel Wrightson wid: bur: 22 July 1642.

1657. John Wrightson buried ye 17 of September 1657.

1658. An Wrightson buried ye 23 of August 1658.

1661. Thomas Wrightson buried the 18 of December 1661.

1679. Ann Wrightson buried May ye 2d.

MARRIAGES.

1573. The 29 of November was Edmund Wrightson and Isabel Winspear maryed.

1616. The 30 day of June was Thomas Nesom and Isabel Wrightsone maried.

1631. October 2 was Thomas Browne and Dorothye Wrightson both of this parish maryed.

1649. Thomas Wrightson and Anne Robinson mar: 29 Nov: 1649.

1649. Edward Wrigston (*sic*) and Jane Barnet mar: 13 Decemb: 1649.

(N.B. The above entry is in a good but strange hand ; and probably refers to Edmund Wrightson.)

BAPTISMS.

1574. The 19 of September was a childe of Edmund Wrightsones baptized and named Elenor.

1576. The 7 day of March was a childe of Edmund Wrightsones baptized and named John.

(N.B. The above entry stands at the head of all the Baptisms in the historic year 1576.)

1580. The 19 of February was a childe of Edmund Wrightsones baptized and named Isabell.

1581. The 23 of March was a childe of Edmund Wrightsones baptized and named Thomas.

1585. The 2 of February was a child of Edmund Wrightsones baptized and named Joan.

1588. The 19 of May was a childe of Edmund Wrightsones baptized and named Dorothy.

1611. The 15 day of December was a child of John Wrightsones baptized and named John.

1615. The 30 day of July was a childe of John Wrightsones baptized and named Thomas.

1630. August 26 was Edmund the son of John Wrightson of Eriholme bapd.

1631. Feb. 19 was Robert the son of John Wrightson of Eriholme baptised.

1651. Dorothy daughter of Edmund Wrigtson (*sic*) baptised the 2 of August 1651.

(N.B. The above entry should be compared with the marriage on 13 Dec. 1649.)

1654. William sone of Edmund Wrightson baptized the 16 of May 1654.

(N.B. The population of this parish is indicated by the fact that in fifty years, commencing with 1575, there were only 233 Baptisms, being less than five per annum.)

I hereby Certify the above 32 extracts to be true Copies of Entries in the Registers of the Parish of Eryholme and Diocese of Ripon. Extracted this twenty fourth day of September in the year of Our Lord One Thousand Eight Hundred and Eighty Eight. By me, Walter Edward Stewart.

Vicar."   Stamp.

Uncertified Copies of Miscellaneous Entries in same Registers.

1590. The 17 of Aprill was Rowland Spenc buryed.

1574. The 8 of March was James ffreer buryed.

1590. The 28 of Aprill was George Blakey buryed.

1590. The 13 day of December was William Blakey buryed.

1575. The 13 of October was a child of John Winspeares baptized and named Rowland.

1593. The 1 day of August was Thomas Winspeare buryed.

1627. March 26 was Thomas the son of William Winspere of Eriholme bapt.

1629. Maye 2 was William Winspere of Eriholme buryed.—
    who had ye Estate at Eriholme.

1650. Thomas Winspear was bur: 21 March 1650.—*son to*
    Wm. Winspere Deceased.

1653. Grace daughter of Tho. Winspear buried March 9 1653.
    —*Qr. She was Heire to Winspire Frehold: at her*
    decease it fell to her Fathers Sister Eliz: who was
    Wife of Geo: Harrison of New Castle Weuer.

1633. November 10 was faith Ricabie the daughter of John
    Ricabie of Eriholme bapd.

1631. Julie 4 was John Calverley the son of Mr. John Calverley
    of Eryholme buryed.

1642. ffower soldiers belonging to captaine Wrey slaine by
    Mr. Hotham troupe bur. 28 Novemb. 1642.

1642. Anthony Coatsworth of Mr. Hothams troupe slaine bur:
    29 Novemb: 1642.

1644. Thomas Cole a soldier under colonel Jackson bur:
    11 April 1644.

[N.B. The above additions, printed in italics, have been
made by the same hand that added the note to the burial of
Edmund Wrightson.]

Earliest successive Vicars mentioned:—

Sir John Emerson	buried 3 May 1571
Sir Edward Smithson	„ 5 Oct. 1576
Mr. Thomas Rivington	„ 16 July 1586
Mr. Francis Rivington	„ 25 Mar. 1618
Mr. John Idson	„ —— 1639
Mr. Lancelot Langhorne	„ 31 Aug. 1651

XXXIV. RICHMOND REGISTERS.

"Certified Copies of Entries in the Parochial Registers of
Richmond, co. York.

(The whole of the below mentioned years commenced on
the 25th of March; hence for example 16 March 1650=
16 March 1651 New Style.)

Baptisms

1650. Elizabeth the daughter of Thomas Wrightson March 16
1652. John the son of Thomas Wrightson May 23
1654. Thomas son of Thomas Wrightson Jan. 14
1660. Maria filia Thomas Wrightson decimo die Martii
1665. Will: son of Tho: Wrightson Dec. 25

Marriages

1697. John Wrightson and Ann Simpson Jan. 22
1699. Tho: Heslop and Mary Wrightson April 30

Burials

1717. Thomas Wrightson Aug. 26
1729. Thomas Heslop Nov. 16
        (Churchwarden of Richmond 1703.)

I hereby certify the above nine Extracts to be true Copies of Entries in the Registers of the Parish of Richmond and Diocese of Ripon. Extracted this twenty seventh day of October in the year of our Lord One Thousand Eight Hundred and Eighty Eight

        By me Richard Earnshaw Roberts M.A.
Rector of Richmond, Rural Dean, and Hon. Canon of Ripon."
                              Stamp.

Uncertified Copies of Miscellaneous Entries in same Registers.

1655. Ann, daughter of William Heslop baptized, July 22.
1659. Ann, daughter of William Heslop buried, Sep. 1.
1687. Henry Wrightson and Else Buck married, Sep. 3.
        [App. D]
1690. Lionel, son of George Vane Esq. baptized, Sep. 11.
1692. Walter, son of George Vane Esq. baptized, Feb. 16.

PEDIGREE OF THE FAMILY OF WRIGHTSON

AS CONSTRUCTED BY THE

Rev. W. G. WRIGHTSON, M.A. Cantab. 1894.

Arms :—Or, a fesse invected chequy azure and argent, between two Eagles' heads erased in chief sable, and a Saltire couped in base gules.
Crest :— In front of a Saltire gules a Unicorn salient or.
Motto :—Veritas Omnia Vincit.

 LTHOUGH this Pedigree extends no further back than the combined pedigrees of the family preserved at the College of Arms (under references " Norfolk," xv, p. 43 and xvii, p. 9), yet it contains a few more names and much more information ; and is so constructed as to exhibit all necessary proofs of descent. The record of each male, shown to have left descendants, is not indented ; but, where his male descendants have failed or vanished, his record is unaccompanied by the thick black line, which indicates the line of continuing family life. The numeral attached to each name is useful for reference, and establishes connection with the subjoined Outline Pedigree. The following are the signs and abbreviations used :

acc.	=	according
afsd.	=	aforesaid
bap.	=	baptized or baptismal
bur.	=	buried or burial
co.	=	county
dau.	=	daughter
Dom. Peds.	=	Domestic Pedigrees
Exch.	=	Exchequer
Exör	=	executor
G. R. O.	=	General Register Office
Jno.	=	John
lg.	=	living
= or mar.	=	married or marriage
M. I.	=	Monumental Inscription
MSS.	=	manuscripts
prob.	=	probably
P. R. O.	=	Public Record Office
?	=	Query
R. B. G. Ped.	=	Pedigree by Sir R. Bigland
reg.	=	register
s. pr.	=	*sine prole*, without descendants
Tho.	=	Thomas
Wm.	=	William
W.	=	Wrightson

First Generation

1 :—JOHN WRIGHTSON of Eryholme [1] in the Wapentake of Gilling-east, North Riding, co. York ; born prob. about 1460.[2]   In the records of an Exchequer Suit he is described as *" great-grandfather"* of *Edmund* Wrightson, the Plaintiff, and

---

[1] That the family was settled in Eryholme before his time is proved by a document of the year 1459 which speaks of a " Richard Wrightson *late of* Eryom," co. York (see a Plea of Debt in " De Banco Roll, Easter term, 37 Hen. VI., membrane No. 232," at P. R. O.).   This makes it certain that the Wrightsons were in Eryholme as far back as the earlier half of the 15th century.

[2] This approximate date of birth rests on the following considerations. If his great-grandson, Edmund, was 23 at his marriage in 1573 and 80 at his death in 1630, he would be born in 1550.   Allowing 30 years for each of the three preceding generations we arrive at 1460.

is stated to have handed over to Ninian Markenfield, lord of the Manor, a certain portion of his freehold lands in Eryholme in exchange for a quarter of the Westfield estate also in Ery- holme (see "Exch. Bills and Answers, Eliz. York, No. 385,"—"Exch. Depositions, Miscellaneous, 32 Eliz. Mich. No. 1946, Durham,"—"Exch. Decrees and Orders, Eliz. Series I. No. 17, folio 211,"—at P. R. O.).

Second Generation

CHILD OF JOHN (1)

2 :—RICHARD W. of Eryholme, described as "*son*" *of Jno. W. afsd.* in afsd. suit; born prob. about 1490. In the afsd. suit it is stated that, about 1564, he demised, not only his Westfield property, but "all other his Freehold lands in Eryholme unto Thomas his younger son . . . . . . for the term of twenty years." In the Homberston Survey of 1570 (see vol. ii, p. 145, at P.R.O.) he stands at the head of both the Copyholders and Freeholders, and his freehold is described as "one tenement built, with divers lands, meadows, and pastures, all and singular which premises the said Richard holds freely by Charter in free socage by service of — part of a knight's fee." Bur. at Eryholme 22 July 1578.

Third Generation

CHILDREN OF RICHARD (2)

3 :—JOHN W. of Eryholme, described as "*son and heir*" *of the afsd. Richard* in afsd. suit ; born prob. about 1520. In 1562 he, along with Agnes his wife, sold 170 acres of Wright- son property in North Cowton, near Eryholme (see "Feet of Fines, co. York, Mich. Term, 3 and 4 Eliz." at P. R. O.). In 1569 he engaged in the abortive Rising of the North, and on 1 Jan. 1569-70 [1] was a prisoner at Durham in the hands of Sir

---

[1] The 25 March was our legal New-year's day till the 1 Jan. 1752, when the present form of the year (already in frequent use) was universally

George Bowes knt., Provost Marshal of the North (see Bowes
MSS. vol. xiii, at Streatlam Castle). Bur. at Eryholme 19
Feb. 1585-6 = Agnes . . . . .; mar. prob. about 1549; bur.
at Eryholme 5 Jan. 1587-8.

> 4 :—Thomas W., described as the afsd. Richard's
> "younger son" in the afsd. suit. In 1569 he was
> somehow concerned in the afsd. Rising of the North
> (see afsd. Bowes MSS. vol. xiii). Bur. at Eryholme
> 22 July 1579; his will (now lost) was proved at
> Richmond same year = Agnes . . . . . ., a defendant
> in the afsd. suit in 1590.

Fourth Generation

Child of John (3)

  5 :—EDMUND W. of Eryholme, described as "*son and
heir*" of the afsd. *John* in afsd. suit; born prob. about 1550.
In 1575 he, along with Isabel his wife, sold 111 acres of
Wrightson property in North Cowton afsd. (see "Feet of
Fines, co. York, Mich. Term, 17 and 18 Eliz. Part 2." at
P. R. O.). In 1590 he commenced the afsd. suit for the
recovery of the afsd. Westfield property, which had been seized
on the attainder of Thomas Markenfield, lord of the Manor, of
high Treason. About 1690 the following note was appended
to his burial register,—"who ought [to have had] the Freehold
now Rickerby's and Lister's, and was cheated out of it after.
Qr. They have a bad Title." Bur. at Eryholme 10 Apr.
1630; his will, dated 13 Feb. 1629-30, was proved at Richmond 28 Sep. 1630 = Isabel Winspere; mar. at Eryholme 29
Nov. 1573; (? the "Isabel W., widow" bur. there 22 July
1642).

adopted in England. When a date, lying between and including 1 Jan.
and 24 Mar., is evidently written according to the old form of the year, the
true modern historic year ought always to be indicated, as here, after a
hyphen.

Fifth Generation

Children of Edmund (5)

6:—Elenor W., bap. at Eryholme, as a "child of Edmund W.," 19 Sep. 1574.

7:—JOHN W. of Eryholme, bap. there, as a "*child of Edmund W.*," 7 Mar. 1575-6; mentioned in his father's will. In 1632 he is mentioned in a Bill of Complaint, as living at Eryholme, and as in contention with Sir John Calverley, lord of the Manor, touching the afsd. Westfield property (see "Exch. Bills and Answers, York, 7 Charles I., No. 235" at P. R. O.). Bur. at Eryholme 17 Sep. 1657 = (1st wife) Elizabeth . . . . .; bur. at Eryholme 20 Apr. 1618, by whom John and Thomas = (2nd wife) Margaret . . . . .; bur. at Eryholme 3 Aug. 1623 = (3rd wife) Barbara . . . . .; bur. at Eryholme 7 Mar. 1631-2, by whom Edmund and Robert.

8:—Isabell W., bap. at Eryholme, as a "child of Edmund W.," 19 Feb. 1580-1; mentioned in her father's will = Thomas Nesom; mar. at Eryholme 30 June 1616.

9:—THOMAS W. of Eryholme, bap. there, as a "child of Edmund W.," 23 Mar. 1581-2; mentioned in his father's will. In 1632 he is mentioned in the afsd. Bill of Complaint as "brother" of the afsd. John, and as "of Eryholme." Bur. there 18 Dec. 1661 = ...

10:—Joan W., bap. at Eryholme, as a "child of Edmund W.," 2 Feb. 1585-6.

11:—Dorothy W., bap. at Eryholme, as a "child of Edmund W.," 19 May 1588; mentioned with great tenderness in her father's will = Thomas Browne; mar. at Eryholme 2 Oct. 1631.

Sixth Generation

CHILDREN OF JOHN (7).

12 :—JOHN W., bap. at Eryholme, as a "child of Jno. W.," 15 Dec. 1611.

13 :—THOMAS W. of Eryholme and Richmond, co. York, bap. at Eryholme, as a "*child of John W.,*" 30 July 1615 (twenty-seven years before the outbreak of the Civil War); mentioned traditionally in two of our Dom. Peds., as in "the Army"; remembered traditionally in the family as "Captain Wrightson of Eryholme," to whom certain old weapons, preserved till 1810, were said to have belonged. He evidently [1] went to live at Richmond before the birth of his eldest child in 1650-1 ; but was not bur. there=Anne Robinson; mar. at Eryholme 29 Nov. 1649 (ten months after the execution of Charles I.); (? the "Ann W." bur. there 2 May 1679).

14 :—ANN W., mentioned, as "daughter of John W.," in the will of Edmund W. in 1629-30; (? the Ann W. bur. at Eryholme 23 Aug. 1658).

[1] Writing in 1800 John (33), the aged grandson of John (20) of Spring House, prefaces his Domestic Pedigree with the words,—"Tradition goes no further back than about the year 1620 or 30, when Two Brothers were living at Eryholme in Yorkshire. The Elder lost a pretty estate there by contending with the lord of the Manor; married and left two sons, John the owner of Spring House and Richard," etc. This tradition has lost a generation by confusing Thomas (13), the father of John (20) of Spring House, with John (7), the elder of the two Eryholme brothers, who had the contention with Sir John Calverley, lord of the Manor. And that Thomas, the son of (7), is the same person as Thomas, the father of (20), is confirmed, when we notice the three following points,—

1st, that, while Thomas, the son of (7), has left *no trace* at Eryholme after his marriage there, Thomas, the father of (20), is found spending his early married life at Richmond only ten miles from Eryholme.

2nd, that the two eldest children of the latter *bear the names* of the two parents of the former.

3rd, that the eldest child of the latter was *baptized just fifteen and a half months after the marriage of the former.*

15:—EDMUND W., bap. at Eryholme, as a "son of John W.," 26 Aug. 1630 (?=at Eryholme, 13 Dec. 1649, Jane Barnet).

16:—ROBERT W., bap. at Eryholme, as a "son of John W.," 19 Feb. 1631-2.

CHILDREN OF THOMAS (9)

17:—THOMAS W. ⎱ mentioned in the will of Edmund
18:—EDMUND W. ⎰ W. in 1629-30.

Seventh Generation
CHILDREN OF THOMAS (13)

19:—ELIZABETH W., bap. at Richmond, as "dau. of Thomas W.," 16 Mar. 1650-1.

20:—JOHN W., described, as "of Spring House," in the parish of Long Newton, co. Durham, in the bur. reg. of his son William,—as "of Hardstones," in the parish afsd., in the marriage settlement of his son John,—and as "of Eryholme" in our R. B. G. Ped. (*i.e.* a Wrightson pedigree of 1770 at the College of Arms, contained in the MSS. of Sir Ralph Bigland, Garter King of Arms, vol. iv, pp. 38-9); bap. at Richmond,[1]

---

[1] The identity of John W. finally of Spring House with John W. formerly of Richmond is proved as follows:—

In the first place, John of Spring House was (acc. to one of our Dom. Peds.) born "about 1655." He had (acc. to all our three Dom. Peds.) a brother called Richard. He had, according to a mar. settlement of 1711, a wife then living called Ann. He was (acc. to two Dom. Peds.) connected with the Heslops of "about Richmond." He had (acc. to the bap. reg. of a grandson in 1717-8) a son described at that time as "Thomas W. of Spring House." He spent the latter portion of his life at Spring House, and (acc. to parish reg.) was buried at Long Newton in 1723.

In the second place, John of Richmond was (acc. to the Richmond registers) bap. in 1652. He had (acc. to a family will) a brother called Richard. He was, acc. to a Richmond register of 1697-8, then married to a wife called Ann. He was (acc. to Richmond registers and a will) brother-in-law to Thomas Heslop of Richmond. He had (acc. to Richmond registers and an Administration) a brother, whose effects were ad-as "*son of Thomas IV.*," 23 May 1652; bur. at Long Newton 16 Sep. 1723=(1st wife) . . . ., by whom John, Thomas, and William=(2nd wife) Ann Simpson; mar. at Richmond 22 Jan. 1697-8 (13 years before the marriage of her husband's "son and heir"); mentioned in the afsd. marriage settlement of 1711 as "Ann his now wife."

> 21 :—THOMAS W., described, as "of Richmond," in his will,—and, as a "Free Burgess," in the Richmond Municipal lists for 1679, 81, 85, and 1705; bap. at Richmond, as a "son of Tho. W.," 14 Jan. 1654-5; bur. there 26 Aug. 1717; his will, dated 3 Jan. 1715-6, proved at Richmond 9 Sep. 1717; *s. pr.*
>
> 22 :—MARY W., bap. at Richmond, as "dau. of Tho. W.," 10 Mar. 1660-1; lg. 1729=Thomas Heslop, a Free Burgess of Richmond and Churchwarden there in 1703; he was Exör to the will of his "brother-in-law," Tho. W., in 1717; mar. at Richmond 30 Apr. 1699; bur. there 16 Nov. 1729; his will, dated 27 Oct. 1729, was proved there 29 Jan. 1729-30.
>
> 23 :—WILLIAM W., bap. at Richmond, as a "son of Tho. W.," 25 Dec. 1665; but not bur. there. The Administration to his effects was granted at Richmond, 3 Nov. 1714, to "Thomas W. of Spring House, co. Durham" with Thomas Heslop of Richmond standing as surety to the Bond.

24 :—RICHARD W., referred to as a "brother" in the will of Tho. W. of Richmond in 1715-6; but not necessarily as then alive.

CHILDREN OF EDMUND (15)

> 25 :—DOROTHY W., bap. at Eryholme, as a "dau. of Edmund W.," 2 Aug. 1651.
>
> 26 :—WILLIAM W., bap. at Eryholme, as a "son of Edmund W.," 16 May 1654.

ministered to in 1714 by "Thomas Wrightson of Spring House." He can only have spent the earlier portion of his life at Richmond, and has left no further trace there after 1677-8.

Eighth Generation

CHILDREN OF JOHN (20)

27:—JOHN W., described, as "John W. the younger, *son and heir of John W.* the elder," in his Marriage Settlement dated 28 Mar. 1711,—as "of Middleton Erow alias One Row," in a Release dated 15 July 1720,—and as "of Spring House," in our R. B. G. Ped. According to our three Dom. Peds. he was 'born in Yorkshire about 1686'; bur. at Long Newton 23 May 1727 = Margaret, a dau. and coheir of Thomas Robinson of Middleton St. George, co. Durham (whose will was proved at Durham 8 Mar. 1733); bap. there 8 Mar. 1687-8; mar. there 1 May 1711; mentioned in her father's will; bur. at Long Newton 10 June 1766.

28:—THOMAS W. of Over-Dinsdale in the parish of Sockburn, co. York, of White House, and of Sedgefield, co. Durham; described as the *second son of Jno. W. of Spring House* in our three Dom. Peds.,—as "*great-grandfather of Thomas W. of Neasham Hall,*" in a deed of conveyance of White House dated 12 June 1828,—as "of Eryholme" in our R. B. G. Ped.,—as "of Spring House" both in his Administration to Wm. W. of Richmond in 1714 and in the bap. reg. of his eldest son in 1717-8,—and as "Thomas W. the elder of White House in the parish of Middleton St. George in the county of Durham, Gentleman," in the Marriage Settlement of that property upon his second son in 1754. Parish books show that he was Churchwarden of Long Newton in 1714 and of Sockburn in 1726. On his Dinsdale estate he built, about 1720, and for long occupied the house now known as Rose Hill; but he finally lived on his Sedgefield property in the large old House on the west side of the Village green. According to our three Dom. Peds. he was born 'in Yorkshire about 1691'; and according to a list containing 29 Wrightson dates (in the hand-writing of his grandson (42), and of which this is the only unverified date) he was bap. 15 Mar. 1691; died

5 Nov. 1768; bur. at Sedgefield = Elizabeth, younger dau. and coheir of the afsd. Thomas Robinson; bap. at Middleton St. George 29 Mar. 1696; mar. there 18 June 1717; mentioned in her father's will; died 10 Apr. 1774; bur. at Sedgefield.

> 29 :—WILLIAM W., described, as "son of Jno. W. of Spring House," in his bur. reg. According to our three Dom. Peds. he was 'born in Yorkshire about 1693 and died unmarried in Newcastle'; and according to our R. B. G. Ped. he was a "merchant." Bur. at Long Newton 31 Oct. 1714.

CHILD OF RICHARD (24)

> 30 :—RICHARD W., mentioned in the will of Tho. W. of Richmond in 1715-6.

Ninth Generation

CHILDREN OF JOHN (27)

> 31 :—THOMAS W., bap. at Middleton St. George, as "son of John W.," 25 Mar. 1712; Churchwarden of Long Newton in 1734; bur. there 28 Jan. 1736; unmar.

32 :—WILLIAM W. of Cockerton Hall, near Darlington, co. Durham; described as "of Spring House . . . . gentleman," in an Indenture dated 12 July 1740,—and as "of Cockerton" in a Marriage Settlement dated 31 Oct. 1754 and in his bur. reg.; bap. at Middleton St. George, as a "*son of John IV.*," 6 Feb. 1714; bur. at Long Newton 10 Apr. 1806, "aged 92" = Ann, dau. of the Rev. Thomas Beckett, M.A. Cantab. (who was instituted Rector of Kirby Wiske, co. York, in 1722, and bur. there 10 Sep. 1751); bur. at Long Newton 1 Dec. 1787, "aged 76".

CHILDREN OF THOMAS (28)

33 :—JOHN W. of Over-Dinsdale afsd.; described as "of parish of Sockburn" in mar. reg., and, as "late farmer at Little

Smeaton, but now of Easingwold, gentleman," in his bur. reg. ;
there is an Estate Map of 1756 at Dinsdale Rectory marking
his lands with his name ; he was evidently the writer in 1800
of the oldest of our three Domestic Pedigrees ; bap. at Long
Newton, as the "*son of Thomas and Elizabeth W. of Spring
House,*" 23 Mar. 1717-8 ; died 12 Nov. 1803; bur. at Birkby,
co. York = Ann, dau. and coheir of John Cornforth of Coxhoe,
co. Durham ; mar. at Kelloe, co. Durham, 19 Apr. 1748 ; died
at Little Smeaton, co. York ; bur. at Birkby 15 Aug. 1762,
where also two of her sisters are buried.

34:—THOMAS W. of White House; described, as "Thomas
W. the younger of White House in the parish of Middleton St.
George, gentleman, *younger son of the said Thomas W. the elder,*"
in the Marriage Settlement of this property on him, dated 31 Oct.
1754; bap. at Long Newton, as the "son of T. and Eliz. W.,"
23 Feb. 1719-20; died before his father; died 4 Nov. 1767;
bur. at Middleton St. George = Margaret, a dau. of William
Garmonsway (*alias* Garmondsway) of Great Burdon in the
parish of Haughton le Skerne, co. Durham ; bap. there 17 Sep.
1719; mar. there 19 Nov. 1754; as a widow she possessed
farms in Haughton le Skerne, Sadberge, Cowpon, and Wolviston, building in the village of Haughton the large house next
the Rectory and another on her Sadberge farm called Newton
Grange ; died 21 Jan. 1797 ; bur. at Sadberge.

35 :—WILLIAM W., described, as "of Sedgefield in the
co. of Durham, gentleman," in his will,—as "an
eminent surgeon," in Surtees' *Hist. of Dur.* vol. iii,
pp. 59-60; bap. at Sockburn, as a "son to Tho.
W.," 25 June 1723; he had his father's property at
Sedgefield ; bur. there 7 Apr. 1810, "aged 87 "; his
will, dated 5 Jan. 1808, was proved at Durham 23
May 1810 = Mary White from Lincolnshire ; bur.
at Sedgefield 20 Oct. 1790; *s. pr.*

Tenth Generation

CHILDREN OF WILLIAM (32)

36 :—ANN W., bap. at Darlington, co. Durham, as " dau. of Mr. Wm. W. of Cockerton," 24 Dec. 1747 ; bur. at Long Newton 4 Apr. 1748.

37 :—NANNY W., bap. at Darlington, as "dau. of Mr. Wm. W. of Cockerton," 1 Feb. 1752 ; she was sole heiress to her father and possessed his Spring House, Middleton-one-Row, and Cockerton Hall estates, on the last of which she lived all her life ; died 1 Dec. 1829, "aged 79" ; bur. at Darlington ; her will, dated 7 July, 1827, was proved at Durham 12 Dec. 1829 = John Garth of Wolsingham, co. Durham ; mar. at Darlington 20 July 1794 ; died 29 Mar. 1810, "aged 88 " ; bur. at Darlington ; *s. pr.*

CHILDREN OF JOHN (33)

38 :—JOHN W. of Thirsk, co. York ; described, as "Coroner and Attorney-at-Law in Bedale," co. York, in his dau. Margaret's bap. reg.,—as "of Easingwold, Coroner, *son of John W. of Dinsdale*," in his son Richard's bap. reg.,—as "one of the Coroners of the North Riding, of Thirsk," in his bur. reg.,—as " my nephew John W., eldest son of my late brother John W.," in the will of Wm. W. of Sedgefield,—and, as " my cousin John W. of Thirsk," in the will of Wm. W. of Neasham Hall ; born at Over-Dinsdale ; bap. at Sockburn, as the "son of John W.," 24 May 1749 ; bur. at Birkby 7 Apr. 1817, "aged 69 " = (1st wife) Margaret, dau. of James Mewburn of Hurworth on Tees ; bap. at Croft 29 Aug. 1749 ; mar. at Bedale 11 Sep. 1775 ; bur. at Bedale 21 Apr. 1780 ; by whom three children = (2nd wife) Dorothy, dau. of Michael Hardcastle of Haughton le Skerne ; mar. at Bedale 8 Sep. 1783 ; bur. in the Grey Friars, Edinburgh, 26 Jan. 1828, "aged 73 " ; by whom four children.

39 :—ANN W., described, as "my niece Ann Price, the wife of Liscombe Price of the City of London, Attorney-at-Law," in the will of Wm. W. of Sedgefield; bap. at Sockburn, as dau. "of Jno. and Ann W.," 27 Aug. 1751 = as above; issue.

40 :—ELIZABETH W., described, as "my niece Elizabeth W." in the will of Wm. W. of Sedgefield; bap. at Sockburn, 17 Feb. 1757; bur. at Easingwold 17 July 1823, "aged 66."

41 :—THOMAS W., described as "my nephew Thomas W., younger son of my late brother John," in the will of Wm. W. of Sedgefield,—as "of Easingwold, Attorney," in his bur. reg.; bap. at Birkby, as "son of John W. and Ann his wife," 15 Aug. 1762; bur. at Northallerton, co. York, 26 June 1823, "aged 60" = Frances, dau. of Jno. Wade of Northallerton; mar., acc. to old note, 19 Nov. 1808; bur. there 31 Aug. 1846, "aged 79"; *s.pr.*

CHILDREN OF THOMAS (34)

42 :—WILLIAM W. of Neasham Hall in the parish of Hurworth on Tees, of Haughton le Skerne, White House, Newton Grange, etc., etc., co. Durham; described, as "my nephew Wm. W., *son of my late brother Thomas* W.," in the Will of Wm. W. of Sedgefield; bap. at Middleton St. George, as the "*son of Thomas W.*," 4 Oct. 1755; he built the Hall about 1805 on his beautiful Neasham estate, and is mentioned in Surtees' *Hist. of Dur.* vol. iii, p. 258; died 8 July 1826, "aged 71"; bur. in the church at Hurworth on Tees; M.I.; his will, dated 21 Jan. 1803, with codicils dated 4 Nov. 1803 and 8 Feb. 1814, was proved at Durham 11 Feb. 1828 = Mary, eldest dau. of Robert White of Norton, co. Durham, and sister of Anthony White, twice President of the Royal College of Surgeons; bap. at Norton 8 Feb. 1768; mar. there 23 July 1795; died 20 Jan. 1818; bur. at Hurworth on Tees, "aged 49"; M.I.

43 :—MARGARET W., bap. at Middleton St. George, as "dau. of Thomas W.," 21 Sep. 1758; died 23 Mar. 1797; bur. at Sadberge; unmar.

CHILDREN OF JOHN (38)

44 :—ANN W., bap. at Bedale 15 Nov. 1777; bur. at
   Croft 16 Feb. 1802, "aged 24"; unmar.

45 :—MARGARET W., bap. at Bedale 14 Oct. 1778 = at
   Easingwold 1 Jan. 1806 to John Brown of Sunder-
   land.

46 :—JAMES W., bap. at Bedale 21 Apr. 1780; *s. pr.*

47 :—CORDELIA W., born 18 June 1784; bap. at Easingwold = Patrick McGregor of Edinburgh; mar. at
   Guisborough, co. York, 5 June 1828; he died in
   London 16 Oct. 1854, aged 73 (G.R.O); *s. pr.* He
   and his wife were parties to the Chancery Suit of
   "Topham and Wife *v.* McGregor and wife," first
   tried at the Durham Spring Assizes 1844, and then
   on Appeal before the House of Lords July 1850.

48 :—JOHN WILLIAM W., born 4 July 1785; bap. at
   Easingwold ; *s. pr.*

49 :—CATHERINE SUSANNAH W., born 31 July 1787;
   bap. at Easingwold ; unmar.

50 :—RICHARD W. of Cockerton Hall, Spring House,
   and Middleton-one-Row ; described, as '*second cousin
   of Thomas W. of Neasham,*' in the afsd. Chancery
   suit,—as "*my relative Richard W., son of Jno. W.
   late of Thirsk,*" in the will of Mrs. Garth ; born
   11 Sep. 1788; bap. at Easingwold, as a "*son of Jno.
   W. of Easingwold, Coroner, son of Jno. W. of Dinsdale;
   and of his wife Dorithea, dau. of Michael Hardcastle
   of Haughton, Gentleman,*" 22 Dec. 1788. According to
   the afsd. Chancery suit, he was 'an officer in the North
   York Militia from 1812 to 1816,' had "no nephews
   and nieces," and died "without issue." He died
   29 Nov. 1830; bur. at Darlington ; his will (of
   which the validity was vainly contested in Chancery
   and before the House of Lords), dated 29 Dec. 1829,
   was proved at Durham 10 Dec. 1830=(1st wife)
   Caroline, a dau. of . . . . McLean M.D. of Galway,
   Ireland ; bur. at Sowerby, near Thirsk, 6 Dec. 1824,
   aged 38=(2nd wife) Eliza Henrietta, dau. of Rev.

Francis Henson senr., Rector of South Kilvington,
co. York, and formerly Fellow of Sidney Sussex College, Cambridge; mar. in 1827; after her husband's
death she mar. Thomas Topham 15 June 1831, and
died in London 31 Mar. 1853, aged 62.

CHILDREN OF WILLIAM (42)

51:—ISABELLA W., born 22 July 1796; bap. at Haughton
le Skerne; died 6 Oct. 1871; bur. there; M.I.;
unmar.

52:—MARGARET W., born 1 Oct. 1797; bap. at
Haughton le Skerne; died 9 Nov. 1873; bur. there;
M.I.; unmar.

53:—THOMAS W. of Neasham Hall, Haughton le Skerne,
Spring House, and Middleton-one-Row; described, as "my
eldest son," in 2nd codicil of his father's will; born 16 July
1799; bap. at Haughton le Skerne; sold Neasham Hall and
estate to the family of Cookson; died at Haughton le Skerne
12 Apr. 1872; bur. there; M.I. His will, dated 25 Nov.
1859, with codicils dated 3 Apr. 1860 and 10 Sep. 1861, was
proved at Durham 14 May 1872 = Rebecca Gilchrist, a dau. of
the late Wm. Potter of Walbottle House (whose will was
proved at Durham 14 June 1834), and aunt to Baron, Lord
Armstrong of Cragside, Northumberland; born in the parish of
Whickham, co. Durham, 3 Jan. 1803; bap. at St. John's Ch.
Newcastle on Tyne; mar. at St. Andrew's Ch. there 16 June
1834; died 24 Sep. 1884; bur. at Haughton le Skerne; M.I.;
her will, dated 1 Feb. 1884, was proved in London 25 Nov.
1884.

54:—ELEANOR WHITE W., born 2 Jan. 1801; bap. at
Haughton le Skerne; died 1 Oct. 1868; bur. there;
M.I.; unmar.

55:—MARY W., born 27 Aug. 1802; bap. at Haughton
le Skerne; died 23 Feb. 1807; bur. at Hurworth on
Tees.

56:—JOHN W., born 25 June 1804; bap. at Haughton
le Skerne; died 26 Aug. 1881; bur. there; M.I.;
unmar.

57 :—WILLIAM W., born 10 Mar. 1806; bap. at Hurworth on Tees; died 30 Sep. 1878; bur. at Haughton le Skerne; M.I.; unmar.

58 :—ROBERT WHITE W. of Bengal Medical Service, surgeon; born 2 Dec. 1807; bap. at Hurworth on Tees; according to M.I. in Hurworth Church, he "died on the 13 Feb. 1853 on his passage to the Cape of Good Hope on board the Alfred off Saugor Island, where his remains were committed to the deep "= Anna Maria, a dau. of the late John Frederic Lumley of Stockton on Tees; mar. at Hastings, co. Sussex, 2 May 1844; died in London 12 May 1886; bur. at Leamington.

59 :—MARY ELIZABETH W., born 10 Oct. 1809; bap. at Hurworth on Tees; died 13 Jan. 1863; bur. at Haughton le Skerne; M.I.; unmar.

Twelfth Generation

CHILDREN OF THOMAS (53)

60 :—WILLIAM GARMONSWAY W., M.A. Cantab., of the Old Hall, Hurworth on Tees, also of Haughton le Skerne, Spring House, and Middleton-one-Row; sometime (1870-5) Vicar of St. Paul's, Beckenham, co. Kent; mentioned, as "*my son*," in his father's will; born 24 June 1836; bap. at Haughton le Skerne; lg. = Priscilla Anne, eldest dau. and coheir of Alfred Head of 13 Craven Hill Gardens, Hyde Park, London (whose will was proved in London 23 Mar. 1880); born 22 Mar. 1840; bap. at St. Peter's Stepney; mar. at Christ Ch., Lancaster Gate, Paddington, 4 Dec. 1866; lg. (For many of her relatives see Joseph Foster's *Royal Descents*.)

61 :—REBECCA INGRAM W., born 16 July 1837; bap. at Haughton le Skerne; lg. = Jeremiah Head, M.Inst. C.E., a younger son of Jeremiah Head of Ipswich, and second cousin of afsd. Priscilla A. Head; born 11 July 1835; registered at the Friends' Meeting House, Ipswich; mar. at St. Andrews, Newcastle on

Tyne, 26 Sep. 1860; lg. at Coatham, Redcar. Three sons and two daughters now living, viz., William Howard H.; Archibald Potter H.; Benjamin H.; Mrs. Mary Campbell; and Kathleen H.

62 :—THOMAS W., M.P., of Neasham Hall, and Norton Hall near Stockton on Tees; mentioned, as "*my second son,*" in 1st codicil of his father's will; born 31 Mar. 1839; bap. at Haughton le Skerne; repurchased Neasham Hall and estate from the family of Cookson; was returned 5 July 1892 in the General Election as the Parliamentary (Conservative) Representative for Stockton on Tees; lg.=Elizabeth, eldest dau. of Samuel Wise of Ripon, solicitor (whose will was proved at Wakefield 17 June 1885); born 19 Sep. 1844; bap. in the Cathedral, Ripon; mar. there 23 June 1869; lg.

63 :—JOHN W., President of the College of Agriculture, Downton, co. Hants; Professor of Agriculture in the Royal College of Science, London; mentioned, as "*my third son*" in 2nd codicil of his father's will; born 9 Sep. 1840; bap. at Haughton le Skerne; lg. = Maria Isabel, only dau. of the late Charles Norleigh Hulton of Little Broughton, near Stokesley, co. York, a younger son of the late Wm. Hulton of Hulton Park, co. Lancaster; born 13 Mar. 1850; bap. at Kirby in Cleveland; mar. at Croft, co. York, 23 July 1872; lg.

64 :—MARY W., born 7 Mar. 1842; bap. at Haughton le Skerne; lg. unmar. at Beckenham, co. Kent.

CHILD OF ROBERT (58)

65 :—LEONARD RAISBECK W., born at Moradabad in India 3 July 1848; died 25 Nov. 1869; bur. at Leamington, co. Warwick; his will, dated 3 ·Nov. 1869, was proved in London 7 May 1870; unmar.

Thirteenth Generation

CHILDREN OF WILLIAM (60)

66 :—ELLEN W., born 26 Nov. 1867; bap. at Christ Ch., Paddington; lg.

67 :—ROBERT GARMONDSWAY W., B.A. Cantab., Barrister-at-Law, born 6 Apr. 1869 ; bap. at St. John's, Paddington ; educated at Marlborough and Trinity College, Cambridge ; called to the Bar at the Inner Temple in 1894 ; lg.

68 :—ALFRED HEAD W. of New Zealand ; born 29 May 1870 ; bap. at St. George's, Beckenham ; lg.

69 :—ISABEL INGRAM W., born 4 Oct. 1871 ; bap. at St. Paul's, Beckenham ; lg.

70 :—LUCY GILCHRIST W., born 20 Dec. 1872 ; bap. at St. Paul's, Beckenham ; lg.

71 :—HARRY W., born 29 Sep. 1874 ; bap. at St. Paul's, Beckenham ; educated at Marlborough College ; lg.

72 :—EDWARD ST. JOHN W., born at St. John de Luz, France, 22 Apr. 1877 ; bap. there ; died 30 Sep. 1877 ; bur. at Montreux, Canton de Vaud, Switzerland.

73 :—PRISCILLA MABEL W., born 26 June 1883 ; bap. at St. Paul's, Beckenham ; lg.

CHILDREN OF THOMAS (62).

74 :—MARY ISABELLA EDITH (" Ella ") W., born 7 Aug. 1870 ; bap. at Norton ; lg. = George Frederick Lloyd Mortimer, Barrister-at-Law of the Inner Temple, son of the late Rev. M. L. J. Mortimer, Vicar of Norton ; mar. at Norton 18 Oct. 1893 ; lg.

75 :—THOMAS GARMONDSWAY (" Guy ") W., B.A. Cantab. ; born 21 Aug. 1871 ; bap. at Norton ; educated at Marlborough and Trinity College, Cambridge ; lg.

76 :—LUCY ELIZABETH WISE W., born 26 Jan. 1873 ; bap. at Norton ; lg.

77 :—CHARLES ARCHIBALD WISE W., midshipman in the Royal Navy ; born 17 July 1874 ; bap. at Norton ; lg.

78 :—WILFRID INGRAM W., born 20 Feb. 1876 ; bap. at Norton ; lg.

79 :—MARGARET JUSTINA W., born 22 Apr. 1877 ; bap. at Norton ; lg.

80 :—GRACE EVELYN SPENCER W., born 5 July 1880 ; bap. at Norton ; lg.

81 :—Rebecca Hope Gilchrist W., born 9 Jan. 1883;
bap. at Norton; lg.

82 :—Jocelyn Bruce W., born 12 Sep. 1887; bap. at
Norton; lg.

Children of John (63)

83 :—Rebecca Elena W., born 27 Oct. 1873; bap. at
Trinity Ch., Cirencester; lg.

84 :—John Frederick Hulton W., born 6 Feb. 1875;
bap. at St. Paul's, Beckenham; lg.

85 :—Alyne Garmondsway W., born 26 Oct. 1876;
bapt. at Trinity Ch., Cirencester; lg.

86 :—Thomas Reginald W., born 7 June 1878; bap.
at Downton; lg.

87 :—Edmund Gilchrist W., born 25 Aug. 1879;
bap. at Downton; lg.

88 :—Hilda W., born 11 June 1881; bap. at Downton; lg.

89 :—Archibald Ingram Hulton W., born 30 July
1882; bap. at Downton; lg.

90 :—Georgiana Maria Hulton W., born 29 July
1884; bap. at Downton; lg.

91 :—Roger Armstrong W., born 1 Mar. 1888; bap.
at Downton; lg.

92 :—Philip Blethyn Hulton W., born 17 Nov.
1890; bap. at Downton; lg.

93 :—Cerdic William W., born 18 Oct. 1892; bap. at
Downton; lg.

OUTLINE PEDIGREE OF THE WRIGHTSON FAMILY.

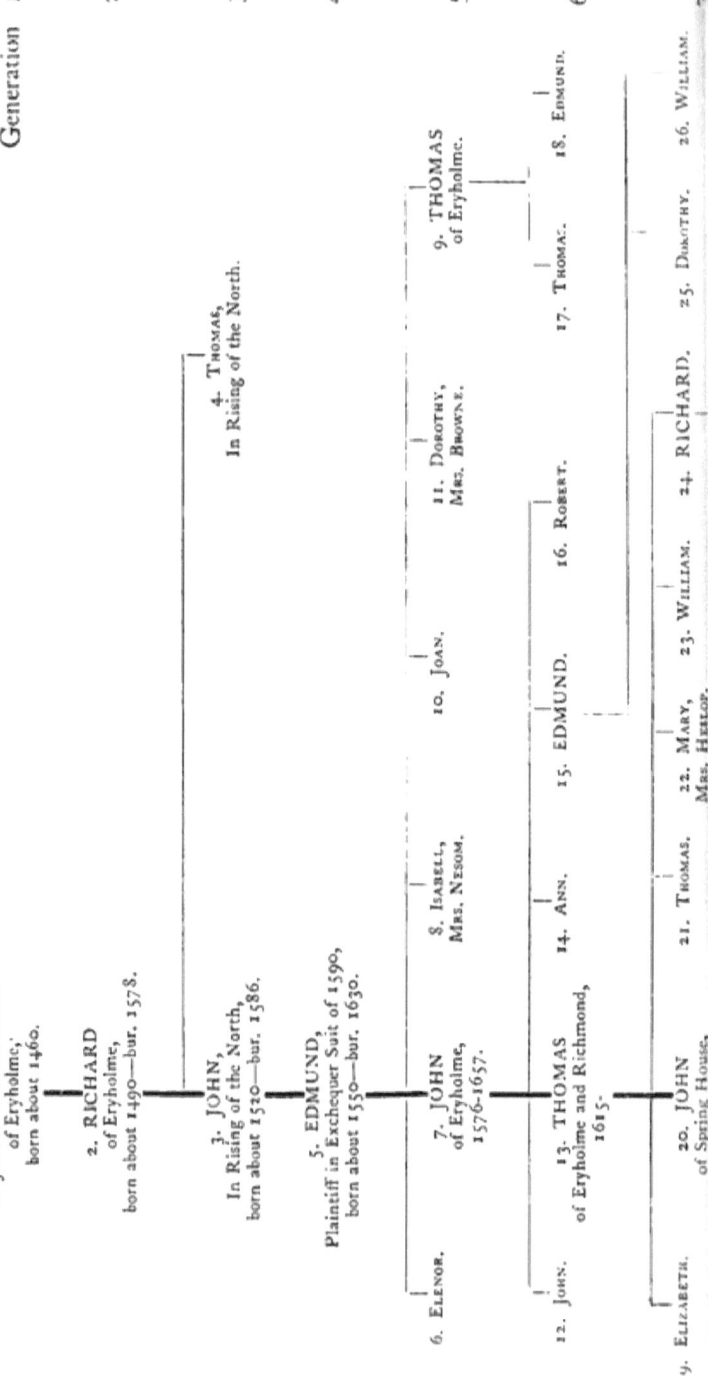

Generation 1

Generation 2

Generation 3

Generation 4

Generation 5

Generation 6

1. JOHN WRIGHTSON of Eryholme; born about 1460.

2. RICHARD of Eryholme, born about 1490—bur. 1578.

3. JOHN, In Rising of the North, born about 1520—bur. 1586.

4. THOMAS, In Rising of the North.

5. EDMUND, Plaintiff in Exchequer Suit of 1590, born about 1550—bur. 1630.

6. ELENOR.

7. JOHN of Eryholme, 1576-1657.

8. ISABELL, MRS. NESOM.

9. THOMAS of Eryholme.

10. JOAN.

11. DOROTHY, MRS. BROWNE.

12. JOHN.

13. THOMAS of Eryholme and Richmond, 1615-.

14. ANN.

15. EDMUND.

16. ROBERT.

17. THOMAS.

18. EDMUND.

19. ELIZABETH.

20. JOHN of Spring House,

21. THOMAS.

22. MARY, MRS. HESLOP.

23. WILLIAM.

24. RICHARD.

25. DOROTHY.

26. WILLIAM.

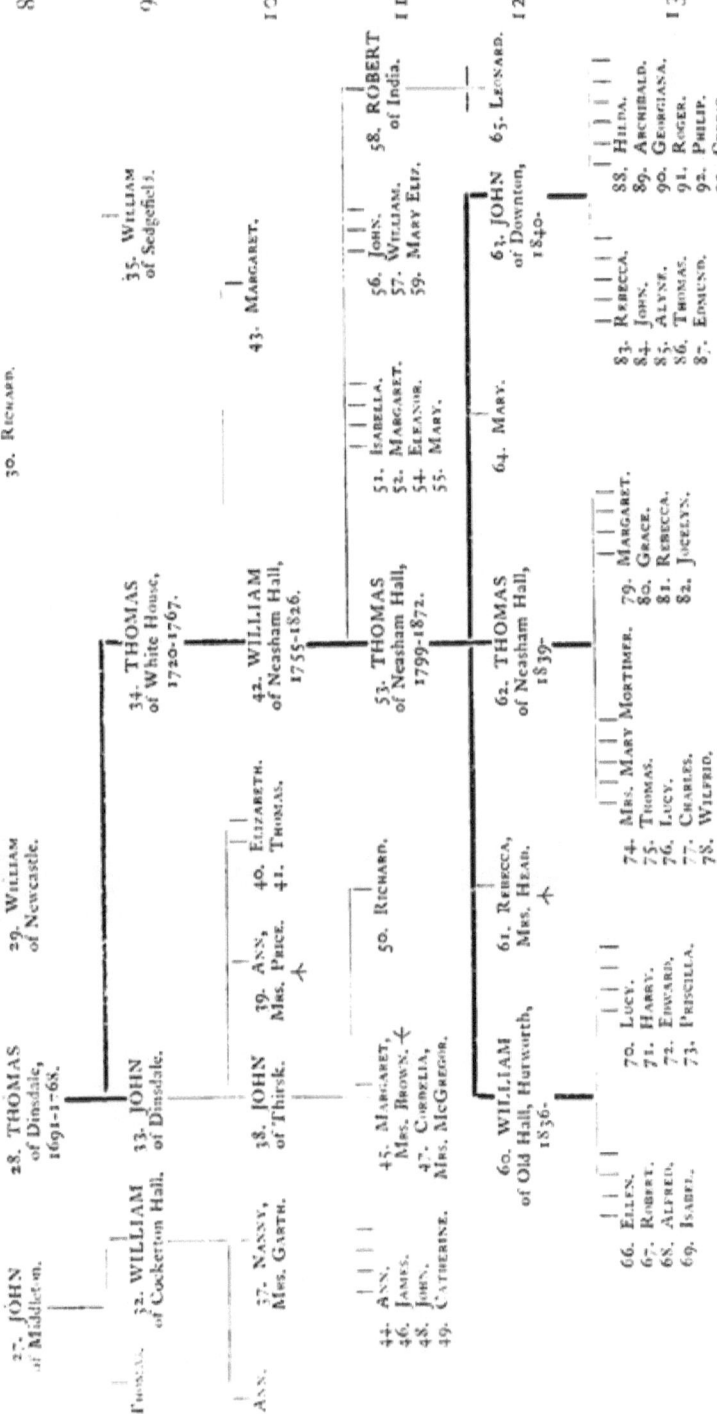

FAMILY OF WRIGHTSON.

THE earliest known records of our family carry our thoughts to Eryholme. It is a small township with a hamlet of the same name, lying on the Yorkshire side of the river Tees, just opposite to Hurworth and Neasham, two very pretty villages in the county of Durham, some three miles from Darlington. The Neasham ford, which at one time served as an important passage between the north and south of England, crosses into Eryholme; and this was the place where each newly appointed Prince Bishop used to enter the County Palatine, and where, surrounded by a vast crowd of mounted gentry, the lord of Sockburn used to discharge his feudal obligation by presenting to the Bishop the dragon-slaying falchion of the doughty Conyers.[1] Bridges and

[1] See Longstaffe's *Hist. of Darlington*, pp. 143, 144.

railways have however turned the currents of life into other channels, and as seen now on a summer's day, Eryholme is one of the greenest, quietest, and most out-of-the-way places to be found in a busy neighbourhood.

In far away mediæval times the Manor belonged to that important family of Markenfield which was finally ruined during the reign of Elizabeth through its participation in the great anti-Protestant "Rising of the North." So closely is the fate of this family associated with our own domestic story, that a brief sketch of its fall and of the abortive insurrection is almost essential to the comprehension of our earlier records: and given at this point such a sketch will be found to contribute largely to the perspicuity of my after narrative.

The Markenfields [1] were one of the oldest of our great Yorkshire county families. Their chief residence was at Markenfield Hall near Ripon, which was built in the reign of Edward II. by John de Markenfield, Chancellor of the Exchequer. I find this family holding lands at Eryholme in 1428; and, after that, in many other places along the south bank of the Tees as far as Romaldkirk. Sir Ninian Markenfield was one of the most prominent warriors at the great battle of Flodden-field in 1513, and it was on that occasion that he received knighthood. As his

---

[1] Authority I.

eldest son married a sister of the celebrated Richard
Norton of Norton-Conyers, his (Sir Ninian's)
grandsons had for their uncle the most ardent
champion of the so-called Catholic party to be
found among the gentry in the north of England.
It is indeed to the personal influence of this uncle
that I ascribe in no small degree the ruin of his
nephews, and through them the earliest known
misfortunes of our family.

However the case may have stood elsewhere,
our northern counties were slow to get into sympathy with the changes effected during the period
of the Reformation.   Except in the bustling little
towns of the West Riding, where persecuted
Protestants from the Netherlands had settled,
there was but little interest felt in the doctrinal
teachings of the Reformers.   The higher and
broader aspects of the change were as yet invisible
to the uneducated and half barbarous inhabitants.
To the vast majority of these the Reformation
meant the ruthless destruction of magnificent and
hospitable Abbeys, and the transfer of Church
property from kindly and considerate to hard and
grasping landlords: it meant the scornful attack
on ideas, ceremonies, and even amusements, en-
compassed by the halo of far and affectionate association : it meant the establishment of a new and
therefore distasteful order of worship, forced on
the acceptance of parishioners in stripped and dis-
figured churches under penalties, which, during
the latter half of Elizabeth's reign, included
ruinous fines, deprivation of property and work,

and even long years of imprisonment in loathsome dungeons like the Kidcotes on York bridge or the Block-house at Hull. Even in the time of Henry VIII. the indignation of the North-country folk led them to rally round the banner of the " five wounds" and join in the Pilgrimage of Grace; but by the eleventh year of the reign of Elizabeth the accumulated forces of discontent had attained a power sufficient, if wisely directed, to have upset the government and, for a time at least, to have restored the old form of religion.

The claim of Mary Stuart, Queen of Scots, to the English throne is well known; and it was round her that the enthusiasm of the Catholics and their well-wishers surged up in innumerable intrigues and plots. As early as 1564 the curse of God and of the Pope was threatened against all who would not assist by money or otherwise the cause of Mary Stuart. A few years later her greatest enemy, the Regent Murray, travelled north from London bearing on his person documents which it was of the utmost importance to the Queen of Scots to have captured or destroyed. He seems at one time to have intended to cross the Tees at Neasham ford, for it was said to have been somewhere " about Northallerton " (as Eryholme might roughly be described to be) that the Nortons, Markenfields, and some others, arranged to kill him,—as was soon after done by Hamilton of Bothwellhaugh. The whole country was indeed on the verge of an explosion, when the de-

feated and beautiful Queen of Scots was brought,
virtually as a captive, to Bolton Castle scarce
fifteen miles south of the river Tees. Her arrival
there precipitated matters, and brought about
a catastrophy of which the details must be read in
history. By far the most vivid narrative I know
is that by Mr. Froude in his History of England.[1]
That brilliant and picturesque historian seems
actually to lead one into the circle of impetuous
young gentlemen,—the romantic and impassioned
knights-errant of the warlike north. We see
them hovering round, or seeking to gain admittance to the now famous castle; while he, who
could catch a kind glance or kinder word, became
for evermore the slave of one, whose rank and
beauty—whose abilities and woes—still render it
impossible to regard her with the calm eye of dis-
passionate justice. Conspicuous among these
brave young gallants were the sons of old Richard
Norton and their cousins the two Markenfields, of
whom John was but a boy still in his teens. By
the aid of Mr. Froude we can watch young Kit
Norton winning his way into the bewitching presence of the captive Queen: and, in the gloom of
the long past wintry day, we too can stand within
the castle hall; and, while servants arrange the
dishes and custodians are absorbed in a game of
chess, we see him at her side,—nay, actually holding her embroidery, while with soft skeins of silk
and softer eyes she binds the hands and heart of

[1] See also Surtees' *Hist. of Durham* (General History),
vol. i.

the poor youth, who two years later will lie beneath the executioner's knife at Tyburn for her sake.

If at this time the weak and hesitating Duke of Norfolk had boldly unfurled his banner as the champion and the husband of Mary Stuart, he would soon have had a gallant army at his back, and there can be scarce a doubt would have succeeded in placing her upon the English throne. But after exhibiting a hesitation almost equal to his own, Elizabeth was roused at last to a full sense of the need for action. She struck hard and quick. Norfolk was clapped into the Tower, and Mary Stuart removed from Bolton. The plot for the restoration of the old religion was however not yet extinguished. It still smouldered; and finally burst into flames, when (either by way of testing their loyalty or securing their persons) Elizabeth summoned to Court the disaffected Earls of Northumberland and Westmorland. On the 10th November 1569 the former virtually gave the signal. Accompanied by Norton, Markenfield, and others, he at once united himself with Westmorland; and in a few days they entered Durham and called the north to arms. With small effort we can realize the scene in Durham cathedral, when, in the fading light of that winter's day, there rolled up beneath its echoing arches the tramp of the armed multitude surrounding the two Earls, and headed by old Richard Norton, with a great gold crucifix hung round his neck and in his hands the long-preserved banner of the Pilgrimage of Grace with its cross, and streamers, and five wounds. The next day they moved south to Darlington, gathering force like a snow-ball; and at cross-road and village green, in town hall and in pulpit, made known their purpose to the world. A few days later their advanced horse were well across the Ouse; and they actually got within little more than fifty miles of where the Queen of Scots was lodged. Her liberation from Elizabeth was indeed the achievement on which success depended, for the possession of her person would have brought many of the most powerful members of the nation into the Earls' camp. But such was not to be the case. Another day or night and the rescue of the illustrious captive would have been attempted; but on the 23rd of November a courier dashed in from London, and the orders which he bore swept Mary Stuart beyond the reach of friendly hands, and virtually sealed the fate of the great Rising of the North. After a few days' pause the Earls and all their followers turned back upon their steps. Those, who still clung to Lord Westmorland, achieved a temporary success in driving Sir George Bowes out of Barnard Castle, and for a few more days retained possession of the fords across the Tees. But the rebellion was seen to be a failure; and, as the forces of Elizabeth approached, all its most conspicuous leaders fled, leaving their unhappy followers helpless and scattered over the whole country side.

The chief representative of the Government in the disturbed districts was the Earl of Sussex, Lord President of the Council of the North; but by far its most active partizan was the above mentioned Sir George Bowes[1] of Streatlam Castle and of South Cowton near Eryholme,—father-in-law to Mr. Conyers of Sockburn, whose younger brother Robert and nephew John Sayer of Worsall were both among the rebels. Although surrounded on every side by the retainers of the Earls, Bowes made his mind up at the very commencement of the Rising; and it was in recognition of his great services that he was made Provost Marshal of the North.

Never in her life did Queen Elizabeth exhibit herself in a more repulsive aspect than after the collapse of this rebellion. The magnitude of her late danger is her sole excuse. Amidst the thirst for vengeance, her constitutional avarice is seen at its very worst. Death by martial law would not touch property, but she was bent on securing forfeitures. Hence the declaration of her pleasure that neither the Earl of Sussex nor Sir George Bowes should execute any freeholder or wealthy person. Among the rest Bowes was, within certain limits, left to use his own discretion as to the selection of victims for execution.[2] By the 23rd January 1569-70 he reported that he had put six hundred to death, besides those disposed of by Lord Sussex: and yet Elizabeth's vengeance

[1] See Surtees' *Hist. of Durham*, vol. iv, pp. 101-18.
[2] Authority IV.

was not appeased. Froude speaks of her, as "possessed by a temper unlike any which she ever displayed before or after." In February the Crown Prosecutor was obliged to tell her plainly that, if she were obeyed, many places would be left naked of inhabitants, and that she would do well to grant a general pardon.

The family of Markenfield was of course entirely ruined; and its many estates reverted to the Crown. Its two rebel brothers are alone possessed of any interest to us. The last I see of John is in Durham gaol, where he lies a prisoner in the hands of Sir George Bowes. Mr. Froude says he had "some right in the estates,"—I presume some reversionary interest in the family property,—and that he "was attainted only to bring his title to his brother's lands to the Queen." About the same time Thomas, the head of the doomed family, is to be seen flying towards Scotland. The Nortons and he are in a party which gradually dwindles down to some twenty men and three ladies,—forlorn fugitives, riding through cutting wind and driving snow into the Debateable Land, where they spend their dismal Christmas in the dens and lurking places of such outlaws and moss-troopers as Black Ormiston (one of the murderers of Darnley) and John o' the Side, at whose vile abode the unhappy ladies were robbed of their horses. Thomas Markenfield is next encountered in company with the Earl of Westmorland at Fernihurst, the stronghold of the fierce Kers near Jedburgh; and the last glimpse I catch of him is on the Continent in the service of the King of Spain.

Although in their time the Markenfields were by far the most distinguished people connected with Eryholme, yet among the actual residents the family of Wrightson was the most important. It is indeed a very old family in the sense of having been in possession of landed property for a very long time; and the legal documents connected with that possession afford not only proofs of descent, but also supply evidence of relative social position. For example, in the year 1570 official lists were made both of the freeholders and the copyholders of the manor of Eryholme, and it is the same aged member of our family who ranks first in each list. Again, as both his eldest son and eldest grandson came into possession of neighbouring properties otherwise than through their wives, it is (in absence of any record of purchase) almost certain that these properties had been derived from Wrightsons of whom I as yet know nothing. The lands that I have discovered as formerly belonging to our family in Eryholme may have amounted to 600 acres, and in the adjoining township to nearly 300 more; so that, if some common ancestor held the greater part of this, he must have been a substantial man of considerable importance in so retired a locality. "At the beginning of the fifteenth century, according to Fortescue, almost every small village had its

knight, squire, or frankelyn,—the last a substantial freeholder who ploughed his own acres,
bore his own produce to market, mustered the
young men of the parish to the customary exer-
cises of the long bow, lived without wish for
London life, but was on the whole content with
the career which the village, the manor courts,
and the commission of the peace afforded him." [1]
The frankelyns occupied that social zone which
lay immediately below, and not infrequently rose
into that of the so-called County Families. Below them came the yeomanry. At the present
day the frankelyns would be described as "country
gentlemen," or as "gentlemen farming their own
land;" but they were of immensely more importance, both politically and socially, when England was almost a purely agricultural country.
It is to this class that I think our mediæval
ancestors,—at all events in the main line,—belonged. But, though many of our standard
families have sprung from the sturdy frankelyn
stock, many of the younger sons passed readily
and naturally into the ranks of the yeomanry.
One of these is the very earliest relative of whom
I have as yet found mention. His name was
Richard Wrightson; and he is referred to in a
De Banco roll of 1459 as "late of Eryholme." [2]
Where he went to, or what became of him, I do
not know; but the fact of his having come from
Eryholme before 1459 proves most conclusively

---

[1] W. Denton's *England in the 15th Century*, p. 250.
[2] Authority II.

that our family must have been settled there at all events as early as the first half of the fifteenth century.

JOHN WRIGHTSON (1) of Eryholme is the first of our family who finds a place in our proved pedigree. He must have been born about 1460 during the Wars of the Roses, something like a quarter of a century before the accession of the House of Tudor; and he owes the preservation of his memory to a law-suit initiated by his great-grandson. So far as I can piece together the fragmentary documents that have come down to us from these far times, it seems that some ancient copyholds had lapsed into the hands of the Markenfields as lords of the manor of Eryholme. Such a circumstance is not surprising, when we remember the awful destruction of life that went on almost continuously during the hundred and eighty years following on the death of Edward I. The Wars of the Roses, which lasted about thirty years, are supposed directly or indirectly to have destroyed one tenth of the population. This civil war had been preceded by the Hundred-years War with France. And this again had been preluded by the terrible invasions of the victorious Scots. But great as was the mortality wrought by war, it was small compared with that arising from more than twenty outbreaks of the plague; of which one, known as the Black Death, is actually reckoned to have carried off over half the population of England in a single

ear.   During the whole of the sad period, of
which I speak, our previously prosperous nation
was in a state of decay, and nowhere more so
than in our northern parts.   After the disastrous
defeat at Bannockburn there were many fearful
invasions of the Scots.   At one time Northallerton
and Ripon were sacked.   At another the Earl of
Murray and James Douglas came to Darlington,
and from thence went forth to waste the country,
—the one towards Hartlepool and Cleveland, and
the other towards Richmond.   The marches of
the two warring kingdoms were reduced at length
to a state of destitution like that in the time of
William the Norman.   I have read that the
famine was so terrible that children were eaten
by their parents, and " thieves that were in prison
did pluck in pieces those that were newly brought
among them, and greedily devoured them half
alive."   The old twelfth century church at Eryholme used to present the appearance of the
patched-up ruins of some once larger edifice.
When in 1889 it was renovated, the whitewash
was cleared from the old arches, and the rough
floor lowered some sixteen inches to what had
been its original level.   The contractor told me
that there were many marks of fire, not only on
the arches, but also between the more recent and
more ancient pavement, for between these he
found various fragments of charred beams mingled
with what seemed human bones.   These remains
have now been swept away; but in the fact of
their recent presence I seem to discern the dim

outline of a fearful tragedy, when the church had been the last refuge for the villagers, and had then been burnt above their heads.

With the memory of such historical circumstances before our minds we cannot wonder that, in the period before our family first comes in sight, large numbers of copyholds fell, simply for want of claimants, into the hands of the lords of the manors.[1] But when a copyhold, or customary tenure, had vanished, and the underlying freehold had reverted to the lord, he might, if he chose, at any time regrant it,—not as a new copyhold, but on exactly the same terms as those on which it had been previously held. In respect of such a voluntary grant there was however full discretion given in fixing the amount of the admission fine; and thus the lord had a means for adjusting any change of value that had grown up through change of times.[2] The most natural explanation of the earliest known circumstance in our family history, is that the Markenfields had become possessed of some of the ancient copyholds on their manor of Eryholme. These may have been in their hands, as part of their freehold, for a hundred years or more; but now, swayed probably by a desire to rectify some boundary, Sir Ninian Markenfield (who became lord in 1497) determined to regrant a part of this copyhold land to our ancestor John Wrightson, receiving in return

[1] I think it probable that the Eryholme Court Roll perished, like many others, during this troublous period.

[2] Authority V, Obs. 2.

(doubtless as the substantial portion of the admittance fine) a fraction of the freehold land already held by the said John Wrightson. The copyhold, which thus passed to the Wrightsons, is described as " a fourth part of all those lands called Westfield," for which, in lieu of the old villein service, a payment of "thirty five shillings" a year was rendered. A fourth part of what now bears the name of Westfield in Eryholme falls not far short of a hundred acres; and, though I have no means for recovering the old boundary lines, I am willing provisionally to assume this as the area of John Wrightson's copyhold.

RICHARD WRIGHTSON (2) was the son and heir of the aforesaid John. In the Homberston survey, made when he was an old man in the time of Elizabeth, he stands at the head of both the freeholders and copyholders of Eryholme. His freehold is described as " one tenement built, with divers lands, meadows, and pastures, which the said Richard holds freely by charter in free socage by the service of — part of one knight's fee, and renders therefor by the year at the feast of Martin only three shillings and four pence,"—a quit-rent which I take to be the ancient commutation into money of the still more ancient feudal obligation of military service. His copyhold consisted of the previously mentioned quarter of the Westfield estate. It is almost certain that he had no more than two sons: and it is in connection with these that what little more I know about him comes to light.

JOHN WRIGHTSON (3), the elder of these two sons of Richard, is one of the persons already referred to (p. 72), as affording indirect evidence of the existence of otherwise unknown relatives. During his father's lifetime he came into possession of, and in 1562 sold, nearly two hundred acres of land in North Cowton.[1] That he did not acquire it by marriage is clear, for the warrant on the sale is made out, not as against the heirs of his wife, but as against his own heirs : and, if he had purchased it himself, the record of such a purchase could hardly have escaped my search. His case is paralleled by that of his son Edmund,[2] who came into possession of another North Cowton farm of more than a hundred acres. It is almost certain that these two properties were derived from some dying-out branch of the Wrightson family connected with, or residing in, North Cowton, a township which approaches within a mile and a half of the Westfield of Eryholme. The particular John Wrightson, of whom I am speaking, is the ancestor, who beyond all others plunged his family in misfortune, but who is nevertheless an object of continuing interest. His life was cast amidst most perilous and perplexing circumstances, and unfortunately he took a wrong, though by no means a dishonourable

---

[1] Authority III.   [2] Authority VII.

course. We must remember that he was born
before the first abolition of the Pope's authority
in England: and that he was a vigorous young
man when the passions of Yorkshiremen were
roused by the destruction of their glorious
monasteries. His life embraced the whole period
of the English Reformation ; and every known
circumstance concerning him goes to prove that
his sympathies were on the Catholic side. As to
the state of the Church in Eryholme, the registers
show that until 1576 the parish priests retained
the old pre-Reformation title of " Sir,"—for in
the days of chivalry the priest was fellow with the
knight and ranked above the squire. And, when
we remember that the final rupture between the
Pope and Queen did not take place till after the
Rising of the North ; and that, during the earlier
part of Elizabeth's reign, the vast majority of
benefices were held by clergy ill-affected to the
Reformation ; I do not think we shall be wrong,
if we assume Sir Edward Smithson, the parish
priest, to have been one of the old sort,—in secret
sympathy with the Markenfields and with all who
wished for the restoration of the old Church order.
I have already (p. 66) described how that in 1564
the cause of Mary Stuart began to be taken up
with extraordinary vigour by the leaders of the
so-called Catholic interest ; and it was at this very
time, that I find old Richard Wrightson taking
the likewise extraordinary step of settling by some
sort of lease the whole of his property for the next
twenty years upon his younger son. The old man

was evidently preparing for some serious contingencies,—providing against some great danger to the family property ; and this danger was in some way connected with his eldest son, who was nevertheless not to be disinherited. Seen in the light of after events, it seems to me as clear as day that his eldest son (who was now in middle life) had become a dangerously active man among the disaffected, and that the aged father was contriving means to save the property in case of the failure of the plot. As the time for the great Rising of the North drew near, it seems as if the face of young John Markenfield must have become familiar in Eryholme and at Westfield. If it had not been so, I think it would have been difficult to gain, at a somewhat later time, even a moderate credence for the manifestly absurd tale that he had held the property,[1] described in the still earlier Homberston survey as Richard Wrightson's copyhold. At this time John Markenfield was indeed only a boy under twenty years of age; but, as brother of the lord of the manor and as possessing a reversionary interest in the same, he would command an attention altogether disproportionate to his years. From what I gather he was a gallant and impetuous youth ; and I like to think of him at Eryholme pointing (as I am sure he must have often done) to the long flat back of that Pen-hill, which marked where Bolton Castle lay. It is a lofty hill visible from almost every district in the north of York-

---

[1] Authority VI.

shire; and, as he pointed to its far blue outline,
I can imagine him rousing the enthusiasm
of his hearers with such tales of the Royal
Captive there, as he had gathered from his cousin
Kit Norton and other romantic champions of the
Queen of Scots. Some such personal influences
must have been used, for, when the Rebellion
took place, the Markenfields were joined by a
group of brave, if misguided, men from Eryholme. Among these was our ancestor John
Wrightson. The description I have already given
of the Rising of the North enables us fully to
realize his surroundings at the time. We can
think of him amidst that exhilarating rush to
reach the Queen of Scots, and amidst the de-
moralized retreat of the baffled host. For a time
we can only imagine his position; but in the
January of 1569-70 we come full upon him, in
company with John Markenfield and many more,
as a prisoner in Durham gaol.[1] They are all
there in the hands of Sir George Bowes, the
terrible Provost Marshal of the North. But
besides the list of these unhappy captives, there is a
second list preserved at Streatlam Castle, which
contains the names of many more, who (rightly
or wrongly) were believed to have been in some
way parties to the insurrection. In spite of all
old Richard Wrightson's neat arrangements for
securing the family property, this second list
contains the name of his younger son Thomas,
not as a prisoner, but as one who had been

'joined with the rebels at some time during the rebellion.'

One of the most repulsive features to be seen in the civil wars of former times is the fierce and even wolf-like rush invariably made upon the possessions of the vanquished. In respect of what had belonged to the Markenfields, it is obvious that Sir George Bowes was eager to secure their Eryholme property, either as an addition to his neighbouring estate in Cowton, or for his son-in-law at Sockburn. With such an object before his mind it was of course desirable to make out the area of the land affected by the Markenfield attainder as large as possible; and the simple fact of our Westfield property being (through the unfortunately directed caution of old Richard Wrightson) a twenty years' leasehold, may at first have made Bowes honestly imagine it held by lease under Markenfield, and therefore at the close of the lease bound to lapse into the Markenfield's forfeited estate. When we remember that at this very time Bowes received an authority, which placed the lives of both Richard Wrightson's sons entirely at his mercy (p. 70), we can conceive the old man's paralysis of helpless terror on learning that the Provost Marshal was bent on taking possession of his copyhold. What was the use of asserting his rights to the property, if thereby he insured the execution of those he wished to leave it to? In such an evil case, the Wrightsons must have been absolutely helpless in the strong man's hands.

Treating the Wrightson copyhold, as if it were wholly and entirely part and parcel of the forfeited Markenfield estate, Sir George Bowes made use of one of his servants or bailiffs, called Rowland Spence, and so managed that this servant received from the Queen a twenty-one years' lease of the whole of Westfield and much more. Spence was only the stalking-horse of his master; for, after the death of that master, he (to use his own words) declared that he held his lease simply "in trust for the benefit of Sir George Bowes." It is important for us to notice that in the Wrightson family itself there was an interest, which coincided with the wishes of Bowes; for Richard Wrightson's younger son might actually be advantaged by the destruction of the copyhold tenure. He had only the remainder of the twenty years' lease granted to him by his father; and, if a new owner could only be induced to grant him a new and extended lease at the old rent, he would of course secure the possession of the estate for a longer time. I must say I find no trace of Thomas Wrightson himself having acted in any underhand way; but this was the principle on which his wife seems to have managed a nefarious business. According to the statement of Rowland Spence himself, the wife of Thomas Wrightson got at Sir George Bowes, paid him money, and secured an order by which Spence was obliged to let her hold, occupy, and enjoy, the said Westfield property till the end of his lease. By doing this she secured the property on terms, that added ten years to her husband's tenure ; but at the same time she made it extremely difficult, if not impossible, for his family ever to reclaim it again. There is an obscure point of law, of which it is very unlikely any of the Wrightsons of Eryholme ever heard. It is as follows, and has a bearing on the present case. If the lord of a manor (who was in this case the Queen) demised the freehold of a copyhold tenement for a term of years, and the lessee (in this case Rowland Spence) assigned the term to the copyholder, the copyhold interest would be extinguished, and at the expiration of the term of years what had been copyhold would be found to have merged in the freehold of the manor.[1] In this case old Richard Wrightson was really the copyholder ; but, if he was cajoled or terrified into being a party to the new lease granted to Thomas, I assume that such action would suffice to extinguish his customary tenure : and to those, who were ignorant of the terrible danger of his two sons, it would moreover appear incredible that he had ever possessed a customary or copyhold tenure on what he allowed to be treated in such a way. Sir George spared both the brothers.   John lived just long enough to become possessed of,—but hardly to enjoy,—the freehold still belonging to the family at Eryholme ; and Thomas left a will, which, if it had not unfortunately been lost, might not only have thrown some new light on the few facts I have tried to interpret, but also have shown whether he left any children.   There

---

[1] Authority V, Obs. 2.

is one old relic of this time which I do not like to leave unmentioned. It is the silver chalice at Eryholme church, which bears the London Hall-mark for 1570, and the same Maker's-mark as is seen on the chalice at Greatham, county Durham. As I have held the Eryholme chalice in my hand and raised it to my lips, I have felt in touch with my far distant ancestors, when, under the pains and penalties of recusancy, they were forced to drink from that same cup,—for we may be sure that their religious proclivities had not greater licence after participating in the abortive effort to set a Popish Queen upon the throne of Elizabeth Tudor.

EDMUND WRIGHTSON (5), the son and heir of John, was married in 1573 to Isabel Winspere, who was almost certainly the daughter of one of his father's comrades in the then recent rebellion. During his father's lifetime he had come into possession of over a hundred acres in North Cowton; but this he sold in 1575. After his father's death he seems to have entered into quiet possession of whatever remained of the family property. This doubtless consisted of a part, if not the whole, of the old freehold of the Wrightsons mentioned in the Homberston survey. In his will [1] Edmund chances to give the names of some of his fields. I read these names to a very aged resident in Eryholme, but with the exception of one they were all forgotten. This one name

[1] Authority XI.

however the old man remembered to have heard in childhood, as belonging to a field or fields, midway between the present Westfield House and the steep scar or cliff made by the Tees in the Yorkshire banks just opposite to Newbus Grange. If, as is very probable, the Wrightson freehold extended to the brow of the cliff, it assuredly comprised one of the prettiest portions of the township. Unlike his father, Edmund was branded with no stigma of rebellion ; and, having nothing to fear from the scrutiny of his past life, he determined to make an effort to recover the Westfield property. He was supported to some extent by the depositions of the aged Thomas Winspere,[1] who was probably his wife's grandfather, and whose memory of events extended backward to the time of Sir Ninian Markenfield. Edmund filed a Bill of Complaint in the old equity division of the Court of Exchequer,[2] and described therein how that, by virtue of the Exchange of property effected between Sir Ninian Markenfield and his own great-grandfather, this portion of Westfield formed part and parcel, not of the forfeited Markenfield estate, but of that belonging to the Wrightsons. The defendants were at first Rowland Spence and Agnes, now the widow of Edmund's uncle Thomas ; but, as Spence died soon after the commencement of the suit, Agnes Wrightson was left to continue it alone. The absence of any reference to the Court Roll of the manor makes me almost certain it must have

---

[1] Authority IX.   [2] Authority VIII.

perished before that time; although, if it had
been producible, there can be no doubt the copyhold tenure had been extinguished. It had indeed
become freehold, and on all sides it seems to have
been spoken of as such. In absence of the Court
Roll, this is less surprising than might be supposed, for the existence in the north of England
of those so-called tenant-right estates, which were
a sort of customary freeholds, could not do otherwise than tend to blur out the usually clear dis-
tinction between a freehold and a customary
(*i.e.* a copyhold) estate. It would require the aid
of an accomplished legal antiquary to fill up and
interpret the fragmentary records of this suit; but,
so far as I can see, the extinguishment of the
customary tenure would deprive Edmund Wrightson of any real ground of claim. At the same
time I am not sure that I have grasped the whole
bearings of the question; and everything seems
to prove that in his own, and also in his son's
lifetime, Edmund was believed to have a 'case.'
So far as his appeal to the Exchequer was concerned, it was ended after something like a year's
delay, by an Order[1] to the effect that the question
was to be tried in an action of trespass at the next
Assizes. I have as yet found no trace of the con-
tinuance of this particular suit elsewhere; and I
think that a practical acquaintance with the cost
of litigation may have been sufficient to induce
Edmund to leave his aunt in quiet during the few
remaining years of her tenure of the place; just

[1] Authority X.

as, after the close of her lease, he may well have
hesitated about commencing a struggle with the
rich and powerful county family into whose
hands Westfield and the whole of the manor of
Eryholme had passed.

Whatever may have been the aims and hopes
of Sir George Bowes with regard to this manor,
they had been disappointed. For a time Queen
Elizabeth hesitated, but at last ended by bestowing
it, not on Bowes, but on Thomas Calverley,[1]
Chancellor of the county of Durham. He was
a member of that great Yorkshire family,[2]
which was at one time represented by the
infamous man who was slowly " pressed to
death " after murdering his children, and at
a later time by the attractive original of Mr.
Addison's " Sir Roger de Coverley." The son
of Thomas Calverley was Sir John, and the
son of Sir John was John Calverley esquire of
Eryholme. This branch of the Calverley family
seems to have lived chiefly at Littleburn in the
parish of Brancepeth ; but the registers prove that
they must often have resided in the Old Hall at
Eryholme, and the tomb of one of them is in the
church. Of the old Hall, which stood midway
between the church and the ford, there only now
remain a few relics. These consist of some
massive foundations level with the ground, and a
piece of wall, which, while utilized to form the

---

[1] Authority VIII.
[2] See Joseph Foster's *Pedigrees of the Yorkshire County
Families.*

back of some cottages, contains two built-up door-
ways with red stone jambs and lintels of the
Tudor period. There is also a huge barn that
evidently formed part of the outbuildings; and all
is surrounded by a perfect labyrinth of ancient
earthworks, which carry one's thoughts back to
the grim days of northern warfare. I think it
probable that this was one of the gentlemen's
houses which suffered much in the great Civil
War; but in comparatively recent times I am
told that it formed a sort of quarry, from which
materials were drawn for almost any amount of
building in its neighbourhood.

That Edmund Wrightson did not venture to
bring his claims to a legal issue with the Calverleys
is I think clear, both from my failure to discover
any record of his having instituted fresh legal
proceedings, and also from the fact that during
his lifetime his eldest son was living quietly at
Westfield as a tenant of the Calverleys. But,
whatever the losses of our family may have been
through the previous law-suit and misfortunes of
his father, Edmund's will proves that he had not
sunk below the rank of an independent freeholder
of respectable means, for he describes himself as
having already given Portions to his children, and
he leaves his widow provided for out of his landed
property.

JOHN WRIGHTSON (7), the eldest son of
Edmund, and his younger brother Thomas both
lived at Eryholme. If I may judge from the

little I know of their conduct, they were ill-
pleased at their father's apparent acquiescence in
the loss of the Westfield property. Speaking of a
time before the old man's death, Sir John Calverley represents John Wrightson as occupying
the said property at a certain rent, although (for
reasons on which he does not choose to enter) the
farm was " of far greater " annual value than the
said rent. He then goes on to tell how that soon
after the father's death, not only was he unable
to obtain any rent, but that, when he tried to
induce the elder brother to deliver up the premises,
' the said John Wrightson by the animation of the
said Thomas Wrightson utterly refused to do so.'
The contention between the lord of the manor
and the two brothers became so violent, that in
1632 Calverley filed a Bill of Complaint in the
Court of Exchequer ; and it is from this Bill that
I gain my information.[1] This action on the part
of Sir John Calverley seems to have had the effect
of checking the brothers in what was really a very
rash course of conduct ; for, though I have
searched through the whole of the Exchequer
Decrees, Orders, and Depositions for Yorkshire
to the end of the 10th of Charles I., I have failed
to discover any further reference to the above
matter of dispute. But though the Wrightsons
appear to have felt themselves unequal to the
prosecution of a costly suit, yet there is an almost
certain proof that the Calverleys had found it
advisable to look into and place on record their

[1] Authority XII.

title to the land; for they hunted up the Homberston survey, and after the death of Sir John Calverley his eldest son had the part concerning his Eryholme property copied into the Roll known as the Queen's Remembrancer, where it may still be seen with a note stating that it had been entered there " at the instance of John Calverley esquire." [1] I think this extract from the old survey would be enough to prove how that, by the destruction of the copyhold tenure, our Westfield property had really become part of the estate of the Calverleys. They were in no sense to blame for the way in which our rights had been destroyed; but there is a most singular piece of evidence as to the popular judgment and sympathy having been on our side. The same hand, which in and about 1690 made various regular entries in the Eryholme registers, has added sundry notes to several earlier entries. Perhaps the most curious of these notes is one appended to the burial register [2] of Edmund Wrightson in 1630. It runs as follows :—" who ought [? to have had] ye Freehold now Lister's and Rickaby's and was cheated out of it after. Qr. They have a bad Title."

Up to this point our family history has been compiled exclusively from documents, which during many years I have discovered in various places : but what I have last told dovetails most

---

[1] "Memorandum Roll, Queen's Remembrancer, Hilary Term, 12 Chas. I. [1637]. Roll No. 17." Pub. Rec. Office.
[2] Authority XXXIII.

beautifully into the earliest portion of previously known family tradition.

There exist three copies, or rather three slightly different editions, of a Domestic pedigree[1] of our family. The earliest of these was made in 1800 by John Wrightson of Dinsdale, the very aged grandson of one whom we always remember as John Wrightson of Spring House: and the latest was copied by my father about 1815. Each of these pedigrees is prefaced by an almost, but not quite, identical paragraph, recording what is simply traditional. It is in this paragraph that we come unmistakably in contact with the two Eryholme brothers, who about 1630 had the contention with Sir John Calverley, lord of the manor, touching the Westfield property.

" Tradition," says the earliest of these pedigrees, "goes no further back than about the year 1620 or 30, when Two Brothers were living at Eryholme in Yorkshire. The elder lost a pretty estate there by contending with the lord of the manor: married and left two sons, John owner of Spring House and Richard the younger who died young at sea.—The younger Brother went as a Captain in King William's expedition to Ireland; married there, from whom sprang Alderman Wrightson of Dublin's family.—So far tradition only."

The memory of the aged writer of the above traditional paragraph was clearly at fault; both in respect of John Wrightson of Spring House, who

[1] Authorities XXIX, XXX, XXXI.

was the grandson, and not the son, of the elder of the two Eryholme brothers; and also in respect of the younger of the brothers, who, living at Eryholme "about the year 1620 or 30," could not possibly have gone in 1690 to fight and get married in Ireland. But at the same time it is obvious that the old man was placing on record a true picture of what remained on his mind from the talk of those who had long passed away. Indeed the inaccuracies of his detail go to confirm the general faithfulness of his impression.[1]

[1] If I had succeeded in proving the connection between our family and that of the Dublin Alderman, this is the point at which I should have introduced in smaller type a not uninteresting sketch of "The Irish Wrightsons." But, though our own proved pedigree supplies no trace of evidence in support of the thrice repeated tradition of relationship, yet such is not the case with the Irish pedigree (see Appendices A and B). In that pedigree we see the great-grandfather of the Dublin Alderman is an Anthony Wrightson, who in 1613 was in the service (probably as Steward or Estate Agent) of a certain Richard Aldborough of Ellingthorpe Hall, about half a mile from the residence of William Aldborough of Aldborough Hall near Boroughbridge. Now the eldest son of this latter gentleman was the Arthur Aldborough who from 1607 to 1612 owned, and I believe lived on, my property at Middleton-one-Row. He must have become acquainted with many people in our neighbourhood, and one of his sisters married the Rector of Long Newton. Hence I have discovered a ready means by which some member of our family (most likely living outside of Eryholme) might be introduced to a situation on the Ellingthorpe estate. Such a discovery lends no inconsiderable support to the traditional relationship first placed on record by John Wrightson of Dinsdale,—especially when we bear in mind that, after his death, his grandson was received as a relation by the family of the Alderman. The absence of the name of Anthony from our proved pedigree ought to occasion no surprise, inasmuch as we

THOMAS WRIGHTSON (13), the eldest son and heir of the elder of the two Eryholme brothers, was the real father of " John Wrightson of Spring House " : and the father of John Wrightson of Spring House was, according to two of our domestic pedigrees, in " the Army." There was however no regular army in existence at that time in England, so that such a statement, if it be correct, can only mean that he was engaged on one side or the other in the great Civil War of the time of Charles I. Among old members of the family, who have now passed away, I used to hear him spoken of as " Captain Wrightson of Eryholme " ; and my father has often described to me various old weapons said to have belonged to him. One of these was just such a long straight cut-and-thrust sword, with a profusion of guards around the hilt, as I have seen in collections of weapons dating from that time. These so-called relics of his ancestor were often examined by my father when he was a boy ; but they were put aside as being dangerous, and then entirely lost sight of during the engrossing troubles of my grandfather's declining years. My father often referred to the day-dreams roused by these ; and he loved to associate them with Cromwell and his Ironsides, with Marston and with Naseby. With such long past talk still fresh upon my memory, I was one day startled by coming across the name of a Wrightson, who had been Quarter-

know few of those far distant names, save such as chance to be preserved in the old legal documents I have discovered.

Master to the Lord Protector's own immortal
Regiment of Horse : he was however not one of
our family, but a Richard Wrightson of Beverley,[1]
whose will was proved in London in 1657.
Such military traditions nevertheless fit perfectly
with all the facts I have discovered concerning
the father of John Wrightson of Spring House. A
reference to our proved pedigree will show that
he was, as I have before said, a Thomas Wrightson,
who was just seven-and-twenty years of age at the
outbreak of the war, and who did not marry till
1649, when, by the execution of the King, the
war seemed to have been terminated.   Even
if the misfortunes and impoverishment of his
family did not impel him to join the discontented
portion of the nation, there were both inducements
and opportunities afforded for enlistment at Eryholme.   Mr. Markham, in the eighth chapter of
his *Life of Fairfax*, tells us that in November
1642 young John Hotham, Sir Matthew Boynton,
Sir Henry Foulis, and Sir Hugh Cholmley, were
raising troops for the Parliament among the
moorland villages of Cleveland and Richmondshire, in which last district Eryholme lay.   Co-
incidently with this the Earl of Newcastle was,
according to Longstaffe's *History of Darlington*,
forming the four northern counties into a Royalist
Association.   The line of the Tees inevitably became the scene of various encounters between the

---

[1] A family of Wrightsons lived at Beverley in the 17th
century, and the Testator's mention of a brother there proves
that he belonged to them.

rival parties: and the registers at Eryholme contain some interesting evidences of these earlier struggles in the Civil War. Thus on the 28th November 1642 they record the burial of four Royalist soldiers, for it is specified that they were slain by Mr. Hotham's troop: and the following day there is the burial of one of Mr. Hotham's own men. Indeed the tokens of slaughter do not disappear from Eryholme till just before the Battle of Marston Moor. So far as I can see, there is not the slightest reason to doubt the tradition of this Thomas Wrightson having been a soldier during the great war. What I have learnt about the circumstances of his parish at the time, makes it probable that he fought on the side of the Parliament; but to say more is to trespass on the region of romance. When however I recall the friendliness subsisting afterwards between his family and the Vanes of Long Newton, I like to let myself imagine that he may have served under Sir George, the younger brother of the great and good Sir Harry Vane: and, if so, he is tolerably certain to have taken part in the gallant defence of Raby Castle against the attacks of the Cavaliers. It was, as I have already implied, only a few months after the execution of the king that he was married at Eryholme; but the baptisms of all his earlier children at Richmond prove that he had then removed some ten miles from the ancient family home. The absence of his name from the Richmond burial register however suggests a still later change of residence, although some of his children remained in Richmond all their lives. With him, or at all events in his time, a change in the family fortunes clearly commenced; for, while his father and uncle are seen struggling at Eryholme amidst narrow means with a powerful landowner, his son was in such easy circumstances that he bought my present Spring House farm, and I am told also the adjoining farm of White House, which ultimately descended to my father. It is possible that like many others he may have secured substantial advantages during the war, or there may have been relatives (unmentioned in our pedigree) who had bequeathed money to him or to his children. But whatever may have taken place, it is a fact that from this time forward I find our family overcoming old misfortunes, and rising again in wealth and social consideration.

JOHN WRIGHTSON (20) of Spring House, the eldest son of this our traditionally military Ancestor, was born during the Commonwealth, and had two sisters (of whom one married a Thomas Heslop of Richmond) and several brothers. I have discovered that he was twice married. The maiden name of the second wife was Ann Simpson of Richmond; but the name of the first, from whom we descend, is I think doubtful. In our Domestic Pedigrees (which only mention one marriage) the wife is described as "Ann Heslop from about Richmond." But there is no trace of any such marriage in the

H

Richmond register, though it is complete from the early part of 1680 to the early part of 1691. It seems to me that those, who knew of only one marriage, may very well have placed on record an erroneous compound, consisting of the Christian name of the second wife and the Surname of her husband's brother-in-law Thomas Heslop. The oldest of our Domestic Pedigrees speaks of the three sons of John Wrightson of Spring House as "all born at Maltby in Yorkshire." This place lies within the parish of Stainton-in-Cleveland, and within a short distance of the parish church of Hilton. The old registers of Stainton however do not mention them, and those at Hilton have not been preserved as far back as the date of their births. But, though the Yorkshire home of John Wrightson after leaving Richmond remains uncertain, he, somewhere about the year 1700, removed into South Durham, and settled on the oldest remaining piece of our family property. This is a farm now [1] known as

[1] The oldest title deed of this property is a marriage settlement dated 28 March 1711, in which, under the name of "Hardstones," it is settled on the son and heir of John Wrightson. Hardstones is however the name of the adjoining farm still held by the Vane family in the person of the Marquess of Londonderry. Old Mrs. Hind told me that 'when Spring House first came into possession of my family, it bore the name of Hardstones; but that Mr. Vane induced Mr. Wrightson to change this to Spring House,—a name suggested by the little spring that used to rise in a receptacle at the end of the old vaulted cellar, till my father drained it away.' This change of name must have been before 31 Oct. 1714, for on that date John Wrightson is described as "of Spring House" in the Long

" Spring House " near Sadberge, although at that time always described as " in the parish of Long Newton." The adjoining landowner in that parish was Lionel, the son of the before mentioned Sir George Vane: and I have noticed that in some old parish books it is only to the names of Vane and Wrightson that the title " Mr. " is attached. The two families came to be on such kindly terms that the right-hand seat of the ancient carved oak ' settle '[1] at Spring House was familiarly known as " Mr. Vane's seat ; " and old Mrs. Hind (p. 103) was fond of telling how that, ' when her mistress Mrs. Garth (then Miss Wrightson) was a young lady at a boarding school in Durham, there was only one Sunday that the Vanes did not send their carriage to fetch her to spend the day with them.' Her kind entertainer was most likely Henry Vane, who

Newton registers. I myself feel very confident that Spring House farm originally formed part of Hardstones ; and I think it probable that this part had been sold by Sir George Vane or his son Lionel to my ancestor. The particulars of our acquirement of this property doubtless exist among the Fines, Recoveries, and Feet of Fines for the county of Durham, now at the Public Record Office, and referred to in the Deputy Keeper's Report for 1869, p. 45. But until these are indexed, the labour is too great and the matter too unimportant to justify a search through so vast a pile of ancient documents.

The name " Hardstones " was I believe derived from some huge boulders or blocks of whinstone, long since broken up and carted away.

[1] It was afterwards taken to Cockerton Hall ; and, when it came into my possession, I presented it to my brother Tom, who will doubtless soon remove it from Norton to Neasham Hall along with various other specimens of antique furniture.

was not only Rector of Long Newton but a Prebendary of Durham. After this the Vanes rose into the Peerage, and there was a discontinuance of acquaintance, until my brother Tom's increasing social and political importance brought him into most friendly relations with both the Marquess and Marchioness of Londonderry.

What might be the amount of property held by John Wrightson, besides the Spring House farm, I do not know. White House is an adjoining farm, which Mrs. Hind told me he gave to his second son, who was I know the owner. John Wrightson's brother Thomas left him some more property at Richmond. And when we notice that in Sir Ralph Bigland's pedigree of our family he is described as "of Eryholme," the most natural explanation seems to be that he still possessed some portion of the old Wrightson freehold there. He died in 1723; and soon after that time his descendants are found, for about a century, to be divided into three branches, of which the eldest and also the second in seniority died out, leaving it to the third or junior branch to continue the family name.

THE FIRST EXTINCT BRANCH OF THE FAMILY.

JOHN WRIGHTSON (27) of Middleton-one-Row, son and heir of John of Spring House, stands at the head of this earliest extinct branch of our family. He was born in Yorkshire, but was brought as a boy to his father's new home in South Durham. In 1711 he married Margaret, one of the co-heiresses of a Mr. Thomas Robinson of Middleton-one-Row, a very lovely village in the parish of Middleton St. George, county Durham. It was in connection with this marriage that his father settled the farm, soon afterwards named Spring House, upon him. From the time of his marriage to his death it is clear that he preferred Middleton as a residence; for, even after he came into possession of Spring House, it was occupied by another person, either as tenant or bailiff. He died in 1727, and it cannot have been long after that event that Thomas (31), the elder of his two sons, went to live at Spring House, for in 1734 we find him mentioned as Churchwarden of Long Newton. This Thomas has always been remembered with affection. He was a man of deep piety; and the strong interest in the Church, ever afterwards evinced by this branch of our family, may well have first been roused by his example. I have spent many hours in the library at Long Newton Rectory examining the records of old parochial doings; and it gave me much pleasure to see how, after the early death of this Thomas Wrightson, both his remaining brother and my own great-grandfather co-operated with their Rector in all good works.

WILLIAM WRIGHTSON (32) of Cockerton Hall was the younger of the two children of the above John Wrightson of Middleton-one-Row. After the death of his elder brother, he became owner of all that had belonged to this branch of the family, and was in very easy circumstances. Somewhere about the year 1745,—the year of the last Scotch rebellion,—he married Ann, a daughter of the Rev. Thomas Beckett, who from 1722 had been Rector of Kirby Wiske. It was, I believe, in the following year that he purchased the Cockerton Hall estate near Darlington, and settled there for the rest of his life. He lived to the great age of ninety-three, and was buried at Long Newton.

NANNY WRIGHTSON (37), best remembered as Mrs. Garth, was the only surviving daughter and sole heiress of her father William Wrightson of Cockerton Hall. She received a good education at a once well-known school in Durham, and on her return home found herself welcomed in all the best society of the neighbourhood. She had various offers of marriage; but, after the death of her mother, she devoted herself with the tenderest love to the care of her father. It was not till she was above forty years of age that she married an old Mr. Garth, who, though himself a man of good fortune, was willing to take up his abode at Cockerton Hall, and leave his wife free to continue her prolonged labour of filial love. He only survived her father by about four months, and then Mrs. Garth found herself alone in the world. She shrank from society, and cultivated a privacy of life that became at last almost conventual. As a widow she was perhaps the wealthiest lady to be found in the neighbourhood of the then little country town of Darlington ; and I have heard it said, that hers was one of the two carriages which used then to be seen in its few streets. She possessed all that had belonged to her father, mother, and husband ; and was thus in the enjoyment of nearly 2,500 acres of land, with houses, cottages, and at least £15,000 of investments. Being childless, her power of disposal extended only to what had been derived from her father, whilst the rest had to revert at her death to the families from which it had originally come. For many years her annual income much exceeded her expenditure, and this enabled her to exercise to an unusual extent the natural generosity of her disposition. As an illustration of her conduct, George Hind loved to relate how she dealt with a farm derived from her husband. A man, already somewhat advanced in life, had the reversion of this property ; but she chanced to hear he was in narrow circumstances, and made up her mind to transfer it to him at once. All necessary legal steps were taken. George was ordered to mount his horse. The title deeds were placed in his pocket ; and he was sent off to the poor man with the message that, 'Mrs. Garth thought he needed them more than she !' The Church, the local charities, and the poor around, all found in her a benefactor ; and, in spite of the privacy of her life, she was universally regarded with gratitude and admiration. It is sad to record that a woman of this sort was almost estranged from her nearest relatives. On several occasions she expressed the warmest appreciation of my father ; but unfortunately my grandfather had twice come into such violent collision with the wishes of old Mr. Wrightson of Cockerton, that a breach was opened which never closed again. I do not think that Mrs. Garth ever crossed the threshold of Neasham Hall, or did more than receive a few formal visits from its occupants. The only persons, who really knew her intimately during her declining years, were Jane Fenny and George Hind, her favourite maid and honest man-servant. They became the confidants of her anxieties and thoughts to a degree that would have been dangerous with less trustworthy and devoted servants. A wave of renewed ill-fortune was at that time sweeping over our family, and she felt it keenly. In that family, she, an old and childless widow, was the sole surviving member of the eldest branch : the second branch was represented by Richard, a childless drunkard : and the third, as represented by my father, was seen to be involved in almost hopeless financial difficulties. Great was her perplexity of mind as to the direction of that part of her property over which she had control. For long the balance of decision wavered ; but at last it turned against my bravely struggling, though apparently sinking, father. Richard was sent for ; and it was soon known in whose favour the will was made. Mrs. Garth died at Cockerton Hall on the 1st December 1829. Great crowds attended her funeral, testifying thereby the esteem in which she had been held. " It was an affecting sight," writes my father ; " but to no one more so than to myself, for I knew the change which would take place at Cockerton Hall. I truly was the chief mourner who followed good Mrs. Garth to the tomb ! " She was laid beside her husband in his vault directly under the graceful spire of the old church at Darlington. When the will was opened, it was found that, with the exception of some large legacies, all was left to Richard Wrightson ; although, failing issue from him, the Spring House and Middleton properties were my father's in reversion.

George Hind and Jane Fenny had legacies from their late mistress of a thousand pounds a-piece. They soon after married ; and, with the assistance of some borrowed money, purchased a conveniently situated little farm of about a hundred acres on Haughton Moor, to which they gave the name of Haughton Grange. A few years later my father went to reside a mile south of this in the village of Haughton le Skerne ; and it was not long before George and Jane became very much attached to him. The deep sorrow of George at the effects of Mrs. Garth's will, and his devotion to her family, caused him (after the death of his two little girls) to leave the reversion of his moiety of Haughton Grange to my father,—and so to me. He died the 29th August 1866 aged 77, and his will was proved at Durham 28th February 1867. After the death of my father, who outlived George by about six years, I took care that everything was done for the comfort of old Mrs. Hind. I was seldom able to see her more than once a year; but on these occasions I generally remained for several hours. Such visits were largely occupied in talking over long passed family events. Her memory seemed to have absorbed, and indeed wholly occupied itself with the interests and conversations of her venerated mistress and benefactor: and it is from the stores of her wonderfully retentive memory that I have learned some of the facts embodied in these memorials of our family. She died 15th July 1880 in her 88th year; and her will was proved at Durham on the 27th of the same month. It was through this will that, after paying certain legacies, I came to possess the whole of Haughton Grange. But I am glad that in leaving this property to me, Mrs. Hind has taken care to state her reason for so unusual an act on the part of an old servant. Both the act and words reflect honour on a family which could thus awaken an almost feudal spirit of devotion. "I devise, bequeath, direct, and appoint," says she in her will, "all the rest, residue, and remainder of my real and personal Estate and effects whatsoever and wheresoever and of what nature, quality, or kind soever, to the said William Garmonsway Wrightson his heirs executors administrators and assigns, to and for his own absolute use and benefit in testimony of my respect for and gratitude to his relation the late Mrs. Garth of Cockerton."

The Second Extinct Branch of the Family.

In common with the surviving portion of the family, this second extinct branch descends from Thomas (28) of Dinsdale, the second son of John Wrightson of Spring House; but, inasmuch as this Thomas is on the direct line of continuing life, it is necessary, if I would avoid a dislocation in my narrative, to defer what I have to say about him till I arrive again at the main text of this work. I shall therefore for the present pass on to his eldest son, who was the immediate ancestor of this extinct branch.

JOHN WRIGHTSON (33) of (Over-) Dinsdale, Little Smeaton, and Easingwold, was born under his grandfather's roof at Spring House in 1718; and while still an infant was taken to the new house his father had just built on his property in Over-Dinsdale,—a township in the Yorkshire portion of the Tees-divided parish of Sockburn. At thirty years of age he married Ann Cornforth of Coxhoe near Durham. Her father, I have been told, held the then important and valuable post of Agent to the Dean and Chapter of Durham, and seems to have been living at Coxhoe Hall,—a place which however did not belong to him. It was no doubt in connection with this marriage that John Wrightson was put in possession of the Over-Dinsdale estate belonging to his father. There is at Dinsdale Rectory an old Estate Map of 1756 in which this property is marked as " John Wrightson's." The land extends along the west side of that which bears the name of " Hugill "; and this reminds me that my father used to speak about John Wrightson having been led into injurious extravagance by his friend General Hugill of Hornby Grange. Such an intimacy may well have been either the cause or consequence of this John Wrightson's removal, apparently about 1760, to Little Smeaton within a mile and a half of Hornby Grange; although, by virtue of his own property, he continued still to describe himself as " of Dinsdale." The birth of his youngest child at Little Smeaton was followed so closely by the death of its mother, that there was the touching coincidence of its baptism and her burial on the same day. Although John Wrightson was ultimately brought back to be buried beside his wife at Birkby, all the latter portion of his life was passed, some fifteen miles further south, at Easingwold. So far as I know, he was the first person who interested himself about old family matters; for he was the only member of the family who could have been the writer of our "1800" Domestic Pedigree. Of his four children, the youngest son, Thomas (41), lived as a country lawyer at Easingwold, and was much respected and beloved by all who knew him. The eldest daughter, Ann (39), was married to a Mr. Liscombe Price of Islington near London, the son of a Middlesex County Magistrate; and it was from her great-grandson, Mr. James Dallas, Curator of the Exeter Museum, that I had the loan of the above old Pedigree,—a much valued document, which may well have been compiled at the request of Mrs. Ann Price herself.

JOHN WRIGHTSON (38) of Bedale, Easingwold, and Thirsk, was the eldest son of John of Dinsdale. He was born in 1749, and like his younger brother was a lawyer, though best known as a Coroner for the North Riding. He was settled at

Bedale previous to his first marriage, which was with one of the Mewburns of Croft or Hurworth on Tees,—a family of good position in the neighbourhood. After his second marriage he removed for several years to Easingwold; but at last went to Thirsk, where he remained till his death in 1817. He was a genial, extravagant, and popular man; and was very partial to my father, who as a boy was often invited to stay with him. Of his seven children I need only mention two, viz., Richard and Cordelia.

RICHARD WRIGHTSON (50) of Cockerton Hall was born in 1788, and from 1812 to 1816 was an officer in the North York Militia. During this time he was stationed with his Regiment in Ireland, and while there became acquainted with the family of the late Alderman Wrightson of Dublin. My father says "they called upon him, and claimed relationship. He found them possessed of great wealth and respectability." It is possible that Lady Scott, the daughter of the Alderman, may be referred to; but I think it more probable that he met with her relative, another Richard Wrightson, who about that time held the high, but now abolished, office of Master of Ordnance for Ireland, and was the grandfather of my friend, the present head of the Irish Wrightsons. Poor young Richard of the Militia was naturally of a very amiable and humourous disposition, but was utterly devoid of moral firmness. Habits of intemperance, at first contracted among his gay and reckless brother officers, increased to so terrible an extent, that he became at last a perfect slave to drink,—in fact the one drunkard we have ever had in our family. He was twice married,—first to an Irish girl, and then to a daughter of the Rector of Kilvington near Thirsk. All that had come into his part of the family, either from his great-uncle William Wrightson of Sedgefield or otherwise, had, along with the lovely Dinsdale estate, disappeared amidst extravagance, and Richard found himself in really narrow circumstances. Suddenly, to his great delight and surprise, he and his wife received an invitation to stay for some time with old Mrs. Garth of Cockerton Hall; and the invitation was soon understood to indicate that he was to be treated as her heir. For a short time he was careful in his conduct; but at last there was an uncontrollable outburst, and his sad state was seen and fully realized by Mrs. Garth. It was worse than anything she had imagined; and, as George

Hind told me, "it was too much for her." "I have done wrong," exclaimed she to her two faithful attendants; "all will be ruined,—lost!" She took to her bed. It was too late to alter her will, and she died amidst her agitation on the 1st December 1829. On the 29th of the same month Richard made his afterwards famous will, which left everything, over which he had control, absolutely to his childless wife. Within a year the poor fellow drank himself to death; and in six months more his now wealthy widow was again a wife.

CORDELIA WRIGHTSON (47), who after the death of Richard was the last surviving member of her family, was born in 1784. When her father's establishment at Thirsk was broken up, she accompanied her widowed mother to Edinburgh, and in 1828 married a Scotch lawyer of the name of Patrick McGregor. All seems to have gone on well for some years, until certain suspicious circumstances, touching the making of Richard's will, came to the knowledge of her husband and herself. These circumstances, together with its strange and unusual character, induced them to contest its validity. For many years, in various courts of law, the once famous suit of "McGregor and wife *v.* Topham and wife" dragged on its weary and heart-breaking way,—pouring upon our family a flood of painful notoriety, and involving my dear father in his last heavy pecuniary loss. At length, on the 23rd of July 1850, the celebrated Lord Brougham gave judgment in the House of Lords against McGregor and his wife. They were utterly and entirely ruined by the enormous costs, and both died a few years later dependent on the charity of friends.

THOMAS WRIGHTSON (28) of Over-Dinsdale, White House, and Sedgefield,[1] second son of John of Spring House, is the common ancestor of all the surviving members of our family. He was born in Yorkshire, and the date of his

---

[1] He is also described by Sir Ralph Bigland in our R. B. G. pedigree as "of Aryholme," which may perhaps be taken to indicate that up to his time some portion of the old Eryholme property remained in our family.

baptism, " 15 March 1691," has been recorded
by my grandfather, though I have never yet succeeded in discovering the parish where it took
place. I have heard that his father suffered, I
think from a paralytic stroke; and this probably
accounts for the son continuing to live for some
years after his marriage at Spring House. As a
young bachelor he discharged the duties of Churchwarden at Long Newton, and administered to the
effects of his uncle William of Richmond. And
in 1717 he married Elizabeth, the sister of his
brother's wife, and a co-heiress of Mr. Robinson
of Middleton-one-Row.[1] Old Mrs. Hind told me
that White House was given to him by his father.
This farm adjoins Spring House; but when or
how he came to acquire his Dinsdale and Sedgefield properties I do not know. He was evidently
a man of means; but, as there is no mention of
either of these properties in the will of his father-
in-law, I suppose he may have derived them, or
the money to purchase them, from some member
of the family, with whom, or with whose affairs,
I am as yet unacquainted. To the left-hand side
of the glorious view taken in from the lofty village
of Middleton-one-Row, there is to be seen an
almost ideal English farm-stead, occupying the
crest of a rising ground, and surrounded by groups
of well-grown forest-trees. It now bears the
name of Rose Hill, and was the home built for
himself by my great-great-grandfather about 1720
on his estate at Dinsdale in Yorkshire, or Over-

[1] See Appendix F.

Dinsdale, as it is usually called. His land extended from above the Low Middleton ferry up the picturesque southern bank of the Tees, and for a considerable distance along the Girsby road. To this sweet spot he brought his wife shortly before the birth of their third and youngest child; and here they remained for nearly thirty years,—that is, till it became the home of their eldest son, although the father has always continued to be remembered in the family circle as 'Thomas of Dinsdale.' For a short time he occupied his own farm of White House, and then gave it to his second son, removing finally to his property at Sedgefield. He owned the large handsome old-fashioned house of red brick, which still stands on the west side of the village green. And here under the good care of his youngest and most accomplished son, William (35), he passed the last fourteen years of his life. This, his youngest son, was indeed a highly distinguished member of the medical profession; and through his scientific researches (I believe on hydrophobia) became known throughout the country. I remember once meeting with some learned article by him in one of the magazines of the last century. In Surtees' *History of Durham* (vol. iii. p. 50) he is mentioned as " an eminent surgeon."

THOMAS WRIGHTSON (34) of White House, my great-grandfather, was the second son of the above Thomas of Dinsdale. Almost the whole of the earlier portion of his life was passed on his father's beautiful Tee-side estate ; but, on his marriage with Miss Garmondsway,[1] he received the White House farm and settled there. He preferred a country life, although he had been educated to some extent with a view to the medical profession. According to my father, he was much renowned for the gratuitous advice he used to give to his poorer neighbours in their minor ailments. He died before his father at a comparatively early age, and I have heard that at first his widow was in somewhat narrow circumstances. This must however have been the case for no long time, as even during middle life I find her to have been a lady possessed of ample means. Where her property or money came from I do not know, but she was the owner of four farms of various sizes and of other property besides. For some time she contemplated living in the village of Haughton le Skerne, and built herself the nice old house at the east side of the Rectory, now occupied by my friend Miss Malcolm. This house gave her so much satisfaction, that she built another like it on one of her farms near Sadberge, and to this she gave the name of Newton Grange. In this last residence she spent the remainder of a very active and energetic life, dying there in the thirtieth year of her widowhood.

WILLIAM WRIGHTSON (42) of Neasham Hall, my grandfather, was born at White House

---

[1] See Appendix G.

in 1755, a year after the marriage of his parents.
He was always fond of telling how his first teacher
was an old rebel adherent of the unfortunate
Prince, Charles Edward Stuart, who, in the celebrated retreat of the Highland army in 1745, had
somehow dropped out of the ranks and found a
kindly shelter in the seclusion of South Durham.
The clan to which he belonged was that of the
McCouls, mentioned in the 44th chapter of Scott's
Waverley. When all danger of arrest was past,
Mr. McCoul established a small school for the
children of the farmers and country folk near to
White House. His learning was limited, but his
discipline was strict. Punctuality in particular
was enforced under circumstances which would
daunt most young people of the present day. The
hour for assembling was six in the morning; but
in the depth of winter, and long before the break
of day, young William Wrightson might be seen,
lanthorn in hand, bounding over the crisp snow.
And then, as being the first boy to reach the
school, he received for that day the honoured and
much coveted title of "the Prince;" whilst
others following near behind heard themselves
greeted with appropriate names of honour, all
borrowed from that ill-fated band of warriors
whom old McCoul so loved to celebrate. And
thus Tullibardine, Macdonald, Lochiel, Clan-
ranald, Glengarry, and many more, became as
household words in William's ears, and prepared
him to welcome those works of Scott, which in
his old age became a source of unequalled

pleasure.[1] It was of course for only a short time, and chiefly to keep him out of mischief, that little William was placed under the charge of this quaint old Jacobite, for while still a boy he was sent to a good school at Sedgefield. But the circumstances of his earlier training make one realize how he had been in contact with the last flash-up of the passions of the great Civil War. From that time forward his life, and that of his mother, lay within the most marvellous period of growth our nation had ever known. It was then that Horace Walpole wrote in exultation to a friend, "You would not know your own country. You left it a private little island living upon its means. You would find it the capital of the world!" In this there was no exaggeration; for, on the expulsion of the French from North America and India, we waked suddenly to the fact that of all others in this world the English had become the dominant race. During the previous hundred years elevation of sentiment and

---

[1] Speaking of Jacobite associations, I remember two interesting visits,—one on 17th June 1851,—which I paid to the venerable Mary Benton, who lived at Elton near Stockton. She was born about 1735, or possibly a little earlier, being not far short of 120 years of age. She told me that at the time of the Scotch Rebellion she was a "little lass" and saw the Highland army and the Prince himself pass by. The principal thing, that had fastened on her mind, was the splendid appearance of the Highlanders with their bare legs. The faculties of this wonderfully aged woman were quite as clear as those of the white-haired granddaughter who took care of her. Her portrait was painted by the late Mr. Bewicke of Haughton; and I have a lock of her hair. She died I believe in 1852.

national enthusiasm had almost perished; but now the torpor, following on the Restoration and Expulsion of the Stuarts, was overcome. Wesley and Whitfield were rousing men to spiritual consciousness. William Pitt, in Parliament and out of Parliament, was infusing the whole nation with something of his own glowing patriotism. Brindley was just commencing our system of canals. And Metcalf was beginning to make roads out of what had hitherto been tracks almost impassable in winter. There was all, and more than all, the expansive energy of the old Elizabethan period, without its exuberance of defiant ferocity.

This fresh vigorous tide of national life was pulsating of course in the breasts of thousands, but in few more strongly than in the energetic mother and son with whom we are concerned. Both my grandfather and his mother were in living sympathy with the spirit of the age,—whatever their hand found to do, they did it with all their might, and strove to do it gloriously!

On the death of his father my grandfather was brought home; and, though barely entering on his teens, soon showed that he had inherited his mother's energy and general capacity. So far as I can make out, she never quite gave up the oversight or care of her own property, and was in the habit of herself inspecting what was done on her widely scattered farms. On these occasions she rode upon a pillion-saddle, holding by the belt of a groom, while her son accompanied her on his

own spirited young horse.   In old age he used to
recall these days with peculiar delight,—especially
the homeward journeys, when, 'in the rich
autumnal evenings, he and his mother rode on
through dewy copses and by country lanes, until
from Sadberge hill, or near, they saw the great
harvest moon, like a copper shield, rise slowly
above the Cleveland hills and frosty haze.'   The
mind and character of my grandfather were
strongly influenced by the companionship of his
mother; and, when a boy of only nineteen years
of age, he actually set his heart on occupying by
himself a farm of four hundred acres, called
Morton Palms, in the parish of Haughton le
Skerne.   The assistance and encouragement,
afforded by both his mother and uncle Richard
Garmonsway, show at what an early age he had
begun to inspire confidence in those who knew
him best.

It was during the later years of his residence at
Morton Palms that he married Mary, the eldest
daughter of Mr. Robert White of Norton, near
Stockton-on-Tees.   Mr. White was a man of
good position and considerable wealth.   He had
several sons, who were all very gentlemanly and
agreeable men, although among these Anthony
was by far the most brilliant in his natural capacities and attainments.   On leaving Cambridge
this Anthony went to London, where he rose to
the very summit of his profession, and received
the distinguished honour of being twice elected
President of the Royal College of Surgeons.   He

died 9th March 1849,[1] and in 1877 my brother Thomas, then living at Norton Hall, placed in the church a window to the memory of this his highly-gifted great-uncle. Next to Anthony the best known brother was Thomas, a barrister, whose son Lieutenant-Colonel White of H.M. 22nd Regiment died in 1866.

My grandfather lost both his noble-minded mother and his truly saintly sister in 1797. They died within two months of each other. All that had been theirs now passed to him, so that he became possessed of considerable means. Besides money he was now the owner of five farms. Of these, two lay to the north of Stockton at Cowpon and Wolviston,—another lay at Harrowgate near Haughton le Skerne,—the fourth was Newton Grange,—and the fifth and last was the entailed farm of White House.

In 1803 my grandfather's circumstances were such that he was able to purchase from Sir Charles Turner the Neasham, Morton, and Maidendale estates,[2] for which he gave thirty thousand pounds. After this purchase he was (I have been told) the

[1] A day or two after his death *The Times* newspaper contained a sketch of his career, commencing as follows,—"The medical profession has lost one of its brightest ornaments in Anthony White, the eminent surgeon, who died at his house in Parliament Street, on Friday morning the 9th inst., aged nearly 70. Mr. White was a graduate of Cambridge, where he took an honourable degree. He came to London at an early period, and commenced practice as assistant surgeon at the Westminster Hospital," etc.

[2] See Surtees' *Hist. Dur.* vol. iii, p. 258.

owner of no less than eleven farms: and he knew that his eldest son would probably inherit more from the Wrightsons of Cockerton Hall. To my grandfather it seemed not at all improbable that he might become the founder of a County Family; and there can be no doubt that this was his ambition. The Neasham estate consisted of about four hundred acres, and, both from the beauty of its situation and the richness of its soil, was evidently capable of immense improvement. On this particular portion of his property he resolved to erect the family mansion; and about Christmas 1805 Neasham Hall became the seat of the Wrightsons; and, in spite of what we call " the Cookson episode," it has been successively the home, first of his son, and then of his wealthiest and most influential grandson, Thomas Wrightson, M.P., the present owner.

At the time of which I am speaking the financial affairs of Europe had passed into an entirely abnormal condition, owing to the gigantic wars arising from the great French Revolution. Partly in consequence of our insular position and splendid fleet,—partly in consequence of James Watt's invention of the steam-engine and the spread of factories,—and partly in consequence of an excessive circulation of paper-money, the increase of the real and fictitious wealth of England became enormous. This increase of wealth was accompanied by a corresponding increase of population, which at that time virtually depended on the produce of the English soil for subsistence. Wheat

rose to famine prices, and the value of land rose
with it. Land, that could never be made to pay
at other times, was inclosed and brought into
cultivation. The income of every land-owner
was doubled, and agriculturists were able to introduce improvements that altered the whole aspect
of the country. So long did this state of things
continue, and so steadily did it increase, that, in
common with many other country gentlemen, my
grandfather regarded the abnormal inflation of the
landed interest as an enduring stage of national
development. In spite of this mistake all might
have gone well, if it had been possible for an
ambitious and capable man of action like him to
have maintained a policy of cautious economy
amidst such stirring times. But this was impossible. The properties he had bought were un-
developed; and the steady rise in the value of
land caused him to ridicule the idea of any danger
arising from debt incurred for the sake of carrying
out well-advised improvements. He entered on,
and persevered in, this almost fatal course of
policy, until his debts reached the alarming figure
of sixty thousand pounds. But nevertheless, until
events disproved his argument, his opinions carried
weight, and he impressed all around him with a
sense of power. I remember hearing how on
one occasion brave old Captain Toppin turned to
his eldest son with the exclamation, "By George,
sir, your father ought to have been Governor
General of India!" To adopt the glowing language of my father, "the hills clapped their hands

before him, and the valleys rejoiced ; and in his
confidence he might reasonably have exclaimed,
I shall die in my nest, and I shall multiply my
days as the sand : my glory is fresh in me, and
my bow is renewed in my hand." For a considerable time my grandfather was convinced that
he was right in thus impetuously hurrying forward the development of his beautiful estates ;
but the collapse of the landed interest, which
followed on the unexpected fall of Napoleon
Bonaparte, served at last to open his eyes to his
one great mistake. He owned that he had gone
" too far," and ordered a valuation of his entire
property. It was set down at no more than ninety
thousand, and, after the passing of the Currency
Bill in 1819, it sank to only sixty thousand
pounds,—which was the amount of his debts !
Thus by a combination of political events abroad
and financial legislation at home, did my grandfather find himself in a most critical position. An
effort was made to realize assets. Some of the
farms were sold. But it was a time when few
people dared to invest in land ; and these forced
sales merely enhanced the difficulties of the situation. In fact the only wise course lay in reducing
expenditure, increasing production, and waiting
for better times. It is at this point that my father
first comes upon the scene. He was still a youth ;
but his lawyer-like cast of mind, and his wonder-
ful capacity of concentrating energy, soon made
him invaluable. With exhausting, but by no
means unfruitful, effort he and his father united

in battling with adverse circumstances. A few years passed over and prospects began to brighten. In 1825 there was such a gleam of national prosperity, that the Chancellor of the Exchequer congratulated the country on having surmounted its difficulties. But, alas! in the winter of that year the darkest clouds overspread the nation. There was a fearful commercial crisis. Misfortunes came thick upon my grandfather. The Bank, in which his much-needed accumulations were deposited, broke,—some of his very largest debtors failed,—and a fire destroyed the most valuable agricultural buildings on the " home " farm, which farm he and my father always kept in their own hands. Twice was my father sent to London during that dreadful winter to try to save something from the general wreck. After days and nights of travelling on the storm-beat tops of the coaches of that time, with spirits crushed beneath a burthen of anxiety, he reached home at last in a rheumatic fever, which laid him for nearly nine months on a bed of agony and permanently shattered his constitution. This accumulation of misfortune broke the old man's heart. Never shall I forget the emotion with which my father once—but only once—described to me the way in which his ever-revered father came and knelt before him, as if in prayer, to ask forgiveness for having (as he fully believed) ruined him and all the family. He had but a short illness and expired at Neasham Hall on the 8th July 1826 in the seventy-first year of his age. His remains lie in his own vault beneath his memorial tablet in Hurworth church. "The crowds," says my father, "that attended his dear remains spoke eloquently of the respect with which he was regarded. That solemn procession from Neasham to Hurworth was like the funeral of a prince. I felt, and still feel, towards him as a Romanist towards his patron saint. . . . . . It is truly mournful to think that a person so highly gifted, so honourable, and good, should have been involved in difficulties so overwhelming. No vulgar ambition defaced the dignity of his sentiments. Usefulness and benevolence were his aim and end. And in the various specimens of skill with which he adorned the country—whether agricultural or architectural—this character is fully manifested.[1] In explaining his views to me he often quoted the well-known lines of Pope,—

> 'Who then shall grace, or who improve the soil?
> Who plants like Bathurst, or who builds like Boyle.
> 'Tis Use alone that sanctifies expense,
> And Splendour borrows all her rays from Sense.' "

THOMAS WRIGHTSON (53) of Neasham

[1] Since his time Neasham Hall has received various additions, and my brother is at present planning more; but the beautiful and artistically arranged woods, and the whole laying out of his Neasham estate, remain as evidences of his taste and benevolently exerted skill. When he bought the property the river banks were almost devoid of timber; and, while building a great part of Neasham village, he took care to add a piece of rich garden ground to every cottage. Even since my return to the parish, I have heard the old people speak of him with enthusiastic admiration.

Hall, my father, was born 16 July 1799. His boyhood was passed chiefly at the once famous school of the Rev. George Newby of Witton-le-Wear. He was to have been brought up to the Bar, but adverse circumstances put an end to such a purpose, and called him home to commence that Battle with Debt, which was to continue till he was nearly fifty years of age. There is no need for me to go into further details touching the sad circumstances of the family at the time of my grandfather's death. But the gradually lowered national conception of family and commercial honour (following in part on the growth of individualism and in part on the increased facilities for evading financial obligations) must impart an air of romantic self-sacrifice to the conduct of my father at this time.[1] He knelt down beside his father's corpse, and devoted his whole life to the preservation of that dear one's memory from stain; and then, in spite of all dissuasions, administered to his father's will, although in doing so he handed over to his father's creditors the only part of the old family property that had been entailed upon himself. For a few years he must really have been insolvent; but his character stood high, and he was never driven to extremity.

---

[1] In a somewhat similar position and at the same period Sir Walter Scott also refused to avail himself of any legal screen. "It is," says he in his Journal for 24 Jan. 1826, "the course I would have advised a client to take, and would have the effect of saving the land, which is secured. But for this I would, in a Court of Honour, deserve to lose my spurs. No, if they permit me, I will be their vassal for life!"

On the death of Richard Wrightson in 1830 he
inherited my present Spring House and Middleton
properties; and, by a mortgage on the former, he
made one more desperate effort to save Neasham
Hall.   But health, spirits, resources, all began to
give way; and at last he found himself obliged to
part with the place he loved as dearly as his life.
With the exception of a heavily mortgaged part
of the village, the whole Neasham estate,—the
last of all my grandfather's properties,—was offered
for sale, and purchased by the late Colonel James
Cookson. "Never shall I forget," writes my father,
" the agony of parting with that dear place.   We
left it with feelings indescribable.   Every field
and tree were interwoven and associated with the
memory of our sainted parent.   His name ' became religion ; ' and the breaking up of the
establishment, which his revered hands had orga-
nized and built, seemed almost an act of profana-
tion.   But filial reverence, local attachment,
youthful enthusiasm, were all in vain.   Stern
necessity compelled a retreat ; and so, after a long
succession of sales, I was obliged to make the last
and greatest sacrifice of all.   On the 7 Dec. 1834
I visited for the last time every room in the loved
mansion—now no longer mine—and after offering
up a short ejaculatory prayer in each, left Neasham
Hall—

> ' But my heart shall not flag,
> And my nerves shall not shiver,
> Though devoted to go——
> To return again never ! '

' Cha till me tuille, ged shillis
McLeod cha till McRimmon,—'
McLeod *may return*, but McRimmon *never !*
' Moritur, et moriens dulces reminiscitur Argos.' "

The half-veiled indication of what I know to
lave been an intense, though almost secret hope,[1]

[1] Strangely enough this hope began to be realized on a distant
anniversary of this agonizing farewell. At all events it was
in the 7 Dec. 1891 that the first document, connected with the
repurchase of Neasham Hall and Estate, was signed by his son
Thomas and by the then head of the Cookson family. A few
days later my brother wrote to me saying that he had met the
Marquis of Londonderry at a ball, "and he was most effusive
in his congratulations on having got back the old family property." I had also a glowing letter from my brother John.
Just to think," says he, "that after all these years the old
place, so associated with those dear faces of our infancy, should
once more belong to the Wrightsons ! It is a most auspicious
and memorable event. Oh, William, to think of that old dream
of ' buying back Neasham ' being fulfilled, and on the very
day when the sorrowing family left it nearly sixty years since.
A God-fearing generation they were, and nothing could be
more in harmony with our dear Mother's belief and feelings
than that in ' the same month, and in the self-same day of the
month ' this wandering in the Wilderness should have terminated so happily. You ought, you know, to have been
here ; but of course you hold the *old* property. I congratulate
you now upon your extraordinary labours in tracing the family
history, because the family from year to year has become more
worthy of being traced. But how few families have found a
man who had the ability, the inclination, the time, and the
means, for carrying out such an investigation. Your work will
last and always command interest ; and it is one which every
member of this large family will always thank you for doing.
As to Tom he has done his part nobly." The action of some
members of the Cookson family however so far impeded matters,
that it was not till 30 June 1892 that the Neasham Hall estate
actually passed into my brother's hands. He had previously
pressed me to purchase it ; but I declined.

seems to me only to intensify the pathos of my dear father's farewell to Neasham. The mournful resolve, indicated also in the same fragment of old Gaelic song, was maintained to the end of life, for, though often visiting his property at Middleton, he could never be induced to pass the crest of Neasham bank, so as again to look upon that lovely view, which, as years passed by, became etherealized into something like the dream of another world. And that in dying he remembered his ' sweet Argos,' as he loved to call it, was perhaps indicated by a last effort, when speech had failed, to grasp a little relic of Neasham which he always carried about his person.

* * * * * * * *

I have now reached a turning point in our family history where the recovery from a long series of misfortunes begins by slow and almost imperceptible degrees to take place. In looking back to this turn, which has led to far more than the repurchase of Neasham, the most trifling incidents appear to me invested with peculiar interest, particularly when they illustrate the way in which a kind Providence works for the good of those who strive to do their duty.

It was in the autumn of 1819 that, in one of their rambles through Dinsdale woods, my aunts Isabella and Ellen Wrightson found themselves near the pretty little Spa. Whilst walking there, they saw an elderly gentleman in company with a young lady, both dressed in the deepest mourning,

nd bearing on their faces marks of grief. Some-
hing happened,—the dropping of a handkerchief
r glove,—which enabled my aunt Ellen to speak
o the young lady; and then the sorrow of the
ne and the tender dignity of the other drew them
ogether. It was the commencement of a life-
ong friendship. The gentleman was Captain
Toppin,[1] a brave old Indian officer residing at
Newcastle-on-Tyne. The young lady was his
last remaining child: and the two were sorrowing
over the recent loss of her beautiful sister Harriet.
There is no need to speak of intermediate events.
It is enough to say that they became extremely
intimate with the Wrightsons and frequent visitors
at Neasham Hall. Some time after the death of
Captain Toppin his daughter married Archibald,
a son of Mr. William Potter, a Northumbrian
Coal-owner, who resided at Walbottle House
about six miles west of Newcastle. My aunts
were bridesmaids, and soon formed a cordial
friendship with the bridegroom's sister Rebecca.
This led to much pleasant intercourse between
the Neasham and Walbottle families, and in time
my father became attached to Miss Potter. Her
father had been twice married, and for the sake
of his second family he, although a very old man,

---

[1] He had been dreadfully wounded at the taking of Seringa-
patam in 1799, and was in consequence sent home. He was a
most fascinating man, and moved in the highest circles of society.
Hugh, Lord Percy, afterwards Duke of Northumberland, was
his frequent guest, and nourished such regard for him, that, on
becoming Duke, he behaved like a near relative to the then
fatherless daughter of his friend.

had recently embarked the whole (
in "sinking" for coal in a new distr
umberland near Cramlington.   Th
which attends all such enterprises, a
ledge of his own sad circumstanc
father hesitate for long in the decl:
sentiments : but the incident, which
him and proved the turning point in
remarkable, that I will give it, ju
often heard it from his lips.

On the very last occasion, that ol
visited Neasham Hall, he was accom
daughter.   When they were about
father stepped into their carriag
approached the gate at the end of tl
he felt that to go further would imp
courtesy.   Fear and affection held
state of most painful suspense.   " O]
himself, " that God would indicate
For some time there had been s
suddenly Mr. Potter (who had evid
religious meditation) turned to hi
words, "My dear sir, the Scriptur
is the accepted time,' and then, as th
to give it greater emphasis, the .
'Now is the day of Salvation.'"   I
speaker imagine the singular appr
his observation. "You are a dear go
said my father to himself, "and a b
to rest on you and yours.   I accep
as a message from Heaven, and wil
this is indeed my day of Salvation f

hitherto uninterrupted misfortune." The limit
of the estate was reached, but the carriage was
not stopped; and so, with a mind resolved, he
continued with them on their way.

Very soon after my father's engagement the
long-sought-for coal was reached at Cramlington;
but to all appearance its quality rendered it in-
capable of being worked at a profit. The shock
of this discovery was too great for Mr. Potter.
He died at the age of eighty-seven, after a very
short illness, on the last night of 1833. His
daughter described to my father the ruin of all
her prospects, and offered to set him free from his
engagement. He however refused to give her
up; and so, on the 16th July 1834, they were
married at St. Andrew's Church, Newcastle-on-
Tyne. In the December of the same year
Neasham Hall ceased to be my father's home;
and then, after a few months' interval, my parents
passed with quiet firmness to a cottage. It was
at Haughton le Skerne, near Darlington, that they
spent almost the whole of the first seventeen years
of their married life. At first they occupied a
small house, which now forms the north wing of
a larger one standing in the angle made by Bell
lane and the road to Darlington; but in May
1839 they moved into a much better house,
situated in the middle of the north side of the
village, and one which possessed the advantage of
a nice garden,—now ruined almost past recognition.

No sooner were my parents settled in "the

cottage," as they always loved to call their earliest home, than they commenced their long-enduring efforts to pay off the heavy debts which still remained after the sale of Neasham. As my father had been brought up to no business or profession, his only course out of difficulty lay in the reduction of expenditure. With the full concurrence of my mother, he laid down the rule "*Never to spend more than One Third of the realized Income.*" To the observance of this rule he always attached the very greatest importance. Speaking of it, whilst yet in the midst of his difficulties, he says, with almost prophetic confidence, " Future generations will look back to it,—or at all events they will *feel its effects!* " Although the most trying period of my parents' lives lies below my own horizon line, yet I well remember the little rededged slate with its careful record of daily expenditure, down to the chance vagrant's penny : and, amidst widely different circumstances, I have looked with strangely mingled feelings at my father's old account books, which invariably commence with his prayers for help to lead an honest and upright life.

The gloom of this sad time was however unexpectedly dispelled by the discovery of the value of the coal at Cramlington. Inferior for household purposes, it was found to be magnificent for generating steam ; and in 1838 a first dividend of profits was made. The amount was only small ; but pit after pit was added to the first, and the affair was continually enlarged, until it became

great collieries of England with an
l of nearly half a million tons of "best"
lst this spring-tide of returning fortune
 debts melted away like snow. The
n Spring House was left to the last.
 off on the 17th May 1847; and then
ee man. I was but a little boy at the
vet I can recall the sense of mingled
ankfulness, when for the first time I
uds of anxiety and grief pass from my
:. Misfortune had not however quite
m, for a couple of years later the
 Chancery suit led to an unexpected
lower" on the part of Richard Wright-
v. This claim, which involved the
ˑ about two thousand pounds, was at
rged; and from that time my father's
one of steadily increasing prosperity.
ı "the cottage,"—in my parents' first
me,—that I (60), my sister Rebecca
ny brother Thomas (62) were born:
uite remember our removal into the
e, where John (63) and Mary (64)
he little family group.
ıe greatest events in our early life was
ɔf our father's four maiden sisters and
ır brothers to live in Haughton. They
 quaint old-fashioned house at the
end of the village. It evidently in-
emains of some more important edifice,
ned fragments of wall some three feet
vas full of all sorts of odd nooks and

K

corners,—mysterious closets,—and unaccountable doors. With a considerable amount of truth, our childish imaginations conceived it to contain an almost limitless supply of cakes, tarts, and preserves. We were diligent, and not unsuccessful, explorers after such 'hid treasures': and our mother's anxious warnings against 'too many good things' were as readily forgotten by us, as they were disregarded by our hospitable aunts. My aunt Isabella disliked such cautionings. When our mother left us there, we were lost in admiration to see how my aunt used to ruffle her feathers up; and, with a half-humorous indignation in her tone, exclaim to her sister, " I think, Ellen, that we know how to entertain our visitors! "

I need hardly say that my dear aunt and godmother, Isabella Wrightson (51), appeared to us, as she really was, the most prominent person in this our 'other home.' At an early age she had been called upon to take the place of a mother in the family: and, with a sunny indomitableness of disposition and a by no means unlovely pride, she assumed and maintained her position amidst circumstances which would have crushed the spirits of more ordinary people. Her fine, elastic, health-suggesting *physique*, seemed capable of inspiring all around with cheerfulness and vigour. But, even while her large-hearted sympathetic nature wakened a widespread sense of affection, there was a sort of imperious straight-forwardness about her, that made her the centre of authority in the little village circle of acquaintances. Ten years

after her death, when making arrangements for
the funeral of the last member of that household,
I found that they were still " Miss Wrightson's "
opinions and views, which ruled amidst the kindly
neighbours who offered their assistance. " Your
aunt Isabella," observed the old Rector with some
asperity, " would have made a capital Empress."

My aunt Ellen Wrightson (54) was graceful in
figure and lovely in face. Her bearing was gentle,
calm, and dignified. She was not learned, but
possessed a natural culture and imagination, which,
in her company, made it a delight to pour forth
all one's best thoughts and newest information.
She had declined several offers of marriage, and
might, if she had chosen, have occupied a leading
position in county society ; but an early disappoint-
ment had turned her heart from marriage, and
left a shade of chastened sadness, which did not in
the least take from, but rather added to, the charm
of her attractive presence.

A near approach to a portraiture of these two
dear aunts may be seen among the exquisitely
delicate word-paintings in Mrs. Gaskell's celebrated *Cranford*. As I peruse that book, I seem
again to breathe the atmosphere of my aunts'
village home,—to see them act, and hear them
speak.

When I was a little boy and they still vigorous
women, I enjoyed with them innumerable rambles
in the country. One of the most delightful of
our longer expeditions used to be to the Old
Hall at Hurworth-on-Tees. Some of the maiden

sisters of my father's friend Colonel Colling lived there, and my aunts liked to visit them. It is a spacious residence on the south side of the village green,—in fact, the choicest house in the place; and its grounds embrace about five acres of a particularly sheltered portion of the north bank of the Tees. On the side away from the village, the flower garden consists of a succession of beautifully laid out terraces, which gradually lead down to a fine bend of the river. The gardens, or rather the whole of the grounds, were my delight, for they included a paddock, a pretty little waterside copse, and even afforded a glimpse of Neasham Hall a mile and a half away. Into these grounds I was never long in escaping from the staid company of my elders. From the more lofty gravelled walks, as indeed from all the south windows in the house, I remember how the many-tinted trees and shrubs and flowers in front,—the stretch of sparkling water beyond,—and the Yorkshire fields and plantations of Eryholme in the background, seemed like some lovely picture in my eyes. Little did I imagine that in the decline of life this same sweet spot would become my home!

Of my two uncles resident in Haughton, William (57) was my favourite. He was very fond of fishing, and often took me on his expeditions, whether along the banks of the sluggish Skerne or to the rippling Tees. He was one of the most earnest God-fearing men I ever met. After a somewhat careless youth, he became deeply religious; and in spite of the opposition of his sisters joined the Wesleyans. As years passed over, his genuine piety won him a place of high esteem. Among rich and poor he was ever welcomed, but never more so than in a time of sorrow. I visited him shortly before his death. After tea we went up to his room, as usual, for a little prayer. While there he spoke with deep emotion of the way in which he had been allowed to minister by the death-beds of all his sisters and my father. When about to separate, he stood up, and laying his hand upon his heart said, in a tone of mingled joy, thanksgiving, and triumphant hope, "William, it's all right here!" A month later he was found lying dead in bed. From the undisturbed position of the body, and the perfect serenity of the countenance, it was evident that death had been instantaneous. At the funeral almost every blind in the village was drawn down, and many of the working men came to the grave dressed in their Sunday clothes. He was the friend of all.

The only one of my father's brothers, who was engaged in any special calling, was Robert (58). He was a most accomplished medical man, who, during the latter portion of his life, occupied a high official post at Delhi in the service of the old East India Company. In person and disposition he was extremely like his sister Isabella: and during his visits to England I conceived a great affection for him. He married a niece, and virtually adopted daughter, of Mr. Leonard Raisbeck, the most wealthy and influential solicitor in Stockton-on-Tees, from whom she inherited a handsome fortune.

The foremost figure in our proper home was undoubtedly my Mother. She was a woman gifted with an admirable constitution both of mind and body; but, though good-looking, her face derived its greatest charm from its ready expression of lively and sympathetic feeling. At an earlier period she and her two half-sisters, Jane Potter and Mrs. Armstrong, had been regarded as among the most accomplished and intellectual women to be found in or near Newcastle-upon-Tyne. But a new bias was given to her mind by a sermon she chanced to hear in London. It was preached at the Caledonian Chapel by the celebrated Edward Irving, the friend of Carlyle the historian. From that time religion was the controlling power in her life; but it was a religion which shaped itself into almost exclusively practical forms. Except on rare occasions she evinced no interest in Ecclesiastical questions; and never participated in the passions of Theological disputants. It was to her Bible alone that she looked for instruction, as it was in the Bible alone that she saw the outline of that Saviour, from whom she drew the light of a life full of buoyant hopefulness, unconscious self-sacrifice, and patient well-doing. Her intense anxiety, as to the conduct and up-bringing of her children, was appreciated by us all; and the fear of paining her was our most powerful dissuasive from evil. Through a long vista of years I can

to occasions, when, after a ‘naughty
in my little crib to see my mother
r-light, bending like a white angel
silent prayer.   And I was much
in later life, I came across a so-
ıct Journal," filled with notices of
failure in rising to higher things;
ıese early struggles after righteous-
ıecessity a childish aspect, yet they
ity from the intensity of the feeling
hey were recorded.   My mother
ersion to the early forcing system of
ıich in presence of more modern
:aminations has now become almost
ıhe sought to infuse our minds with
ıusiasm after knowledge,—trusting
ıiasm to carry us on irrespective of
choolmasters.   There is no doubt
right in regarding the repulsive
school as frequently destructive of
ıt interest in the subjects taught;
ıe time there are insuperable objec-
ıeferring to commence a subject till
imagination.   Her own modesty
· from seeing that, except for her
sm, our imaginations might never
uck at all.   I shall however never
le range of information she imparted
ʒhton walks.   A group of wild
avel pit,—a heap of broken stones,—
to supply a theme.   And there is a
which even yet I can never traverse

without thinking of the Saxon Heptarchy, so vivid
was the impression she created while walking
there. As I look back to those early days, I
recall the discovery of Nineveh, with the marvellous reopening of so many long-closed avenues
into the past;—the sudden outburst of Geological
science, which flooded each dull rock and glacial
bed with glorious interest;—the finding of gold
first in California and then in Australia, followed
by the wide expansion of our English race;—all
these, and many kindred events, as seen through
the medium of our mother's mind, assumed an
almost gorgeous hue. What the emotions of the
younger ones might be, it is impossible for me to
say with certainty; but, speaking for myself, I
felt as though looking over some wide expanse
of sea at a glorious sun-rise. It seemed to me
the sun-rise of the World's youth;—it was but
the sun-rise of my own!

The description of my Father (53) is almost
co-extensive with the concluding portion of Part
First of these Memorials; but I must not close this
little gallery of Haughton family portraits without
according him the place of special honour.

My Father's ruling passion was Love of Family;
and his whole life was ungrudgingly devoted to
the support or insurance of its character, honour,
and prosperity. In him an almost inflexible will
was associated with a highly-strung sensitive
organization, quivering (in spite of his reserve)
with intense emotion. I need hardly say that,
amidst his peculiar circumstances, such a con-

stitution laid him open to intense mental suffering.
The earliest impression he has left upon my mind
is that of a sad retiring form, with an age of
anxiety and sorrow silvering too soon the once
raven blackness of his hair. Even though I was
then too young to comprehend his misfortunes,
he was surrounded by such an atmosphere of sup-
pressed grief, that I remember weeping passionately
at the mere thought of him,—I knew not why.
There is no doubt that his sympathies and interests
were in their range as narrow, as they were intense;
but, amidst the secluded and yet tragical surroundings of his early life, a character like his
could hardly have developed otherwise. The likeness of my dear father was taken in 1845. It is
now in my possession. The artist[1] has failed to
catch the imaginative and exquisitely humorous
glance of the eye; but he has nevertheless very
faithfully depicted my father as he appeared, when
rapidly improving circumstances were beginning
to restore his naturally serene and courteously
dignified expression of face.[2]

---

[1] Mr. William Bewicke of Haughton, a most interesting
man and valued friend, whose story is related in Longstaffe's
History of Darlington, pp. 342-7.

[2] Shortly before his death he gave me his manuscript account
of our family. From his mention of the traditionally known
Eryholme brothers to the death of his father this account would
fill forty pages of the main text of this book, although one half
of these would be occupied with the story of his father. This
manuscript has been extremely useful to me in respect of
family circumstances during the 18th and earlier portion of the
19th century; and on various occasions I have introduced
extracts from it.

Before I pass on from our early ʋ
is perhaps worth while to record ;
most vivid Reminiscences associated

One of these is connected with
great power as a reader. He was aɪ
admirer of the works of Sir Walteɪ
do not think the author himself couḷ
his conceptions more vividly before
father did. We were quite at homᵉ
gallery of characters, which this greą
bequeathed to posterity; and the ;
varied panorama in which they moʋ
as real as the scenes amidst whiɕ
After one of these books my father ʋ
us the history of the period in whiɕ
had been aroused; and in doing so, h
more nor less than repeating in ouɪ
what had been taking place in the ɕ
large. Indeed the ignorant and fierᵉ
which the Middle Ages had been t
writers of the eighteenth century,
away in presence of the genial intere
by Scott. A century ago names anɕ
as familiar as household words, had ḇ
of to an extent that would appear alɱ
to the rising generation. And iʰ
atmosphere of sympathetic interes
Scott, that our new, brilliant, anɕ
exact, school of historians arose,—s
and stimulating yet more, the histoɪ
of innumerable Englishmen. Sḷ
utilized in the same way by my

though much more difficult than Scott, was brought within our reach, for I am glad to find that they were really the finest passages of humour, pathos, and high sentiment, that my father's reading stamped upon my mind, when I was a little boy between ten and fifteen years of age.

In the Ecclesiastical sphere the most stirring event belonging to this period was the great High Church revival. That revival expressed the natural and inevitable reaction against the principles of the French Revolution and the unspiritual Utilitarianism of the eighteenth century. Protestantism had become almost paralyzed on its positive side; and was in fact little more than a protest against all obtrusive dogmas or ecclesiastical usages. Among cultivated and ardent Churchmen like John Henry Newman, Hurrell Froude, Keble, and Pusey, such a state of things was intolerably dreary, and was certain to incite to action. The mediæval direction of the movement associated with these names was largely influenced by the mental current set in motion by Scott. Pusey used often to refer to this in conversation; and Newman in the third chapter of his *Apologia* distinctly tells us that such was the case; for by 'stimulating the mental thirst of his readers,—feeding their hopes,—and setting before them visions, which, when once seen, were not easily forgotten, —Scott had silently indoctrinated them with ideas, which were afterwards appealed to as first principles.' At the time when this High Church revival commenced, the general tone with regard to

religion was that of the mild contem
Mr. Thackeray's *Vanity Fair*.   Th
heard the great Irving preach, my
to wonder how any person of strengtl
could be religious.   But this conten
was quickly changed for one of astoɪ
It was not long before the nation see
gone mad with terror lest it should s
itself converted to Romanism against
the " No Popery! " cry was raised ɪ
single improvement which delight
generation of church people.   My mɪ
disturbed, contented herself with re
efforts to make us good Biblical scl
if we had been left to our parents, it
we should have been almost oblivioɪ
mendous tumult raging in the countɪ
the visits of our grandmother Pott
ever gained a most alarming glin
was going on.   As the descendan
Covenanters, she had no love for tl
England, and a perfect loathing of
feasted us with stories of the " bl
house," and strove to fortify our
with the sight of highly seasone
where repulsive portraits of recen
were alternated with hideous pictu
in the Inquisition.   No vituperative
of language seemed at that time to
to win the commendation of even r
people.   My dear old grandmotl
cause for spiritual satisfaction in r

sons; but she was much refreshed on hearing the testimony borne by one of them to the effect that 'The religion of the Pope was the Religion of the Devil.' " You see, my dear," said she to me with her pretty Scotch accent and intonation,— " you see your uncle's no that fair from the kingdom o' Haiven!"

But the one great spectacle, which never failed to arouse our keenest interest, was the Rise of the Railway System, with its attendant development of engineering works. We might be said to live in the very cradle of that system. The line connecting Stockton and Darlington ran past the house where I was born; and the laboured snortings of the " No. 1 " Locomotive must have been amongst the first sounds that fell upon my infant ear. This, the very earliest of all the railways in the world, had been opened no more than ten years, when my parents went to Haughton; but by that time it had more than justified the expectations of its energetic promoters. As a natural consequence, the previous distrust of such like undertakings gave place to an almost insane eagerness to invest money in the construction of lines wherever and whenever the opportunity occurred. We saw much of what was going on, for at this time the connection between London and the North was made through Darlington. I was never weary of escaping to the bridge near Harrowgate toll-bar to watch the innumerable " navvies " tumbling " the dirt " into long lines of tilting waggons, while the very earth seemed to melt away before their flashing spades: and it was a memorable day, when, on the 18th of June 1844, I saw from this same spot the railway opened, with old George Stephenson acting as engine-driver on the first locomotive that traversed the now finished work. Great as was the effect upon us of what we saw, that which we heard aroused a still more lively interest. Indeed the stories of early intercourse between our grandfather Potter and George Stephenson,[1]—the achievements of the younger Stephenson,—and the news of great inventions by our cousin, afterwards Lord Armstrong,—served to cast round Engineering the halo of romance, and to suggest to my parents a likely path for the advancement of their sons.

And so the first experiment was tried on me; and, at the very zenith of England's unrivalled commercial supremacy, I was sent as a premium pupil to a great Tyne-side shipyard, where amidst ridicule and opposition the novel material of *iron*, instead of wood, had been adopted for the construction of floating bodies!

The Haughton life of my parents came to a

---

[1] In 1815-16 Stephenson invented his Safety-lamp, and my grandfather warmly advocated its superiority to the Davy lamp. He asked George to dine with him at Walbottle one day, and little Robert Stephenson was brought in with his father. My uncle Archy would not sit down at table with the "workingman"; but my mother took her accustomed place, and well remembered the timid fair-haired boy, who ate in silence, while Mr. Potter and his father sat discussing schemes, which a quarter of a century later served peacefully to revolutionize the world. I may mention that George's father had lost his sight while working at the Walbottle colliery.

close a few months after my departure. For the sake of his children's education and advancement, my father resolved to take what to him at least was a painful step. He decided to remove to Newcastle-upon-Tyne ; and on the 28th of April 1852 we there found our new home. It was not long before my brother Thomas commenced his wonderfully successful engineering career at his cousin Armstrong's magnificent Elswick Works. And at a somewhat later time my brother John was placed with a leading Tyne-dale farmer at Corbridge, where he laid the foundation of his great agricultural knowledge.

My Mother's Relatives were very leading people in Newcastle ; and, as we naturally came much in contact with them, it is fitting at this point of my narrative to introduce a Sketch of those in whom we felt the greatest interest.

My Grandfather Potter always said that the real foundation of his own and his family's success, was to be found in the effect produced upon him, at the early age of seventeen, by a sermon, which he heard preached on the 20th of May 1764, outside the old Pandon Gate at Newcastle, by the great and good John Wesley. He was twice married. By his first wife he had several children. Among these Addison, his eldest surviving son, lived on his own estate at Heaton Hall ; and his daughter Ann, after marrying Mr. Armstrong, became the mother of the present Lord Armstrong of Cragside, Northumberland, and of the wife of the late Baron (Judge) Watson. By his second wife my grandfather left, not only my mother, but my four uncles,—Archibald Gilchrist, who married Miss Toppin,—Edward, the manager of Cramlington colliery,— Henry Glasford, a medical man in Newcastle,—and William Simpson, a bachelor, whose headquarters were in London.

My Grandmother Potter was, during the few remaining years of her life, by far the most attractive figure among our Newcastle relatives. She was the prettiest, and certainly one of the most aristocratic looking old ladies, I ever saw. Although

Gilchrist in name, she was both on her father's and mother's side of the Ingram [1] stock, which linked her with the great events of the Civil War in England and with the struggles of the Covenanters in Scotland. In very early life she heard John Wesley preach; and years later, along with her friend Lady Maxwell, became one of a small group of his higher class followers in Edinburgh. After her death, a sketch of her life was written, which, in a much mutilated form, may be seen in the *Wesleyan Magazine* for August 1856.

Sir William, afterwards Lord Armstrong, was undoubtedly our most distinguished relative; but his memory needs no embalming here. A man, who was pronounced by Robert Stephenson to be the greatest mechanical genius of his time,—whose inventions in hydraulics and artillery are now used in every portion of the world,—who formed the vast Elswick Works,—who entertained the Prince and Princess of Wales,—and, who, since building his magnificent residence at Cragside, has presented a large portion of his Jesmond property as a Park to Newcastle,—will for many centuries be remembered in his native city.

But by far the most striking member of my mother's family was her much-loved brother William. He was certainly the most superb man I ever saw. His face was extremely handsome,—his figure grand,—his bearing *distingué*,—his voice rich and deep,—his powers as a picturesque talker unrivalled,—while his disposition overflowed with large-hearted generosity. From beginning to end his life was that of a Childe Harold; and, alas! through no inconsiderable portion, that also of a Don Juan. Indeed the first outbreak of his romantic and passionate nature was in connection with Lord Byron's call to "arm for Greece." From that time his career was one long series of adventures, which (to a great extent before the vulgarizing aids of steam-ships and of railways) carried him round the entire world, and from Tierra del Fuego in the south, to Finland in the north. He was for long among the Arabs, where his reckless daring earned for him the startling sobriquet of "the son of Satan." He fought upon the barricades in Paris. He risked his life among the Italian Carbonari. And he emerged from the recesses of Nubia with his faithful little Hassan, whom he had rescued from some cruel fate. At a later time he was scouring

[1] See Appendix H.

across the Pampas of South America,—then revelling amidst the scenes depicted in Prescott's *Conquest of Mexico*,—and next among the Mormons at Utah. Age could not tame his ardour; and, when about seventy, he wove a web of travel over India, China, and Japan. In England his bachelor home was at the Reform Club: and with his peculiarly popular qualities he became a well-known man in society. When the Prince of Wales was in India in 1875-6, my uncle became acquainted with him through their mutual friend the Duke of Sutherland. The Prince was so much interested and delighted, that he afterwards called on him at his private rooms in London and sat for hours in conversation with him. I think the proudest moment in my uncle's life was, when he was introduced by the Prince to the Princess of Wales as ' the most extensive traveller he had ever known.'

My uncle Archibald Potter, and his wife, my ever dear aunt Bessy, were the closest and most constant friends we found among my mother's relatives. At the time of our removal to Newcastle he was living, as an independent gentleman of fortune, some six miles to the west, at Walbottle House,—my grandfather's old residence. It was a comfortable rambling place, with good gardens, well-covered fruit-walls, and excellent vinery. The Roman Wall and foss, from which Walbottle (*i.e.* the Wall-dwelling) derives its name, had passed within a few yards of the north side of the house; and the deep indentation in the ground is an actual relic of that ancient work. The view over the valley of the Tyne from Walbottle is both extensive and beautiful: and, about a mile below the House, there is the scene of the Battle of Newburn, where in 1640 the advanced portion of the army of Charles I. was defeated by the Scotch Covenanters under Leslie and Montrose. My uncle's house was a second home to me; for I was always welcomed and happy there. Never in my life did I meet with a man possessed of such gay *insouciance*,—such exuberance of animal spirits,—and such sanguine intrepidity. Nothing annoyed him more than the expression of a doubt as to everything going on in the most prosperous and brilliant way imaginable: and it was impossible to be in his company without finding the *couleur de rose* shed over every prospect, past, present, or future. My frequent visits to Walbottle, when I was about seventeen or eighteen years of age, afford some of the most vivid and delightful of my youthful reminiscences. I was fond of walking out in time for my uncle's afternoon dinner and returning the next day in one of his carriages. Even as I now write, there are scenes painted upon my memory, as though by the brush of a Meissonier or Gerard Dow. Again I feel, or rather see myself, within that low square entrance hall, shaking the snowflakes from my cloak, with a soft wintry light falling through painted glass on old oak furniture. There stands my uncle's portly form, so filling up his study door that only a side glimpse can be obtained of the long lines of well-bound volumes on their shelves. There comes the vivacious little figure of my dear aunt Bessy with welcome in every look and gesture. And, as my eye follows a well-dressed man-servant, I see through an open door that the cloth is spread, and that already the silver dish-covers are flashing in the light of a real north-country fire. And so, through the long interval of years, I can faintly feel again something of the rapturous enjoyment of that hungry youth, who had just ended his long winter's walk in this home of luxurious comfort, abounding hospitality, and overflowing kindness.[1]

On settling at Newcastle my parents found themselves surrounded by wealthy and extravagant relations. Their actual income was equal to what some of these were spending; but, with a resolution to live at one third of this, they appeared comparatively poor. It is not surprising that in some quarters their conduct caused considerable annoyance; for relatives as much resent an economy which can never benefit them in the

---

[1] My uncle and aunt Archibald Potter left Walbottle and went to live near London in June 1861. He survived his wife by ten years, dying 26 April 1878. By his will he left me his late wife's share in the beautiful Newlandside Estate near Stanhope, which I sold for something near five thousand pounds. His share of Cramlington colliery was equally divided between myself and my two brothers. And a very considerable sum of money in Railway investments, etc., went to my sisters; though Mary, as residuary legatee, had much the larger portion.

future, as they applaud an expenditure that reflects some credit on them at the present. A man possessed of my father's concentration of purpose was however not likely to be influenced by the superficial opinions of such persons. His own temporary social environment counted for absolutely nothing with him, if only he could see the way honourably to replace his family in the position my grandfather had lost. Thirty years later one of the oldest of my mother's relatives exclaimed to me, " Oh, Mr. Wrightson, how little, how very little, did we appreciate your father's conduct at Newcastle!" He was however soon left to lead a life as retired as he chose. He went little into society ; but he often visited his sisters at Haughton, where he would sometimes stay for many weeks at a time, engaged in building, draining, and other business. Each year he increasingly felt the strength arising from his economic rule, and in 1857 he commenced a long and wonderfully successful series of railway investments. These enabled him not only to help his children, when they needed capital ; but also, finally, to leave his wife more than the entire amount she had handed over to him in his times of adversity.[1]

[1] Under my Father's will the whole of his personal property passed absolutely to my Mother. With powers of direction, but not of disposal, I came in for the whole of his real estate, although various annuities and charges made it of little value to me for many years. On the 16 June 1891 I added to and much improved my Middleton property, by purchasing for £1,000 a house and premises that broke through my line of frontage.

To my dear Mother the life and stir of Newcastle was very delightful. Freed to a great extent from her earlier domestic and financial anxieties, she engaged herself in various useful and religious works. I think her most successful effort was made among the poor, neglected, and degraded factory girls. For years a good night school was kept going at St. Lawrence's Quay, where reading, writing, religious instruction, needle-work, and even simple cookery were taught: and there must be many humble homes, where the higher morality and superior degree of comfort are owing, under God, to the energy and benevolence of my mother. Among her own relations also she became a blessing. It was she who led both her brother Edward and her nephew Charles of Heaton Hall to God; just as, at a much later time, her influence seemed to prevail over her brother William, after long years of earnest prayer and compassionate remonstrance.

Although our parents went very little into company, we of the younger generation saw a good deal of our friends. My sister Rebecca was very popular. Like her brother Tom, she had a fine voice and genius for music, so that our house became a sort of musical centre, and we were welcomed in all directions. It was a happy period of our lives; and the greater part of it was passed at 3 Jesmond High Terrace, a most pleasantly situated block of buildings, which at that time marked the extreme limit of Newcastle towards the north. Our parents were much pleased, not

only with the class of young men with whom we
associated, but also with the various subjects on
which we occupied ourselves in leisure time.
Thus I was one of about twenty more who got
up a Literary and Scientific Association. We
met at each other's homes or houses, and every
member was expected to read a paper, or lead a
discussion, on some topic of general interest. The
first meeting I attended was on the 19th of
January 1854, when a paper on Acoustics was
read. It was held at the rooms of one of Robert
Stephenson's favourite engineering pupils, with
whom I became acquainted that night for the
first time. His name was Jeremiah Head; but
little could I have imagined that the friendship
thus commenced was ultimately to lead to my
own and my eldest sister's marriages, and to my
brother Tom's important business partnership.

Our connection with the Family of Head has been a matter
of so much importance, and so largely swayed my father's course
of action, that it is well to say a few words about it at this point,
although in doing so I must speak as with the knowledge of later
years.

There were two branches of the Heads,[1] distinguished for the
time being from one another, as " the Jeremiah Heads of Ipswich,"
and " the Alfred Heads of London."

Old Jeremiah Head, who was a first cousin of Mr. Alfred
Head, was a much respected member of the Society of Friends,
and for some time Mayor of Ipswich. He had a large, clever,
and energetic family. Of these I need only mention two, viz.,
Jeremiah, and his younger brother Arthur. The former is
now a well-known Consulting Engineer, who in 1885-6 was
President of the Institution of Mechanical Engineers. The

[1] See Appendix I.

latter, next after my brother Tom, is by far the largest shareholder in the Engineering Works of Head, Wrightson and Co. at Thornaby-on-Tees.

Mr. Alfred Head had no sons, and his family consisted of a wife and three daughters. He was a born-member of the Society of Friends; but, after the example of his good mother, had been baptized and joined the Church of England. His mother was first cousin, not only to Mrs. Elizabeth Fry and Joseph John Gurney, the great philanthropists, but also to Samuel Gurney, Mrs. Hoare, Lady Buxton, and a number of the Hanburys; so that his connections included some of the most famous people in London for vast benevolence and wealth. By a most singular coincidence, both he and his wife could show lines of royal descent from King Edward the Third.[1] He was the most charming, and altogether most loveable old gentleman I ever knew. I have heard him compared to one of the brothers Cheeryble in Dickens' *Nicholas Nickleby*,—and, if a few slightly grotesque features be removed from those captivating twin characters, I think the likeness is admissible. In his great Counting House he was adored by every clerk,—from old Mr. Pindar (his "Tim Linkinwater"), who was there for near fifty years, to the youngest who found himself in the employ of one, whose great capacities for business were associated with thoughtful benevolence and sweet tranquillity of disposition. His wife was good, benevolent, and intellectual. And my life-long intimacy with the daughters has enabled me to estimate at its true worth the varying, but in each case harmonious, development of the best qualities derived from both their parents. When I first became intimate with Mr. Alfred Head, he was living in handsome style, with a country house at Epsom and a town house near Hyde Park. He was a generous giver to the Church and to innumerable charitable objects. But his business income increased so much more rapidly than his expenditure, that, at the close of his long partnership, it was found he had made what most people would call a large fortune.

The break-up of our family circle commenced in 1860 with the marriage of my eldest sister to my friend Jeremiah Head, and my own almost

[1] See Appendix K.

simultaneous departure to Cambridge. After this, it was not long before my parents found themselves with no one left save Mary. But though they never saw us again, except as casual visitors, they followed our widely different paths with sympathizing love and wisely rendered aid. Thus in 1863 they were rejoiced and proud to see their son John appointed Professor of Agriculture at the Royal Agricultural College, Cirencester. And in 1866 my father was able, not only to advance money to his son Thomas to join Jeremiah Head's brother in Works that have since become large and splendidly successful, but also to assist me in arranging for my most happy marriage with Priscilla Anne, the eldest daughter of Mr. Alfred Head of London.

At last the long sojourn of my parents in Newcastle came to an end. As far back as 1861, my uncle Archy Potter and his wife had gone to live near London ; and, by removal or death, the most valued of my mother's relatives and friends had disappeared. The house felt empty. The quietness became oppressive. There was no object in remaining longer. And so, without any very definite plans, they broke up their establishment in 1869, and along with Mary paid a prolonged visit to my uncle Archy, who was sorrowing over the recent loss of my dear aunt Bessy.

Soon after this I received my appointment to the Vicarage of St. Paul's, Beckenham ; and, as my parish lay within driving distance of my uncle's house at Clapham Common, my wife and I saw much of my dear parents at this time.

In 1871 they went north again, and took temporary lodgings at Redcar near to their daughter Mrs. Head. It was there that I last visited my father. He had become quite the aged man. We had much conversation, and he told me that his work was done, and that with God's help he had more than fulfilled the vow he had taken nearly fifty years before. All anxiety on account of his family had passed away, and he surveyed the progress and position of its various members with honest pride and heart-felt thankfulness. He saw me, not only as a Clergyman with a beautiful church, an attached congregation, and a peaceful parish ; but also married to his utmost satisfaction, and with a new generation springing up around me. He saw his daughter Rebecca, a happy wife and mother, with a high-principled and accomplished husband. He saw Tom settled at Norton Hall with a charming wife and family, rising by honourable means to a wealth and influence that swept all previous misfortunes of the family into oblivion. He saw John occupying an important scientific position, and accepted as one of the highest of agricultural authorities. And lastly he had Mary, still disengaged and free to bestow the kindly sunshine of her presence,—either on him, or on her much loved uncle,—just as she most could make herself a help or blessing.

The last time I ever saw my dear father in life

was at a quarter past ten on the morning of
November 10th 1871, and he was waving his
hand to me as my train passed out of Redcar
Station on the journey south. In the following
March he and my mother went to stay a few
weeks with his last surviving sister at Haughton
in the dear old house he still continued to rent
for her, and in which he had told me he would
like to die. My mother had seldom seen him
happier than he was the day before his sudden
illness. He had been in Darlington calling on
one of his most intimate and valued business
friends; and he had heard the characters and
positions of all his children spoken of in very
glowing terms. He was greatly excited, and
kept recurring again and again to what had been
said. Indeed, as he reached the close of life,
everything had assumed its brightest hue. His
own circumstances, and still more those of his
children, were such as would in the earlier days
of his Haughton life have appeared absolutely incredible. And then, as if to set a crown upon the
whole, the Spring burst forth upon the scene,
clothed with surpassing loveliness. But the wealth
and beauty of the world were not for him. He
saw them, but as from some Pisgah height, and
unselfishly rejoiced at the thought of those, whom
by constant self-denial he had honourably guided
through nearly forty years of difficulty. With the
exception of a cheque to help the Sadberge
schools, almost the last words he penned may be
taken to express the deep and solemn feelings

stealing over him. With failing hand he wrote Newman's well-known hymn, beginning,—

> Lead, kindly Light, amid the encircling gloom
> Lead Thou me on ;—
> So long Thy power hath blessed me, sure it still
> Will lead me on.

And then for the last time he walked out into the glad sunlight of the morning, and engaged in his favourite pursuit of gardening. After an early dinner, and while my mother was dressing in order to accompany him in a call on the widow of his old friend Colonel Colling of Red Hall, he was seized with sickness. It continued all night, and then the worn-out frame gave way. The mind began to wander, and the speech became confused. With solemn dignity he lay with his fine Roman face and expressive eyes towards heaven. And so, with my mother's hand clasped firmly in his, and his brother William's prayers accompanying him, he calmly and almost imperceptibly passed into another world.

It was on Friday the 12th of April 1872 that my ever-revered father thus died, just where he wished to die. On the Tuesday following, in the presence of his widow and of all his children, except Mrs. Head, he was buried at Haughton-le-Skerne, side by side with his noble-hearted sister Isabella and his still more beloved Ellen, in the family burial-place he had purchased there. The little spot of ground lies on the extreme north side of the Church-yard, some fifty yards to the west of the old tower; and it is marked by a large grey granite headstone and surrounding curb. The law no longer permitted the use of the old family vault beneath the Church at Hurworth; but, by the addition of a few lines on my grandfather's memorial tablet and the erection of a painted window, my father has also a memorial in the parish to which he belonged, when his home was at Neasham Hall.

The last twelve years of my dear Mother's life were, I am sure, the most serenely happy she had ever known. After she became a widow, I had little difficulty in persuading her to settle in the parish where I was vicar. A comfortably arranged and well-built villa-house, on a half-acre of ground, was purchased. We had it beautifully furnished; and I planned and directed the laying out of the garden with the greatest pleasure. And then on the 17th November 1873 she arrived, along with Mary, at her new home (now 21 Brackley Road, Beckenham), to spend the eventide of her life, so near my Church, that the setting sun cast the long shadow of the spire across her lawn.

She was welcomed from the first; and, as years passed by, was looked at with ever-increasing love and veneration. So far as we could see, her powers of intellect and imagination never knew any diminution. But to the vivacity of thought, which we usually associate with accomplished women in their prime, she added the sweet, ready, and almost tremulous sympathy, which forms one of the most graceful features in a refined and ripened Christian.

For some years her income was exceptionally large; but she never raised her expenditure: and, without at all reducing her capital,[1] she gradually distributed, during her lifetime, more than twenty thousand pounds among her children. I knew she was generous elsewhere; but it was not till after she had passed away, that I learned how much good she had been doing by a continuation to the last of her unobtrusive self-denial.

My mother had no fear of Death, but a very considerable fear of dying. To her Death bore no other appearance than that of removal to an infinitely wider and brighter sphere of life; but in presence of the thought of dying,—that is, of the possibly prolonged suffering and final physical collapse,—her sensitive spirit shrank. She spoke to me of the depth of gratitude she should feel, if from "the other side" she could look back to a painless exit from this lower world. And this dread was, I know for a fact, the only dark shadow that ever crossed her sunny mind.

Accompanied by her daughter and maid, my mother used to pay periodical visits to Bournemouth, Hastings, Worthing, and other accessible seaside places; but in 1884 the little party took a bolder flight and went to Redcar. Although in her eighty-second year, she was bright and buoyant; and, in the last (unposted) letter she ever

---

[1] Under my Mother's will, her share in Cramlington colliery passed equally to me and my two brothers. Each of her five children received not far short of six thousand pounds in money. And in addition Mary had her house and furniture.

wrote, describes " a delightful trip and pilgrimage to Newcastle." Along with Mary she had gone for a few days to see old scenes and faces,—had been most cordially received by her few remaining friends and relatives,—had gone with pleasure over the " Armstrong Park,"—and then, returning by Haughton on the Saturday, had taken tea with her old friend Miss Malcolm, and visited her husband's grave, little imagining that she herself would be laid beside him that day week. The following Wednesday, September 24th, she was up and dressed as usual at half-past seven ; but at breakfast complained of a slight pain in her chest, and was induced to take her book and go to bed again. She had been meditating on her text for the day,—" This is the Victory, that overcometh the World, even our faith,"—and on the accompanying verses, I think by Frances Havergal,—

> Increase our faith ! On this broad shield
> All fiery darts be caught !
> We must be Victors in the field
> Where Thou for us hast fought.
>
> Increase our faith, that we may claim
> Each starry promise sure,
> And always triumph in Thy name,
> And *to the end* endure.

There was a slight sense of sickness, and she asked for a drink of water. My sister stepped across the room to get it ; and, as she did so, heard a cheery voice respond to some remark. She took hold of the glass,—turned round,—and saw her mother lying perfectly dead, with no sound save that of a gentle gush of air from the contracting chest. Not even a finger had stirred between the pages of her book. She had had her wish : and the sweet ministering Angel, first seen as such in the starlight by my little crib, had finished its long course of self-sacrificing love, and folded its wings in the presence of its Lord.

" And we also bless Thy holy Name for all Thy servants departed this life in Thy faith and fear ; beseeching Thee to give us grace so to follow their good examples, that with them we may be partakers of Thy heavenly kingdom. Grant this, O Father, for Jesus Christ's sake. Amen."

END OF PART FIRST.

APPENDICES.

APPENDIX A.

WRIGHTSON OF IRELAND.

AUTHORITIES.

I. IRISH " R. B. G." PEDIGREE of about 1770.

"Wrightson

Arms :—A fess int. 3 cross crosslets fitchy.
Crest :—On a mount a Tiger saliant.

First Generation

Anthony Wrightson, a Cornet of Horse in Ireland, went there after the Restoration. Ob: . . . . . Buried at Cross Loch, co. Monaghan in Ireland. Married . . . . . . related to Rawdon, Lord Moyra, family ; married in the North of Ireland.

Second Generation

CHILDREN OF ANTHONY

1 :—George Wrightson, a Major, married a Massey, issue all dead.
2 :—Edward Wrightson, a Lieutenant Colonel, died unmarried.
3 :—Hector Wrightson, a Lieutenant of Dragoons, killed in Ireland, unmarried.

4 :—Anthony Wrightson, died unmarried.

5 :—Aldborough Wrightson, ob: 1739 æt: 63. Married
. . . . daur. of . . . .

Third Generation

Children of Aldborough

1 :—Carnes Wrightson, eldest son.

2 :—George Wrightson.

3 :—William Wrightson.

4 :—John Wrightson, a Major in the Army.

Fourth Generation

Children of William

Seven sons."

> Obs. :—The above pedigree is contained in one of the
> MSS. of the late Sir Ralph Bigland, Garter-King-of-
> Arms, at the Heralds' College in London, under
> reference " R. B. G. vol. i, 223." It must have been
> constructed after 1750, when Rawdon became Lord
> Moyra, and before " Major " John Wrightson (who
> died in 1779) became a Lieutenant Colonel. I there-
> fore date it about 1770.

II. PEDIGREE OF SCOTT of Ballygannon, co. Wicklow.

"Scott

First Generation

John Scott of Ballygannon, co. Wicklow. Will dated July
1767 and proved 15 Dec: following. Married Mary, dau. of
William Pendred esq. of Braghillstown, co. Carlow.

Second Generation

CHILDREN OF JOHN

1 :—SIR HOPTON SCOTT OF BALLYGANNON aforesaid Knight. Married *Anne, dau. of . . . . . Wrightson* of St. Mary's Parish in the City of Dublin. Marriage licence 3 July 1767.

2 :—John Pendred Scott of Ballygannon, esq. Will dated 7 Feb. 1793 and proved 28 Feb. following. He left a natural son named Robert Thomas Scott.

  3 :—Elizabeth.

  4 :—Martha, unmarried.

  5 :—Mary, unmarried.

  6 :—Catherine, wife of *William Harvey of Dublin, M.D.* She had a son, William Harvey.

Third Generation

CHILD OF SIR HOPTON

Major General Sir Hopton Stratford Scott of the East India Company's Service, was nominated a Knight Commander of the Bath at the Coronation of William IV., 26 Sep. 1831, and was invested 28 Sep. 1831. Married Mary, dau. of Joseph Davie Bassett esq. of Umberleigh, co. Devon.

CHILDREN OF JOHN

1 :—John Middleton Scott, eldest son. Married 21 Mar. 1803, Lady Arabella Barbara Brabazon, dau. of Anthony, 9th Earl of Meath.

  2 :—James Smith Scott, second son.

  3 :—Edward William Scott, third son.

Fourth Generation

CHILD OF JOHN

Elizabeth Ruth Scott, married 30 Jan. 1849 to William, 11th Earl of Devon."

> Obs. :—The above pedigree, having been constructed from Records, etc., in the Office of the Ulster King-of-Arms in Ireland, was forwarded to me by one of the officials in the College of Arms, London, in 1887.

III. REGISTER OF BAPTISM, Delgany, co. Wicklow. "1772 Feb. 21. John Wrightson, son of Hopton and Ann Scott."

> Obs. :—As the Ballygannon of Authorities II and IV is in the parish of Delgany, this is clearly the child of Sir Hopton and Lady Anne Scott, and therefore the grand-child of Alderman George Wrightson of Dublin.

IV. WILL OF ANNE WRIGHTSON, dated 13 Dec. 1800, proved in Dublin 9 May 1803.

". . . . . . I Anne Wrightson of the City of Dublin, *widow of Alderman George Wrightson of the same city.* . . ."

". . . . . to my eldest daughter Elizabeth Nesbit, widow. . . ."

". . . . . . to my grandson Caracross Nesbitt. . . ."

". . . . . . to my grandson James Nesbitt. . . ."

". . . . . . to *my daughter Lady Anne Scott* . . . . . . her late husband's house Great Georges Street and at *Ballygannon.* . . ."

". . . . . . to my grand-daughters Mary Stewart, otherwise Scott, Elizabeth Scott, and Anne Scott . . . . . and Louisa Scott. . . ."

". . . . . . my worthy friend *Doctor William Harvey.*"

V. WILL OF ALDERMAN GEORGE WRIGHTSON, dated 17 June 1783, proved in Dublin 12 Nov. 1783.

"...... I George Wrightson of the City of Dublin Alderman...."

"...... to my dear wife Ann Wrightson...."

"...... to my daughter Elizabeth Nisbitt...."

"...... to my grandson George Nisbitt..."

"...... to my grand-daughter Jane Nisbitt...."

"...... to my grand-daughter Ann Nisbitt...."

"...... to my grand-daughter Elizabeth Nisbitt...."

"...... to *my daughter Ann Scott*...."

"...... to my grandson George Scott...."

"...... to my grand-daughter Mary Scott...."

"...... to my grand-daughter Elizabeth Scott."

"...... to my grand-daughter Ann Scott...."

"...... to my niece Martha Houge."

"...... to my niece Martha Sherlock...."

VI. WILL OF LIEUTENANT-COLONEL JOHN WRIGHTSON, dated 29 July 1779, proved in Dublin 1 Nov. 1779.

"This is the last Will and testament of me Lieutenant Colonel John Wrightson, now residing at Chelsea Cottage in the county of Middlesex...."

"I give and devise all my lands .... in the province of New York in North America .... unto and to the use of my brother Aldborough Wrightson .... and I do hereby appoint *my brother George Wrightson*...."

"...... to *my brother Aldborough Wrightson of Dundalk*, Ireland ...., to his son Thomas Wrightson ...., to *his daughter Sarah Medley*...."

"...... to my sister Anne Wetherby .... to her son Henry Wetherby .... to my niece Amelia Wetherby .... to my niece Agnes Wetherby...."

"...... to my sister Mary Gyles .... to her-daughter Martha Gyles...."

"...... to my niece Frances Coming, only daughter of my *eldest* brother...."

". . . . . . to *my nephew John Wrightson Scott.* . . ."

". . . . . . to my worthy friend Alexander Scott esq. of James Street, Bedford Row. . . ."

". . . . . . to *Martha Clarke, spinster,* now apprentice to and residing with Mrs. Michie and Grame on Ludgate Hill, London . . . . after the 5th January 1786, before which time the said Martha Clarke will, if she lives, have attained her age of twenty one years . . . . to John Clarke a brother of the said Martha . . . . to William another brother . : . . to Margaret a sister . . . . to Elizabeth another sister . . . . during their respective minorities. . . ." [The legacies to this group of Clarke children, apparently orphans residing in London, amount in all to £800. And we note that this was left to them by a grandson of Cornet Anthony Wrightson.]

". . . . . . twenty pounds sterling to be distributed to such poor persons in the parish of *Monaghan* in Ireland as . . . ." [We remember that Cornet Anthony Wrightson was buried in co. Monaghan.]

> Obs.:—The Testator's mention of his nephew John Wrightson Scott proves that his brother George was Alderman George Wrightson of Dublin (see Authority III, Obs.). This will then proves that Alderman George W. had an "eldest" brother,—had another called "Aldborough",—and another who at one time was a "Major John W." feeling interest in "Monaghan." From this it is clear that the "George W." of the third generation in Authority I is no other than Alderman George Wrightson of Dublin.

VII. WILL OF ALDBOROUGH WRIGHTSON, date deficient, proved in Dublin 30 June 1788, with second administation 28 Aug. 1790.

"I *Aldborough Wrightson of Dundalk* . . . . merchant. . . ."

". . . . . to my beloved wife Harriot. . . ."

". . . . . to my sister Ann Witherby. . . ."

". . . . . to the use of my son Thomas Wrightson. . . ."

" . . . . to the two children of *my daughter Sarah* Wright, Thomas Meadley and Harriot Meadley by *her former husband Thomas Meadley* the sum of . . . . due to me by mortgage from my son-in-law John Wright. . . ."

" . . . . . to my nephew and friend Mr. John Page of Dundalk, the younger. . . ."

From the addition made 28 Aug. 1790,—

" . . . . . . Martha Wrightson, the widow and relict and admīx of Thomas Wrightson deceased intestate. . . ."

VIII. COPY OF NOTICE IN A MAGAZINE of 1806, supplied by one of the Irish Wrightsons.

" December 1806. At Lowther Lodge, co. Dublin, James Gildea of Ballinrobe, co. Mayo, esq., to Miss Martha Wrightson, second daughter of the late Thomas Wrightson esq. of Dundalk."

IX. WILL OF CAPTAIN GEORGE WRIGHTSON, dated 1 May 1702, proved in Dublin 31 July 1703.

" . . . . . . I, George Wrightson of Killnegannogh in the King's county, Captain in Brigadier Hamilton's Regiment, being commanded out of this kingdom. . . ."

" . . . . . . to *Mary Wrightson my dearly beloved wife* all my stock with all my household goods and Farms, moveables, moneys due to me as my Arrears for my service in the Army. . . ." [As this was written only seven and a half weeks after the accession of Queen Anne, and as Authority I shows him to have soon received his Majority, he was doubtless a Captain in time of William III.].

" . . . . . . my brother Samuel *Massy* and *Edward Wrightson.* . . ." [The mention of his brothers Edward and Samuel Massy identifies the Testator with Major George W., the son of Cornet Anthony W. in Authority I.]

> Obs.:—To this will is appended in Latin what the widow, as sole executrix, swore to 31 July 1703.

From this we learn that her husband had died "in partibus transmarinis,"—no doubt in connection with the War of the Succession, though he did not live to fight at Blenheim.

X. WILL OF JOHN WRIGHTSON OF LONDON,

dated 10 Mar. 1683-4, proved in London 27 Jan. 1684-5.

". . . . . . I, John Wrightson of the parish of St. Martins-in-the-Fields, in the county of Middlesex, Gent. . . ."

". . . . . . my houses situate in Suffolk Street in the said parish . . . . which I now live in. . . ."

". . . . . . my wel beloved and deare *wife Dorothy.* . . ."

". . . . . . unto my loving *brother Thomas Wrightson* the sume of two hundred pounds, and to my loving *brother Anthony Wrightson* the sum of one hundred pounds by them respectively to be divided amongst *their children.* . . ." [As Thomas is three times mentioned before Anthony it is clear he was the elder of the two.]

". . . . . . to my niece Mary Watsonne and *her children.* . . ." [These were of course the grandchildren of some brother or sister, almost certainly of Mrs. Clarke. But as the Testator was only about 56 at this time, he must have been a younger child of his parents.]

". . . . . . unto *my nephew Benjamin Clarke.* . . ."

". . . . . . to *my niece, his sister, Isabella Clarke.* . . ."

". . . . . . to my godsonne John Clarke. . . ."

". . . . . . to my goddaughter Mary Bowstred. . . ."

". . . . . . my worthy friend and *kinsman* Mr. Richard Pearson Rector of St. Michaels Crooked Lane, London. . . ." [From the London Marriage Licenses we find that on 24 Nov. 1675 this Rector had married Mary Wroughton. Remembering that the grandmother of the Testator's wife was a Wroughton, we see the nature of the 'kinship.']

". . . . . . my *kinsman* Joseph Bowstred of Shefford in the county of Bedford, gent. And John Clarke of the parish of St. Martin-in-the-Fields . . . . my Executors . . . . to whom, for the benefit of *their children* to be distributed as they shall think fit, I devise all the rest of my Estate. . . ." [The former executor appears as "Boulstred" in the administration. The latter is apparently another nephew Clarke with a young family.]

> Obs.:—Although the Testator is not a link, yet it is practically certain that he is a pendant in the Irish pedigree. That his brother Anthony is the same as the Irish Cornet Anthony in Authority I, is I think clear, when we notice how both the Testator and the grandson of the Irish Cornet in Authority VI leave money to the London Clarkes. Besides the Cornet, there was however a younger Anthony W.,[1] a victualler, born only ten years before the Restoration, who lived in St. Margaret's, Westminster.

XI. WILL OF DOROTHY WRIGHTSON, dated 8 Jan. 1686-7, proved in London 21 Jan. 1686-7.

". . . . . I, Dorothy Wrightson of the parish of St. Martins-in-the-Fields . . . widow. . . ."

". . . . . to *John Clarke*, Baker, Tenne pounds for mourning and to his Wife five pounds and to *his children* five pounds apiece. . . ." [No doubt the London executor of her late husband.]

". . . . . to Mr. Richard Person, Minister. . . ."

". . . . . to Robina, the daughter of Richard Person, Minister the sum of one hundred pounds. . . ."

". . . . . to my kinswoman Frances Howard of Norfolk my *sister's* daughter. . . ." [There is no sister mentioned in the Thynne pedigrees.]

". . . . . to my *kinsman* Richard Farrow. . . ."

". . . . . to the Lady Selinger. . . ." [*i.e.* St. Leger.]

". . . . . to the Lady Isabella Bruce. . . ." [Robert, Viscount Bruce of Ampthill, co. Bedford, was created Earl of

---

[1] See Westminster Abbey Registers, Harl. Soc. Publications, vol. 10, p. 18 note.

Aylesbury in 1664. He died in 1685, in which year he was Lord Chamberlain of the Household of Charles II. One of his daughters was the unmarried Lady Isabella Bruce: see Edmondson's *Baronagium Genealogicum*, p. 440.]

". . . . . . to Charles Richards, the sonne of Charles Richards of the parish of Ampthill in Bedfordshire. . . ."

". . . . . . to Mary Crouth of Bedfordshire. . . ."

". . . . . . to my goddaughter, the child of Ann Palmer of Bedfordshire. . . ."

> Obs. :—The Testator's husband is described both in his Marriage License and Will as 'of London,' but in the Thynne pedigrees as "of Ampthill, co. Bedford." I have myself searched the Calendar of Bedfordshire Wills from 1536 to 1700, and I have had the Ampthill parish registers searched with especial care from 1620 to 1640; but in neither does the name of Wrightson occur. The Bedfordshire associations of the Testator and her husband would be accounted for, if he was one of the Gentlemen of the Lord Chamberlain's household; and his house in Suffolk Street was very near the Court at Whitehall.

XII. LONDON MARRIAGE LICENSES, ed. by Joseph Foster.

"Wrightson, John, of St. James, Clerkenwell, gent., bachelor, about 34, and Dorothy Thynn, of the same, spinster, about 30, at her own disposal, at St. Saviour, Southwark, 28 July 1662." [From 1551 to 1700 the only Wrightson or Writson entries in the registers of St. James, Clerkenwell, are the burial of a "Cuthbert W., the elder, householder," in 1593; the baptism of his daughter Rebecca in 1592, and her burial in 1593.]

XIII. THE THYNNE PEDIGREES (Viscount Weymouth and Marquis of Bath).

1. From Edmondson's *Baronagium Genealogicum*, p. 326: " Dorothy, mar. —— Wrightston (*sic*) of Hampthill, co. Bedf."

2. From Collins' *Peerage of England* by Brydges, vol. ii, p. 501 : " Dorothy, the wife of —— Wrightson, of Ampthill in Bedfordshire."

XIV. WILL OF EDWARD ALDBOROUGH of Ellingthorpe, gent., dated 26 July 1613, proved at York 13 Sep. 1613.

" . . . . . . unto Arthur Aldborough gent., Dorathie the wife of Francis Rawdon gent., *Mary Aldborough*, and Jane Aldborough, children of William Aldborough late of Aldborough aforesaid gent. . . ."

" . . . . . . to the said William Aldborough. . . ."

" . . . . . . to every one of the youngest children of William Mauleverer of Arncliff esquire. . . ."

" . . . . . . unto John Brown of Knaresbrough my mother's brother. . . ."

" . . . . . . unto *Anthony Wrightson*, William Barnabie, Robert Watson, and Richard Fensdale, my father's servants. . . ."

" . . . . . . unto *my father, Richard Aldborough of Ellingthorpe* esquire one twilted night cap."

" . . . . . . unto Mistress Aldborough of Ellingthorpe my mother in law [*i.e.* step-mother]. . . ."

" . . . . . . to my sister Annie Aldborough. . . ."

" . . . . . . to Arthur Aldborough or his wife a book called Resolutions, and to Richard Aldborough his son one English Testament."

" . . . . . . to the said William Aldborough and Arthur Aldborough his son, whom I make joynt Executors of this my last Will. . . ."

> Obs. :—Ellingthorpe Hall and Aldborough Hall are only about half a mile apart, so there can be no doubt that it was the above Anthony Wrightson who soon after married Mary Aldborough. Standing first and foremost in the list of so-called " servants," he was most likely the Steward or Estate Manager at Ellingthorpe. The word ' servant ' embraced a much higher class of

employés formerly than now. Thus in 1660 Mr.
Pepys speaks of his sister as his "servant." Again in
1657 occurs an entry in the register of Ottery St.
Mary commencing "Sep. 7. George Trobridge,
Gentleman, servant unto John Vaughan Esq., married
Elizabeth," etc. And a few years earlier Archbishop
Laud speaks of "Mr. Adam Forbes," his steward, as
his "servant." When we notice the marriage
Anthony Wrightson made and the position of his
sons, we at once perceive that the word "servant"
can imply nothing debased in his case.

XV. PEDIGREE OF ALDBOROUGH, see Appendix B.

Obs. :—The connection between this and Authority I is
clear. For Authority I is headed by what is virtually
a modification of the Alborough shield ; it contains
the names of Aldborough, Anthony, and Rawdon ; it
commences with the generation to which the children
of Anthony and Mary Wrightson belonged ; and
lastly the most probable account of the Anthony, who
went to Ireland after the Restoration as a Cornet of
Horse, is that he went to join the Troop of Irish
Horse, which in 1661 was placed under the command
of his first cousin George Rawdon.

PEDIGREE.

First Generation

1 :—ANTHONY WRIGHTSON, mentioned in 1613 as employed
in some capacity by Richard Aldborough of Ellingthorpe in the
parish of Aldborough, near Boroughbridge, co. York = Mary,
a younger dau. of Wm. Aldborough of Aldborough afsd., and
aunt to Sir Geo. Rawdon, Bart., of Moyra, co. Down, Ireland,
the ancestor of Lord Moyra ; bap. at Aldborough 16 May
1590.

Second Generation

CHILDREN OF ANTHONY (1)

2 :—Daughter = ... Clarke ; issue.

3 :—THOMAS W., mentioned in his brother John's will in 1684, as being then a father and great-uncle.

  4 :—John W., described in his mar. license as "of St. James, Clerkenwell, gent., bachelor of about 34,"— in the Thynne pedigrees as "of Ampthill, co. Bedford,"—and in his will as "of Suffolk Street, in the parish of St. Martins in the Fields, co. Middlesex, gent."; born about 1628 ; bur. at St. Martin's in the Fields 8 Jan. 1684-5 ; his will, dated 10 Mar. 1683-4, was proved in London 27 Jan. 1684-5 = Dorothy, dau. of Wm. Thynne, and grand-daughter of Sir John Thynne [1] of Longleate, co. Wilts ; born about 1632 ; mar. by license at St. Saviour's, Southwark, 28 July 1662 ; bur. beside her husband 19 Jan. 1686-7 ; her will, dated 8 Jan. 1686-7, proved in London 21 Jan. 1686-7.

  5 :—ANTHONY W., a Cornet of Horse who went to Ireland

---

[1] This Sir John Thynne, Knt. and Banneret, was twice married, leaving two families.

His first wife was Christiana, sister and heir of the Sir Thomas Gresham who built the Royal Exchange. By her he had 3 sons and 4 daughters. The head of this family became in 1682 Viscount Weymouth, and in 1789 Marquis of Bath.

His second wife was Dorothy, dau. of Sir Wm. Wroughton of Broadhinton, co. Wilts. By her he had 5 sons and 2 daughters. The youngest of these sons was William, who married Alicia Talbot, and by her was the father of 1 son and of Dorothy, wife of John Wrightson. In her will she mentions a sister, of whom I can find no further trace.

The Thynne pedigrees show that Dorothy Wrightson was niece to one of the maids of honour of Queen Elizabeth, and was also first cousin to the grandfather of the Mr. Thynne murdered close to Suffolk Street, 12 Feb. 1682.

after the Restoration of 1660; mentioned in his brother John's will in 1684, as being then a father and great-uncle; bur. at Cross Loch, co. Monaghan = ..., a relative of his first cousin Sir Geo. Rawdon, Bart.; mar. in the North of Ireland.

Third Generation

CHILD OF THOMAS (3)

6 :—Child or children living in 1684.

CHILDREN OF ANTHONY (5)

7 :—George W. of Killnegannogh, King's county, a Captain and finally a Major in the Army of Queen Anne; died on foreign service; his will, dated 1 May 1702, proved in Dublin 31 July 1703 = Mary Massey, who survived him; *s. pr.*

8 :—Edward W., a Lieut.-Colonel; lg. in 1702; unmar.

9 :—Hector W., a Lieut. of Dragoons; killed in Ireland; unmar.

10 :—Anthony W., unmar.

11 :—ALDBOROUGH W., died 1739, aged 63.

Fourth Generation

CHILDREN OF ALDBOROUGH (11)

12 :—CARNES W., eldest son.

13 :—GEORGE W., Alderman of Dublin; living in St. Mary's parish in 1767; bur. at St. Peter's 6 Nov. 1783; his will, dated 17 June 1783, proved in Dublin 12 Nov. 1783 = Anne . . . .; bur. beside her husband 29 Apr. 1803; her will, dated 13 Dec. 1800, proved in Dublin 9 May 1803.

14 :—WILLIAM W., left seven sons.

15 :—John W., Lieut. Colonel, of Chelsea Cottage, Middlesex; his will, dated 29 July 1779, proved in Dublin 1 Nov. 1779.

16 :—ALDBOROUGH W., of Dundalk, co. Louth ; his will was proved in Dublin 30 June 1788 = Harriot . . . .; survived him.

    17 :—Ann W. = ... Wetherby ; issue.
    18 :—Mary W. = ... Gyles ; issue.

Fifth Generation

CHILD OF CARNES (12)

19 :—Frances W.

CHILDREN OF GEORGE (13)

20 :—Elizabeth W., a widow in 1800 = ... Nesbitt. Known issue ;—Caracross N.,—George N.,—James N.,—Ann N.,—Elizabeth N.

21 :—Anne W., lg. 1800 = Sir Hopton Scott, knt. of Ballygannon, parish of Delgany, co. Wicklow ; mar. by license dated 3 July 1767 ; died intestate, administration granted in the Prerogative Court, Dublin, 19 Nov. 1789. Known issue ;—Major General Sir Hopton Stratford Scott, K.C.B.,—John Wrightson S.,—George S.,—Mrs. Mary Stewart,—Elizabeth S., —Anne S.,—Louisa S.

CHILDREN OF ALDBOROUGH (16)

22 :—THOMAS W. of Dundalk ; died intestate, administration 20 Aug. 1790 = Martha . . . . .; lg. 1790.

    23 :—Sarah W. = (1st) Thomas Meadley ; issue = (2nd) John Wright.

Sixth Generation

CHILDREN OF THOMAS (22)

24 :—Daughter, elder.

25 :—Martha W. = James Gildea of Ballinrobe, co. Mayo, mar. Dec. 1806.

Obs. :—The following is taken from a mass of unverified information supplied to me by my friend Mr. Richard Stephen Wrightson, the present head of the Irish Family, assisted by his venerable mother.

Owing to early deaths of parents and removal from old localities their domestic tradition has broken short. But, as they say they are of the same family as the late Alderman Wrightson of Dublin and that their English ancestor came from Yorkshire, they are almost certainly descended from one of the "seven sons" of No. 14 in the above pedigree. In this case one of these seven sons would be the father of Richard Wrightson, the Master of Ordnance for Ireland, who died 1831, his wife having been C. Lyons of co. Westmeath, who died 1817 aged 21. They left two sons, viz., Thomas Richard, Rector of Culfeightrin, co. Antrim, born 1815, died 1874, married 1844 Hetty C. Rice of Mount Rice, co. Kildare : and Richard, Rector of Lusk, co. Dublin, born 1817, died 1875, married 1850 Harriet, dau. of Arthur Nepean Molesworth of Fairlawn, co. Armagh (concerning whom see pedigrees of Viscount Molesworth, especially that in Joseph Foster's *Royal Descents*). The elder Rector left two sons, viz., Richard Stephen, now of Surbiton, co. Surrey, born 1845, married, but childless ; and Edmund, a surgeon at Halesworth, co. Suffolk, born 1849, died 1883, leaving a son Thomas Richard, born 1875, and daughters. The younger Rector also left two sons, Richard Blayney, born 1851, and Arthur Nepean, born 1852.

APPENDIX B.

ALDBOROUGH OF ALDBOROUGH, CO. YORK.

The village of Aldborough, near Boroughbridge, occupies the central portion of the site of the Roman Isurium. The Hall, which stands upon the foundations of the ancient wall near the east gate, was for many generations the home of the Aldborough Family, who also owned Ellingthorpe Hall, about half a mile distant on the other side of the Yore. The decay of this Family was much accelerated during the period of the Civil War. Its final ruin is ascribed by the people of the neighbourhood to the conduct of Sir Richard, "the Royalist," brother-in-law to the redoubtable Cavalier, Colonel Sir John Mallory of Studley Royal. In the sense of ownership I believe that Sir Richard's third son, named after himself, was the last of the Aldboroughs of Aldborough. After his time the manor passed into other hands. In 1887 the owner of the Hall was G. A. Hutton Croft, J.P., who received me courteously, and allowed me thoroughly to examine his beautiful and interesting old Elizabethan mansion. In spite of a savage wrecking by a Puritan mob, the so-called "Aldborough Chapel" in the parish church contains one famous Brass and other family relics, among which is the mutilated monument of William, son of the Richard Aldborough with whom I commence my construction of the latest portion of his ancient pedigree.

AUTHORITIES.

(Vis.) = *Visitation of Yorkshire*, 1584-5 and 1612. Ed. by Joseph Foster.
(Har.) = Harleian MSS. No. 6070, Brit. Mus.
(Wil.) = Wilsonian MSS. in the Leeds Library.

(Reg.) = Parish Registers at Aldborough,—partially searched.

(Tur.) = T. S. Turner's *Hist. of Aldborough and Boroughbridge.*

(Wal.) = J. R. Walbran's *Memoir of the Lords of Studley* (privately printed).

(Sur.) = Surtees' *Hist. of Durham.*

(P. R. O.) = Public Record Office. See 40th Report of Deputy Keeper for 1879, pp. 5 and 489.

(Will E. A.) = Will of Edward Aldborough of Ellingthorpe, dated 26 July 1613, and proved at York 13 Sep. 1613.

PEDIGREE.

Arms :—Azure, a fesse argent between three cross crosslets or.

Crest :—On a torce, or and azure, " an ibex " or.

First Generation

1 :—RICHARD ALDEBURGH of Aldeburgh, lg. 1585 = (1st) Lucy, dau. of Sir Ralph Bourchier of Bourchier, Knt., no issue = (2nd) Eleanor, dau. of Thos. Goldesborough of Goldesborough.

Second Generation

CHILDREN OF RICHARD (1)

2 :—Ellinor A., born 1553 = William Mauleverer of Wothersome, who built the old Manor house at Arncliff.

3 :—WILLIAM A., eldest son, lg. 1612 = (1st) Anne, dau. of Arthur Kay of Woodsome = (2nd) Mary Burdett.

4 :—Francis A.

5 :—Richard A. [He was almost certainly the legatee described by an Edward A. in 1613 as "my father Richard Aldborough of Ellingthorpe" (Will E. A.).]

Third Generation

CHILDREN OF WILLIAM (3)

6 :—William A., bap. 1579.

7 :—Richard A., bap. 1583.

8:—ARTHUR A., son and heir, bap. 1585. In 1607 he and his wife bought the manor of Middleton-one-Row, co. Durham, and land, etc., there (P. R. O.) ; but sold it again in 1612 (Sur. vol. iii, p. 225). In 1630 he is described as " Baron " Arthur A., lord of the manor of Aldborough, and as holding his regular courts of suit and service (Tur. pp. 50, 134). The Wilsonian MS. adds in red ink the following suggestive note, " This Arthur paid £400 to Oliver's Harpies." And in 1649 there is mention of a sequestration for " his delinquency against Parliament " (P. R. O.). = Elizabeth, dau. and coheir of Richard Holland of Heaton, co. Lanc.

9 :—William A., bap. 1588.

10:—Ann A., bap. 1576-7.

11 :—Dorothy A. = Francis Rawdon of Rawdon Hall, near Leeds ; mar. 1603. [Their only son George, great-grandfather of Lord Moyra, was born 1604. He became secretary at Court to Lord Conway,—received grants of land in Ireland,—was first to check the Irish Rebellion in Nov. 1641,—was a distinguished Royalist,—received the command of a troop of Irish Horse 20 Mar. 1661,—was Sergeant Major, a Commissioner for Ireland, Governor of Carrickfergus, and M.P. for Carlingford. He had a seat at the Council Board ; and in 1665 was created Sir George Rawdon, Bart. of Moira. He died in 1684. His second wife was dau. of the above Lord Conway, Mareschal of Ireland (see Lodge's *Peerage of Ireland*, vol. iii, p. 95).]

12 :—Mary A. (Vis.), ' Mary dau. of Wm. Aldborough

bap. 16 May 1590' (Reg.) = "Mr. Wrightson" (Wil.),—"wife of Anthony Wrightson" (Har.). In 1613 he is mentioned by Edward, the son of Richard Aldborough of Ellingthorpe, as in his father's service in some unspecified capacity (Will E. A.).

13:—Jane A., bap. 1591 = Ralph Tunstall, Rector of Long Newton, co. Durham; mar. at Aldborough 23 Jan. 1623-4 (Reg.); bur. at Long Newton 22 Apr. 1659 (Sur. vol. iii, p. 273).

Fourth Generation

CHILDREN OF ARTHUR (8)

14 :—SIR RICHARD A., Knt., son and heir, aged 5 in 1612. Along with Robert Strickland he was returned 7 Oct. 1640 as M.P. for Aldborough in the Long Parliament; but from the Commons' Journal, 12 Sep. 1645, we learn that they were both "disabled to sit," no doubt as Royalists. It was after this he was knighted. The Wilsonian MS. adds in red ink, "In 1642 he gave to the King at York £200, for which his father suffered as above." = Alice, dau. of William Mallory, and sister of Sir John Mallory, M.P. for Ripon in 1640, who, as a Colonel of Dragoons and Governor of Skipton Castle, did efficient service for the King, driving Sir Thomas Mauleverer and his forces out of Ripon (Wal.); mar. at Studley Hall 22 Nov. 1627.

15 :—Arthur A.

16 :—Thomas A.

17 :—Philip A.

18 :—Elizabeth A.

Fifth Generation

CHILDREN OF RICHARD (14)

19 :—WILLIAM A., son and heir, died 1678 = Elizabeth, dau. of John Sykes of Leeds, and widow of Wm. Lodge of Leeds, merchant ; died 1671 (Wil.).

20 :—Arthur A.

21 :—RICHARD A. of Aldborough, brother and heir male of William (Wil.), bap. 17 Dec. 1630 = Mary, dau. and heir of Sir Ingram Hopton, Knt., of Armley Hall, near Leeds, and widow of that Sir Miles Stapleton of Wighill and Armley, who in his burial register of 1668 at Fewston is described as " that quondam almost unparalleled Roialist." [Sir Ingram Hopton was slain 11 Oct. 1643 in the fight at Winceby, after unhorsing and nearly killing Oliver Cromwell.]

22 :—John A., unmar.

Sixth Generation

CHILD OF WILLIAM (19)

23 :—Elizabeth A., dau. and heir of William, died unmar. at Leeds 22 Dec. 1722 aged 69, bur. in St. Peter's choir at . . . . .

CHILDREN OF RICHARD (21)

24 :—Hopton A., died young.

25 :—Richard A., lg. in Jamaica in 1709.

26 :—Alice A. = Robert Hitch of Leathley esq.

27 :—Mary A. = Mr. Broadhurst.

28 :—Arabella A., unmar.

APPENDIX C.

WRIGHTSON OF CRAG, CO. YORK, AND OF OSBASTON, CO. LEICESTER.

From the battlements of the once famous Tees-side fortress of Barnard Castle the view towards the west is terminated by a bold ridge, ending towards the south in a crag, which has given its name to the adjacent lands. The situation is fine. It forms the lofty ground, which divides the romantic gorge of Deepdale from the noble valley of the Upper Tees, and it is situated in the manor of Lartington, which manor, together with others like Cotherstone and Mickleton, are included in the great Yorkshire parish of Romaldkirk. It was in this parish, though chiefly centring round Crag, that what must in the aggregate have come to form a considerable amount of landed property was held by various members of a family called Wrightson,—which family it is just possible may have first been brought from Eryholme by the Markenfields. The name occurs as early as 1415 on the first page of the Lartington court roll; and, among those I noticed in that roll, I may mention the name of a William Wrightson, who in 1457, during the reign of Henry VI., is associated with the most famous Earl of Warwick (the "King-maker"), the Abbot of Eggleston, and Sir Richard Harcourt, in the very limited class of freeholders. Again, while keeping my eyes open for information about the Irish family, descending from the Anthony Wrightson who married Mary Aldborough,[1] I noticed no less than three Anthonies among the Romaldkirk Wrightsons. The first of these was buried in 1602, and was doubtless the

[1] Appendix A.

Anthony " of Lartington," whose will (now lost) is mentioned in the Richmond Calendar for that year. He was probably the father of the second Anthony, who is mentioned among the " tenants for a term of years " in the court roll for the years 1607, 1610, and 1620. The third Anthony has left the trace of his presence in the register of the birth of a child in 1655. The second of these Anthonies was indeed a contemporary of the 'Aldborough' Anthony; but he could hardly have been the same, for he was clearly a Lartington tenant in 1613, at which date we know the 'Aldborough' Anthony to have been in the service of Richard Aldborough at Ellingthorpe Hall, full fifty miles from Romaldkirk. The first clearly noteworthy member of the main line of this family is the Cuthbert Wrightson, who stands at the head of the subjoined Heralds' pedigree of the Wrightsons of Osbaston. He appears also in the Lartington court roll,—in the Romaldkirk burial register,— in the Richmond Calendar of Wills,—and (under the heading of " Lartington ") in the same list of Rebels as contains the name of Thomas Wrightson of Eryholme.[1] He was contemporary with Queen Elizabeth; and in 1569 took some sort of part in the great Rising of the North. The chief agent in punishing the rebels was Sir George Bowes, who was of the ancient family of Bowes of Bowes near Crag. It is probable that through the influence of neighbourly associations, or through some private negotiation, Cuthbert was enabled to evade the full penalty of his offence. The register of his burial in 1593 shows that he was not executed, and the court roll proves that at all events a part of his landed property remained to descend to his eldest son, who in 1596 is described as " Miles Wrightson of the Crag, son and next heir to Cuthbert Wrightson of the Waste, his father." From Miles this property passed to William, and then to Michael, great-grandson of the old rebel.

Michael Wrightson was one of the Ancients of Clement's Inn in London. He is mentioned in the Lartington court roll

[1] Authority IV.

as holding property there, though "residing outside the manor." His name occurs near the commencement of the enormous will of William Hutchinson of Clement's Inn (proved in London 20 July 1698), where he appears as one of the trustees for benefactions in Romaldkirk, etc. He was owner of the Osbaston estates in Leicestershire; and he proved and registered his pedigree at the College of Arms on the 24th April 1695.

Philippa, the only child and heiress of Michael Wrightson of Osbaston, was married about 1689 to the Francis Mundy of Marketon in Derbyshire, who five years later was High Sheriff of that county, and whose descendants are recorded in Burke's *Landed Gentry.*

The following are the chief authorities from which I have gleaned my knowledge of this family—

I. COURT ROLL OF THE MANOR OF LARTINGTON.

Among the muniments at Lartington Hall are certain court rolls of the manor. They are in most cases fragments, probably cut from larger rolls, and the series is far from complete. On the same membranes and papers are records of several other manors, as of Mickleton and Cotherstone. The name of Wrightson has been searched for in all the records relating to Lartington from the earliest, which commences 4 Henry V. After 3 Richard III. there is nothing older than 6 Henry VIII. From the following records only a few extracts have been made. The name of Markenfield has been searched for in all the rolls down to 3 Richard III.

The following brief notes were made for genealogical purposes, and except where otherwise expressed each date refers to a court held at Lartington.

4 Hen. V. [1415-17]. Court of Lord Henry FitzHugh. John Wrightson of Naby holds at the will of the lord 8 acres of land at Naby at 8s. rent.

5 Hen. V. Thomas W. takes of the lord various pastures and meadows.

9 Hen. VI.   William W. and Thomas W. mentioned.

15, 18, 23 Hen. VI.   William W. mentioned.

31 Hen. VI.   William W. senr. and junr. on manor jury.

36 Hen. VI. and 10, 15, 16 Edw. IV. [1457-1477]. Wm. W. is a free tenant of the manor.

1, 3 Richd. III.   Court of Lord FitzHugh. Wm. W. is a free tenant, and Wm. and J. W. are on manor jury.

6 Hen. VIII.   John W. a free tenant.

1596. Cuthbert W. and Jno. W. (deceased) are mentioned in list of free tenants. And among tenants for a term of years are Wm. W.; Tho. W. junr.; Tho. W. senr.; Cuthbert W.; Anthony W.; "Miles W. of the Crag, son and next heir to Cuthbert W. of the Waste his father;" Miles W. of Lartington, son and heir to John W. of the Waste for his lands.

1 James I.   Miles W. of Crag and Tho. W. of Lartington.

1607. Cuthbert W.; Miles W.; Jno. W.; among the free tenants. And among the tenants for a term of years Cuthbert W.; Tho. W.; Miles W.; Anthony W.

1610. Cuthbert W.; Miles W.; Jno. W.; among the free tenants. And among the tenants for a term of years Wm. W.; Jno. W.; Cuthbert W.; Tho. W.; Miles W.; Anthony W. Among those fined another Miles W. and Richd. W.

19 James I. [1620-22]. Miles W. junr.; Tho. W. junr.; among free tenants. And among tenants for a term of years Anthony W.; Richd. W.; Wm. W.; Jno. W.; Tho. W. junr.; Richd. W.; Tho. W. senr.; Miles W. senr.

19 James I.   Cotherstone Manor Court, Tho. W. a free tenant.

1630, 32, 34. Miles W.; Tho. W. senr.; Richd. W.; Tho. W. junr.; among free tenants.

1655. John W., son of Miles W.; Ferdinando W.; Richd. W.; Jno. W., son of Tho. W.; among free tenants. And Wm. W.; Jno. W., son of Richd. W., etc., among tenants for a term of years.

1659. "Leivetenant" Richard W. is mentioned.

14, 16 Chas. II. [1661-5]. Michael W. is mentioned as "residing outside the manor."

The following are the only notes obtained in the name of Markenfield.

36 Hen. VI. [1457-8]. John Merkynfeld, a free tenant of the manor of Mickleton.

14, 15 Ed. IV. [1473-6]. Thomas Markenfield, knt., a free tenant of the manor of Cotherstone.

II. REGISTERS OF THE PARISH OF ROMALD-KIRK.

I have searched these registers from their commencement in 1578 up to the end of 1686, finding 163 entries in the name of Wrightson. Up to the end of 1610 I here give the whole of my notes of entries; but from that date forward only such as possess, or may possess, interest.

BAPTISMS

1585	Sep. 12	John
1594	Oct. 6	Isabell
1595	Nov. 1	Ann
1596-7	Feb. 20	John
1599	Oct. 28	Jane d. of Tho. of Norgill
1599-1600	Feb. 3	Elizabeth d. of Miles of Low Lartington
1600	June 1	Isabell d. of Tho. of Baldersdale
1601	Apr. 19	*Michael s. of Miles of Crag*
1602	Sep. 19	Agnes d. of Reginald of Lartington
1603	Mar. 25	Mary d. of Miles of Lartington
1604	Sep. 16	Elizabeth d. of Jno. of Norgill
1605	May 12	Agnes d. of Tho. of Norgill
"	Nov. 10	Isabell d. of Miles of Lartington
1606-7	Jan. 25	Jane d. of Miles of Lartington
1607	June 14	*John s. of Tho. of Naby*
"	Oct. 11	John s. of Jno. of Norgill

1608	June 19	John s. of Richard of Lartington
1609	Oct. 29	Ferdinando s. of Tho. of Lartington
,,	Dec. 17	Dorothy d. of Tho. of Norgill
1610	Aug. 2	John s. of Miles of Lartington
,,	,,	John s. of Wm. of Norgill
,,	Oct. 7	Thomas s. of Jno. of Norgill
1615	Oct. 22	William s. of Miles of Lartington
1617-8	Feb. 12	*Henry s. of Tho. of Naby*
1618	Apr. 24	Dorothy d. of Miles of Lartington
1621	Apr. 24	Michael s. of Tho. of Norgill, junr.
1624	June 27	Henry s. of Tho. of Norgill [died 1625]
1631-2	Jan. 22	*Jane d. of Wm. of Crag*
1633	Sep. 22	*Michael s. of Wm. of Crag*
1635	Dec. 6	*William s. of Wm. of Crag*
1637	Dec. 3	*Mary d. of Wm. of Crag*
1639-40	Feb. 23	*George s. of Wm. of Crag*
1654	Dec. 3	Margaret d. of Michael of Crag, born.
1655	Dec. 4	Margaret d. of Anthony of Cotherstone, born.
1656	June 27	*Mary d. of Michael of Crag*, born.

MARRIAGES

1584	Oct. 4	Thomas Wrightson and Agnes Wrightson
1592	July 29	Thomas Wrightson and Helene Rayne
1598	Nov. 5	Miles Wrightson and Elizabeth Jackson
1599-1600	Jan. 31	Thomas Wrightson and Mary Temple
1602	Oct. 24	Edward Wrightson and Helinor Taylor
1603	Oct. 10	John Wrightson and Agnes Hugganson
1603-4	Feb. 14	Christopher Rayne and Isabell Wrightson
1606	Oct. 28	Thomas Wrightson and Janeta Jordayne
1672-3	Feb. 6	Michael Wrightson of Crag and Margaret Newby of Briscoe

BURIALS

1586	Apr. 26	John
1586-7	Jan. 9	John
1587	May 28	Matthew
,,	Sep. 29	John
1587-8	Jan. 14	Wife of Miles
1591	Sep. 29	*Wife of Cuthbert of Crag*
1593	Nov. 13	*Cuthbert*
1594	Apr. 16	Agnes
1595	Apr. 11	John
1597	Mar. 27	Widow
1597-8	Mar. 18	Wife of Tho. of Lartington and child
1601-2	Jan. 25	Anthony of Lartington
1602	Oct. 25	Wife of Jno. of Norgill and child
,,	Nov. 30	Thomas of Norgill
1602-3	Jan. 25	Widow of Tho. of Norgill
1603	May 26	Wife of Ralph of Lartington
,,	Sep. 16	Helein wife of Tho. of Norgill and child
1604	Sep. 23	Agnes wife of Jno. of Norgill
1604-5	Jan. 1	Elizabeth d. of Ralph of Lartington
1607	Aug. 2	*Wife of Miles of Crag*
1614	Apr. 12	*Cuthbert of Norgill*
1625	June 15	Henry s. of Tho. of Norgill, junr.
1631-2	Feb. 19	*Miles of Crag*, 'buried in the South Porch.'
1638	Nov. 18	Thomas of Lartington, 'buried in the Church.'
1642	Aug. 14	Dorothy d. of Miles of Lartington
1645-6	Mar. 17	*Margaret wife of Wm. of Crag*, 'buried in the Church.'
1648	May 21	Miles of Lartington
1651-2	Feb. 5	*William s. of Wm. of Crag*, 'buried in the Church.'
1661	May 22	Margaret wife of Jno. of Norgill, 'buried in the Church under her father's stall.'

1661	Nov. 20	Elizabeth widow of Miles of Lartington
,,	Dec. 20	Jennet of Lartington, widow, 'buried in the South Porch under a long stone where John Parkin was buried.'
1664	June 3	Ann d. of Michael of Crag
1664-5	Feb. 1	Margaret widow of Tho., ' Red Tom,' of Norgill
1666	Sep. 2	Agnes wife of Michael of Crag
1671	Apr. 27	Ferdinando of Lartington, ' buried in the South Porch.'

III. WILL OF JOHN WRIGHTSON, dated 22 June 1563, proved at Richmond 27 July 1563. (Bur. at Romaldkirk, Rich. Calendar.)

In this the Testator names his wife Agnes, a son Ralph, and a daughter and grand-daughter both called Elizabeth.

IV. ADMINISTRATION OF MICHAEL WRIGHTSON, late of Crag, co. York. Granted at Richmond 23 Feb. 1684 to Margaret Wrightson of Crag, widow, and Thomas Wrightson of the same place, yeoman, etc.

> Obs. :—The Testator is doubtless the Michael who married in 1672-3 (probably as a second wife) Margaret Newby of Briscoe ; and he was almost certainly the son of Thomas of Norgill baptized in 1621.

V. QUAKER MARRIAGE CERTIFICATE of Henry Boldron of Cotherstone, dated 18 day 1 mo. 1687 [*i.e.* 18 Mar. 1687-8].

Among the 33 witnesses are 7 Wrightsons, viz., 3 Thomases, a Francis, Ann, Elizabeth, and Ann, junr.

VI. PEDIGREE FROM THE COLLEGE OF ARMS, with my own additions placed within square brackets.

First Generation

CUTHBERT WRIGHTSON of Crag [in the manor of Lartington, and parish of Romaldkirk] in Com. Ebor. [mentioned in the Bowes MSS. vol. xiii, as having taken some part in the Rising of the North in 1569; bur. at Romaldkirk 13 Nov. 1593; his will, now lost, was proved at Richmond same year] = ... dau. of . . . . Slater of Bowds [? Bowes] in Com. Ebor. [A wife of Cuthbert's was bur. at Romaldkirk 29 Sep. 1591.]

Second Generation

CHILDREN OF CUTHBERT

1 :—MILES WRIGHTSON of Crag in Com. Ebor., eldest son [described in the court roll of Lartington manor in 1596, as "son and next heir to Cuthbert Wrightson of the Waste his father;" bur. at Romaldkirk "in the South Porch" 19 Feb. 1631-2] = ... dau. of . . . . Rayne of Mickleton in Com. Ebor. [A wife of his was bur. at Romaldkirk 2 Aug. 1607.]

2 :—THOMAS WRIGHTSON [? of Naby, near Crag], second son = ... dau. of . . . . . and had issue.

   3 :—Cuthbert [? Cuthbert of Norgill bur. at Romaldkirk 12 Apr. 1614, and ? the person mentioned in the court roll entries from 1596 to 1610], died *s. pr.*

   4 :—Peter, died *s. pr.*

      Isabel = ... Sanderson and had issue Philip Sanderson, father of Bartholomew and Christopher.

Third Generation

CHILDREN OF MILES

1 :—WILLIAM WRIGHTSON of Crag in Com. Ebor., eldest son = Margaret dau. of John Bolton alias Boughton of Multon in Com. Ebor. [She was bur. at Romaldkirk "in the Church" 17 Mar. 1645-6.]

2 :—MICHAEL WRIGHTSON, second son [bap. at Romaldkirk

19 Apr. 1601] = ... dau. of Anthony Blades of . . . . .
in Com. Ebor.

 Phillis = Henry Douson of . . . . . in Com. Ebor. and
  had issue 1 Thomas, 2 John, and Jane marrd. to
  . . . . . . Morson, clerk.

Children of Thomas

1 :—Thomas
2 :—John [? bap. 14 June 1607]
3 :—Henry [? bap. 12 Feb. 1617-8; and ? the head of the
 Wrightsons of Bowes, see App. D].

Fourth Generation

Children of William

1 :—Michael·Wrightson of Osbaston in Com. Leicest.,
one of the Ancients of Clement's Inn, Com. Middx., eldest son
[bap. at Romaldkirk 22 Sep. 1633; mentioned in the Lartington court roll from 1661 to 1665 as "residing outside the
manor"; registered this Pedigree in 1695] = Philippa, dau. of
Edward Palmer of the Borough of Leicester, Gent.

 2 :—William [bap. at Romaldkirk 6 Dec. 1635; bur.
  there "in the Church" 5 Feb. 1651-2], died *s. pr.*
 3 :—George [bap. at Romaldkirk 23 Feb. 1639-40], died
  s. pr.
 1 :—Jane [bap. at Romaldkirk 22 Jan. 1631-2]
 2 :—Mary [bap. at Romaldkirk 3 Dec. 1637] = Christo-
  pher Mylls, Citizen of London.

Child of Michael

Mary, only surviving child [? born in Romaldkirk parish
 27 June 1656] = ... [leaving] Margaret, only
 surviving child, wife of Robert Harrison of Clement's
 Inn, Gent.

Fifth Generation

CHILD OF MICHAEL OF OSBASTON

Philippa, only child of Michael Wrightson, Gent. =
    Francis Mundy of Marketon in Com. Derb. esqr. ;
    [mar. about 1689 ; was High Sheriff of the county in
    1694 ; and by his marriage acquired the Osbaston
    estates ; his will is dated 21 Apr. 1718. Issue].

Francis Mundy, eldest son and heir apparent.

Edward Mundy, second son.

Philippa, eldest daughter.

Millecent, second daughter.

Entered by Order of Chapter 24th Apr. 1695 per me
    Rob. Dale, Blanch Lion, Coll. Armor Regrarii Deptm.

APPENDIX D.

WRIGHTSON OF BOWES, CO. YORK.

This must have been a junior offshoot of the Wrightsons of Crag,[1] for not only are the two places less than two miles apart, but in the will of the Henry Wrightson of Bowes, who died in 1705, there is a remembrance left to "Thomas Wrightson of Crag." The father of this Henry stands at the head of the Bowes pedigree, and bears the same name as his son. I feel practically certain that he is no other than the Henry who appears in the third generation of the pedigree of the Wrightsons of Crag.

The only permanently interesting member of this group of respectable yeomen is Rodger Wrightson Junr., a youth who seems to have barely survived his twentieth year. His father, Rodger Wrightson Senr., had acquired a handsome competency in addition to a small inherited estate. If my view of his relationship to the Crag family is correct, he was second cousin to the great London barrister who owned the Osbaston estates ; and on this ground alone may well have affected some superiority among the simple villagers. He is found to have been chosen no less than eleven times to fill the office of churchwarden. But that he possessed a hard, grasping, and litigious disposition may be gathered in part from a clause in his brother Henry's will, and in part from his conduct to his son Rodger, whom he evidently wished to make a financially advantageous match.

Unfortunately for the father's plans, the poor youth became passionately attached to a fair young girl of extreme beauty. Her very respectable parents kept the George (now the Unicorn) Inn at Bowes, just as her brother honest "Jack Railton the Quaker" did at the time when he is described in the *Life of*

---

[1] Appendix C.

O

John Buncle Esqr. by Thomas Amory (London 1756 and 1825 [1]). For about a year this courtship was carried on by stealth. At length it became known, and Martha Railton was scornfully "flouted at" by her lover's father, mother, and sister Hannah. He "sickened, and took to his bed about Shrove tuesday, and died the Sunday sennight after. On the last day of his illness he desired to see his mistress. She was civilly received by the mother, who bid her welcome when it was too late. But her daughter Hannah lay at his back to cut them off from all opportunity of exchanging their thoughts. At her return home, on hearing the Bell toll for his departure, she screamed out that her heart was burst, and expired some moments after." This is the touching incident which the poet Mallet, the author of *Rule Britannia*, embodied in 1760 in his famous ballad of *Edwin and Emma*,—commencing, "Far in the windings of a vale, etc." It is related that the two funeral processions simultaneously reached the Church; and that, amidst the deepest emotions, the two faithful lovers were laid at last together in one grave,—on the 15th March 1714-5. The site and the event are alike preserved in memory by the headstone, which stands immediately against the centre of the west end of Bowes Church: and the Vicar told me that even yet, from his study window, he watches lovers come to seal their promises of faithfulness by the grave of Rodger Wrightson and Martha Railton.

Almost the whole of the preceding information and the following pedigree is derived from Frederick Dinsdale's new edition (London 1857) of *Ballads and Songs* by David Mallet.

PEDIGREE.

First Generation

1 :—HENRY WRIGHTSON, yeoman, bur. 11 July 1688 = Elizabeth Alderson. She was bur. 16 Sep. 1686.

[1] In ed. 1825: vol. i, 100, 285; ii, 14; iii, 141.

Second Generation

CHILDREN OF HENRY (1)

2 :—Frances W., bap. 4 Oct. 1662.

3 :—John W., bur. 18 Mar. 1662-3.

4 :—Henry W. of Bowes, bur. 21 Nov. 1705. Will, dated 7 Sep. 1705, proved at Richmond 22 Jan. 1706 = Heloïse (spelt Else in reg., and Aolice in afsd. will) Buck; mar. at Richmond 3 Sep. 1687; bur. 25 Mar. 1729.

5 :—RODGER W., bur. 16 Apr. 1729 = Elizabeth Coates; ir. 26 July 1688; bur. 25 Aug. 1729.

6 :—Isabel W., bur. 19 Dec. 1702. Will, dated 12 Oct. 1698, proved at Richmond 17 Apr. 1703.

Third Generation

CHILDREN OF RODGER (5)

7 :—Elizabeth W., an infant, bur. 31 May 1689.

8 :—Henry W., bap. 21 June 1691, evidently died young.

9 :—Henry W., young child, bur. 7 Jan. 1694-5.

10 :—Hannah W., died at Milby in parish of Kirby-on-the-Moor, co. York; bur. there 13 Jan. 1757 = John Raper of Kirby afsd.; mar. 2 Feb. 1718-9.

11 :—Rodger W., bap. 16 Dec. 1694, died 13 Mar., bur. at Bowes 15 Mar. 1714-5. He was the lover of Martha Railton, and the hero of Mallet's ballad of *Edwin and Emma*.

12 :—Rachel W., bap. 6 June 1695, bur. 22 Sep. 1717.

13 :—William W., bap. 4 Feb. 1699-1700.

APPENDIX E.

(BATTIE-)WRIGHTSON OF CUSWORTH PARK, CO. YORK.

Although this important County Family resides near Doncaster, yet it, as well as ours, holds considerable property in the parish of Hurworth-on-Tees. Hence it is desirable to give so much of their pedigree as may prevent the confusion of names while examining old local documents. I have never attempted to trace back this pedigree, and what I give is compiled in part from published works, and in part from information supplied to me by Mr. Battie-Wrightson in letters and in conversation when I was at Cusworth in October 1893.

First Generation

1 :—WILLIAM WRIGHTSON, referred to in a document preserved at Cusworth.

Second Generation

FROM WILLIAM (1)

2 :—ROBERT W., described in his will (proved at York in 1708) as "of Cusworth," also of Thorpe Arch, Hemsworth, North and South Elmsale, Pontefract, Wakefield, and South Kirby, "attorney at law"; died 1708, aged 79 = (1st wife) Elizabeth, dau. of Tho. Garland of Todwick, by whom three children. = (2nd wife) Elinor Cooper, widow. = (3rd wife) Sarah, dau. of Sir Thomas Beaumont of Whitley Beaumont, knt.; by whom six children.

Third Generation

FROM ROBERT (2) BY 3RD WIFE

3 :—Thomas W. of Cusworth ; bap. 1674 ; High Sheriff
of county York in 1714 ; died 1724 = Jane, dau. of
Sir Paul Barrett of Lee, co. Kent ; *s. pr.*

4 :—WILLIAM W. of Cusworth, heir to his brother, bap.
1676 ; sometime M.P. for Newcastle-on-Tyne ; died 1760 =
(1st wife) Isabel, dau. and heir of Francis Burton of Newcastle,
widow of Tho. Matthews ; *s. pr.* = (2nd wife) Isabella, dau.
and co-heir of Wm. Fenwick of Bywell ; by whom three
children.

Fourth Generation

FROM WILLIAM (4)

5 :—ISABELLA W., sole surviving child and heir, bap. 1727 ;
died 1784 = John Battie of Warmsworth, co. York, who,
in right of his wife, took the surname of Wrightson in 1761 ;
mar. 1748 ; died 1766.

Fifth Generation

FROM ISABELLA (5)

6 :—WILLIAM W. of Cusworth, bap. 1752 ; High Sheriff in
1819 ; sometime M.P. for Aylesbury ; died 1827 = (1st wife)
Barbara, dau. of James Bland of Hurworth-on-Tees ; mar.
1781 ; died 1784 ; *s. pr.* = (2nd wife) Harriot, dau. and co-heir
of Richard Heber of Marton (uncle to Bishop Heber) ; mar.
1787 ; by whom eight children.

Sixth Generation

FROM WILLIAM (6)

7 :—William Battie W. of Cusworth, eldest son and heir, born 1789 ; sometime M.P. for Retford and North-allerton ; died 1879 = Georgiana, only dau. of Inigo Freeman Thomas of Ratton, co. Sussex, by Charlotte his wife, dau. and co-heir of Henry Peirse of Bedale, co. York ; mar. 1821 ; *s. pr.*

8 :—Richard Heber W. of Cusworth, heir to his brother, born 1800 ; died 1891 = (1st) the Hon. Elizabeth de Grey, dau. of Thomas, 4th Baron Walsingham ; mar. 1832 ; *s. pr.* = (2nd) Albinia, youngest dau. of afsd. Inigo Freeman Thomas ; mar. 1877 ; *s. pr.*

9 :—HARRIOT W., died 1864 = (1st husband) the Hon. F. S. N. Douglas, only son of Lord Glenbervie. = (2nd husband) Colonel the Hon. Henry Hely HUTCHINSON, brother of the Earl of Donoughmore ; mar. 1825.

Seventh Generation

FROM HARRIOT HUTCHINSON (9)

10 :—GEORGIANA MARY HELY HUTCHINSON = Rev. Charles THOMAS, Rector of Hemsworth, and youngest son of afsd. Inigo Freeman Thomas and the Hon. Frances Ann, eldest dau. of George, 4th Viscount Midleton.

Eighth Generation

FROM GEORGIANA THOMAS (10)

11 :—WILLIAM HENRY THOMAS, born 1855 ; on the death of No. 8 he, under the will of No. 7, succeeded to Cusworth, and by Royal Licence replaced the surname of Thomas by that

of BATTIE-WRIGHTSON = Lady Isabella Georgiana Katherine, eldest dau. of the 3rd Marquess of Exeter ; mar. 1884.

Ninth Generation

FROM W. H. BATTIE-WRIGHTSON (11)

12 :—Robert Cecil B-W., born 1888.
13 :—Barbara Isabella Georgiana B-W., born 1890.

APPENDIX F.

ROBINSON OF MIDDLETON ONE ROW.

The following fragment of pedigree is constructed from the will of Mr. Thomas Robinson, with dates derived from various parochial registers.

PEDIGREE.

First Generation

1 :—THOMAS ROBINSON "of Middleton one Row," in the parish of Middleton St. George, co. Durham; bur. there 22 July 1732; his will, dated 26 Oct. 1730, was proved at Durham 28 Mar. 1733 = (1st wife) Margaret Wastall; mar. there 15 June 1686; bur. there 22 Sep. 1724; issue = (2nd wife) Dorothy . . . . . . ; mentioned in her husband's will; issue.

Second Generation

CHILDREN OF THOMAS (1)

2 :—Margaret R., bap., as "daughter of Thomas Robinson," at Middleton afsd. 8 Mar. 1687-8; mentioned in her father's will as "my daughter Margaret Wrightson." [See Wrightson pedigree.]

3 :—Hannah R., bap. at Middleton afsd. 28 June 1690; mentioned in her father's will as "my daughter Hannah now the widow of William Richardson late of Great Ayton, co. York" = William Richardson; mar. at Middleton afsd. 8 Oct. 1717.

4 :—Elizabeth R., bap. as "dautr to Thomas Robinson," at Middleton afsd. 29 Mar. 1696; mentioned in her father's will as "my daughter Elizabeth Wrightson." [See Wrightson pedigree.]

5 :—Dorothy R., bap. at Middleton afsd. 14 Apr. 1727; mentioned along with her younger sister in their father's will, as "my daughters Dorothy and Mary," both being spoken of as under age; bur. at Middleton afsd. 26 June 1732.

6 :—Mary R., bap. at Middleton afsd. 5 Apr. 1729; mentioned in her father's will as above.

Extract from the will of the above Thomas Robinson :—

" . . . . . . I do hereby make my good friends Robert Killinghall of Middleton St. George in the said county of Durham Esqr., the Rev : M. William Noble, Rector of Middleton St. George aforesaid, my son-in-law Thomas Wrightson, and my grandson Thomas Wrightson, joynt Executors of this my last will . . . . ."

Obs. :—Robert Killinghall was the squire of the Parish. His pedigree is given in Surtees' *Hist. Dur.* vol. iii, p. 223. The Rev. M. W. Noble was Rector of the Parish from 1722 until his death in 1746. The other two executors are the husband of Elizabeth, and the eldest son of Margaret, the Testator's daughters.

APPENDIX G.

GARMONDSWAY OF SADBERGE AND GREAT BURDON, CO. DURHAM.

The name of Garmondsway has a local origin, and signifies 'the road or way of Garmond.' It must in the first place have been used in connection with that portion of the Roman 'Rycknield Street,' which passed on the east side of the present Garmondsway Moor, about six miles south-east of Durham, and which portion of road is spoken of in old writers as the "Via Garmundi" (see Surtees' *Hist. Dur.* vol. iii, p. 12). According to Camden (see his *Britannia*, vol. i, p. 281, and vol. iii, p. 103 with note) the name 'Garmond' was left in this locality by Gormo, Gormund, or Guthorm, the Dane, in the time of King Alfred.

The ' Vill of Garmondsway ' was doubtless a partially fortified dwelling, somewhat like the home of Cerdic the Saxon as described by Scott in his *Ivanhoe*. It would be surrounded by the cottages of retainers, and was evidently situated in the midst of a very considerable demesne.

After going carefully over the old lists of Norman landowners, I have come to the conclusion that the family, which I have reason to believe owned this Vill in very ancient times, was Anglian or Danish. It was known as De Garmondsway ; and, under the slightly modified forms of Garmondsway, and Garmonsway, has left traces of its continued existence in the records of various neighbouring landed properties, until, after a duration of many centuries, it finally came to an end in my own lifetime.

The following are a few of the proofs of this long-continued presence within a radius of less than ten miles :—

It was in the year 1154 that Hugh Pudsey, the famous Prince Bishop of Durham, and nephew of King Stephen, founded the present Sherburn Hospital near Durham. On the authority of Newbrigensis, it is declared in Godwin's *Bishops* (p. 512) that "this good work was ascribed partly unto other men whom the Bishop enforced to become Benefactors, being loath to be at the whole charges himself." The narrative of one of such transactions was discovered at a comparatively recent time among the title-deeds at Sherburn Hospital, and it may be seen in Burke's *Visitation of the Seats and Arms of the Noblemen and Gentlemen of Great Britain* (vol. i, p. 44). The story tells how there was a dispute as to the ownership of the Vill of Garmondsway, and how the several claimants engaged in a judicial combat, fought under the authority of Bishop Pudsey as Count Palatine. Care was however taken to overwhelm the victor with such enormous legal costs, that in the end he was obliged to compound with the Bishop by surrendering the whole of the property on condition of receiving an annual grant of sixty-four marks,—a sum which shows the large size of the estate. The Vill of Garmondsway was thereupon handed over to Sherburn Hospital and has ever since belonged to it. The point that specially concerns us in this story is that two out of the four claimants bore the name of De Garmondsway, a fact which makes it practically certain that the place had at one time been in possession of the family to which they belonged.

About two centuries later I find (see Surtees' *Hist. Dur.* vol. iii, p. 226 note) that a Garmondsway, who can hardly have been born later than the time of Edward III., had a son called Thomas. This son became possessed of property at West-Hartburn, some two miles and a half south-east of Sadberge. West-Hartburn was an ancient, but now extinct hamlet. It has left its name in a Reconveyance of a part of the Wrightson property, where "West-Hartburn otherwise White House" is described.

After the lapse of about two more centuries we learn (see Surtees' *Hist. Dur.* vol. iii, p. 268 note) that, both in the time of Elizabeth and James I., the Garmonsways were holding land in Sadberge.

And lastly, in 1684 Thomas Garmonsway and the heirs of Richard Garmonsway are mentioned among the freeholders of Sadberge, and Anthony Garmonsway among those of Great Burdon (see Surtees' *Hist. Dur.* vol. iii, pp. 268, 343, etc.).

My father's second cousin, Thomas Waldy of Eaglescliffe, told me that all the property held now or formerly by the Wrightsons near Sadberge, had at one time been included in the Garmonsway estate, for, said he, "it once took in Newton Grange, then called Copy-hill, Spring House and White House, besides other lands." With regard to White House his assertion is supported by one of the above authorities. And with regard to Spring House at all events about thirty acres are proved by one of my title-deeds to have been purchased in 1720 from the Richard Garmonsway and Hannah his wife, whose deaths are recorded on an altar-tomb in Sadberge as occurring respectively in 1764 and 1762.

Margaret,[1] the last of all the Garmonsways, married John Waldy of Yarm. He was a man of good means, and, as she was an heiress with about thirty thousand pound's worth of property, they were in easy circumstances from the first. Their wealth was however immensely increased by successful purchases of land and by moderation in expenditure, so that as a widow she had what was worth between two and three hundred thousand pounds to distribute among, or leave to, her four children. I well remember being taken to see the old lady. She was very kind to me, and was pleased that I bore her family name. Her death took place in 1844; and with her the family of Garmonsway came to an end. It was a family, which had certainly been settled within a radius of ten miles for at least seven centuries; and it is quite possible that its earlier representatives may have occupied the ancient Vill of Garmondsway when Canute passed that way on his bare-footed pilgrimage to

---

[1] She was at one time engaged to her cousin William Wrightson, who failing issue from her was heir to all the Garmonsway property.

St. Cuthbert's Shrine at Durham (see Surtees' *Hist. Dur.* vol. iii, p. 12).

The present representatives of this family, though through females only, are to be found in the families of Waldy, Temple, and Wrightson.

The following pedigree of the latest surviving branch of the Garmonsways has been constructed by me chiefly from a mass of information contained in old letters written on the subject to my father by his second cousin the Rev. Richard Waldy.

PEDIGREE.

First Generation

1 :—ANTHONY GARMONSWAY of Great Burdon in the parish of Haughton le Skerne, co. Durham. One of the three freeholders there in 1684 = Anne Waistell, a dau. of the then lessee of the other portion of Burdon Manor; mar. 12 Apr. 1675.

Second Generation

CHILD OF ANTHONY (1)

2 :—WILLIAM G. of Great Burdon; bap. 23 Feb. 1675-6 = Margaret Thompson; married 9 May 1699.

Third Generation

CHILDREN OF WILLIAM (2)

3 :—William G. "of Great Burdon, gentleman"; "who departed this life June 24th 1775, aged 72 years". M.I.; unmarried.[1]

[1] His silver Tankard was handed down through his sister, my great-grandmother, to her little god-child, my aunt Isabella, who gave it to me as an heir-loom a few years before her death.—W. G. W.

4 :—Richard G. of Great Burdon; bap. 20 Aug. 1713; " died Septr. 19th 1800, aged 87 years." M.I. = Mary Wardell of Blackwell; "died Jany. 12th 1789, aged 68." M.I.

5 :—Margaret G., bap. 17 Sep. 1719; died 21 Jan. 1797 = Thomas Wrightson. [See Wrightson pedigree.]

6 :— . . . . G. = William Harker of Bedale, co. York; issue.

Fourth Generation

Children of Richard (4)

7 :—Ann G., "died May 6th 1764, aged 5 years." M.I.

8 :—Margaret G. of Great Burdon; born 17 Oct. 1761; died 18 Sep. 1844 = John Waldy of Yarm, co. York; mar. 22 Mar. 1791. They left four children, viz., Edward Waldy of Barmpton, born 1791;—Mrs. Mary Temple, wife of the Rector of Dinsdale, born 1792;—the Rev. Richd. Waldy, Rector of Affpuddle, co. Dorset, born 1795;—Thomas Waldy of Eagles-cliffe, near Yarm, deputy lieutenant of the county, born 1801; died 8 Apr. 1886.

APPENDIX H.

THE FAMILY OF INGRAM.

The Ingrams of Temple Newsam, near Leeds in the county of York, commence with a Sir Arthur Ingram, the son of a wealthy London tradesman. As Cofferer of the King's Household in 1615 he was regarded with much jealousy by some of the courtiers, and soon after left London and settled in Yorkshire. His great wealth enabled him to purchase many noble estates, including the manor of Temple Newsam. He was several times M.P. for the city of York,—a member of the Council of the North,—and High Sheriff of the county in 1620.

His eldest brother, Sir William, was Secretary to the Council of the North, and left many grandchildren, of whom one, William, was born about 1622.

There was also a younger brother, who had a son John living in 1623.

It is most convenient to speak of the three surviving sons of this first Sir Arthur Ingram in an order the reverse of their seniority.

The third son of Sir Arthur was Sir Thomas Ingram of Sheriff-Hutton,—M.P. for Thirsk 1640-5,—a Privy Councillor to King Charles II.,—and Chancellor of the Duchy of Lancaster. Through his wife, who was a daughter of the 1st Lord Fauconberg (formerly Sir Thomas Bellasis), he had many interesting connections, for she was sister-in-law to the famous (beheaded) Royalist, Sir Henry Slingsby,—was second cousin to Sir Thomas Fairfax of Nunappleton (3rd Lord Fairfax in 1648), the Commander-in-Chief of the victorious army of the Parliament,—and, through the marriage of her nephew, the 2nd Lord Fauconberg, with Mary Cromwell, she was aunt to the daughter of the Lord Protector.

The second son of Sir Arthur was John Ingram, whose second wife was Dorothy, a daughter of Sir Thomas Fairfax of Gilling Castle (1st Viscount Fairfax of Emley in 1628).

The eldest son and heir of Sir Arthur was, like himself, known as Sir Arthur Ingram of Temple Newsam, and was also a High Sheriff of Yorkshire in 1630. His first wife was Eleanor, a sister of the before mentioned Sir Henry Slingsby; and his second was Katharine Fairfax, a sister of his brother John's wife. He was one of the most devoted Royalists to be found in Yorkshire during the great Civil War. His beautiful town house in York stood in the middle of the lawn, which now covers the north portion of the Minster Yard, his garden extending to the city walls. It was in this house that, on the 19th of March 1642, he received the ill-advised Charles I., just before the commencement of the war. For a few months this house was the home of the King; and it was from here that he set out, not only on his abortive attempt to seize the arms at Hull, but also finally in August to set up the Royal Standard at Nottingham. Sir Arthur did not long survive the execution of his Royal Master; but the favour of Charles II. was bestowed on his son (also an energetic Royalist), who in 1661 was raised to the Peerage as Lord Ingram, Viscount Irwin.

The Ingrams of Glasgow, my Grandmother's ancestors, were no doubt an offshoot of this family. She herself always asserted her relationship to the Lords Irwin; and one of the leading Scotch heralds, whom I once chanced to meet at a dinner table, told me that he had had occasion to look into the Ingram descents, and that the Ingrams of Glasgow and of Temple Newsam were of the same stock. He went into no particulars; but the former may very well have descended from one of the previously mentioned first cousins of Sir Arthur Ingram, the father of Lord Irwin.

According to my grandmother's account, the Ingram, from

whom she descended, accompanied Oliver Cromwell into Scotland in 1650. He was wounded or seized by sickness there,
and never returned to England. He married a Miss Bruce of
Woodhouse in the west of Scotland, who was of the Bruces of
Clackmannan,—the then eldest surviving branch of the great
family to which the Royal Bruce belonged. During the last
century Henry Bruce of Clackmannan was the acknowledged
Chief of the whole family; and on his death in 1772 without
issue, the main line of the family became extinct. His widow
was the well-known and venerable Mrs. Catherine Bruce (*née*
Bruce) of Clackmannan Tower, who entertained Robert Burns,
and delighted him, as much with her Jacobitism, as with the
sight of the helmet and two-handed sword used by King Robert
on the field of Bannockburn. Since the death of this Mrs.
Bruce in 1791, the ancient Tower has fallen into decay; but
the interesting relics of the hero-king have passed into the
keeping of the Earl of Elgin, who is now the head of the family
of Bruce. The Bruces did not forget their connection with
the Ingrams of Glasgow; and, when my grandmother was a
little girl, she was taken by her mother and aunt Simpson to
visit Mrs. Bruce at Clackmannan Tower. In the same sort of
way in which the old lady afterwards spoke to Lord Elgin, she
spoke to my grandmother,—asked if her mother or aunt had
told her how the Royal blood of Bruce was in her veins, and
charged her never to condescend to anything mean or deceitful.

James Ingram, who sprang from this marriage with Miss
Bruce, stands at the head of a short pedigree entered in 1772,
by his great-grandson, at the College of Arms in London. In
it he is described, as "of Carluke in the shire of Lanark," and
as dying "soon after the Battle of Bothwell Bridge, which was
in June 1679." This agrees wonderfully well with the story
told by my grandmother; for she described this her ancestor as
a Covenanter, who became involved in the Insurrection crushed
at that Battle. Indeed, the details of the story she told, present
so many features common with those seen in the hero of Scott's
Old Mortality, that I am disposed to think the novelist had at

P

least some portions of the story of James Ingram before his mind, while sketching the outline of his " Henry Morton." Like Henry Morton, this my great-great-great-great-grandfather was the son of an old Puritan officer,—he also was somehow concerned with Bothwell Brigg,—he also had a very narrow escape, —and he also (if I remember aright) fled for a short time to the Continent. He is however said to have been greatly impoverished through the confiscations carried out by the savage Dalzell. The idea that James Ingram was to some extent the prototype of " Henry Morton " agrees with the topography of the novel ; for Carluke is ten miles from Bothwell Bridge, and just three miles from that Craignethan Castle, which once belonged to the great Evandale branch of the House of Hamilton, and which is stated by Lockhart to have been the original of " Tillietudlem,"—adding the information that *Old Mortality* was the first story in which Scott tried to adhere to actual circumstances so far as they suited his dramatic conceptions. Scott may well have heard the story of my grandmother's ancestor from his friend Campbell the poet, who was a near connection of the Ingrams of Glasgow. *Old Mortality* was published in 1819 ; but it was in 1800 that Scott became intimate with Campbell, only a few months after his explorations in and around Craignethan, and while he was still full of interest as to the locality (see Lockhart's *Life of Scott*, chapters ix, x).

Archibald Ingram, one of the five grandchildren of this old Covenanter (through his son John, also of Carluke), is said to have been born in 1701. He became a very great merchant in Glasgow, and amply redeemed the misfortunes of his grandfather. So highly was he esteemed among his fellow-citizens, that twice, if not thrice, he was elected to the dignity of Lord Provost of that city,—a bronze life-sized statue was erected to his memory,—and a handsome street near the centre of the city still perpetuates his name. His great wealth enabled him to give full scope to his benevolence. The most striking incident, preserved among the traditions of his family, may be told in a few words. A descendant of his grandfather's greatest perse-

cutor,—I presume one of the Dalzells, whose peerage was forfeited in 1715,—had sunk into desperate want. Knowing Mr.
Ingram's character, she, as a last hope, sent to tell him of her
state. He found her in a wretched garret, with some relics of
old finery about her; and was glad to give the assistance she
required. Provost Ingram was twice married to ladies, who
sooner or later connected him with interesting or distinguished
persons. His first wife was Miss Janet Simpson, whose sister
Mrs. Campbell was grandmother to the poet. His second wife
was Rebecca, sister to Henry Glasford of Duggleston, through
whom he became connected with Sir James Nesbit of the Dean
and the Earl of Cromarty. Of his children I need only mention
three, viz., John, Anne, and Agnes.

John Ingram, the eldest son of the Provost by his first wife,
was born in Glasgow 1728. He become a merchant; and, in
the Ingram pedigree, which he entered at the College of Arms,
he describes himself as "of St. Magnus, London." Of his
seven children, Jane, or Jannet, was married to a leading
London merchant called Joseph Travers, whose name still
stands at the head of one of the best known city firms.

Anne Ingram, the youngest daughter of the Provost by his
second wife, married William Simpson of Parson's Green near
Edinburgh, a Director of the Bank of Scotland, and a very
wealthy man. It was she who took my grandmother to Clackmannan Tower, and it was at her house that my orphan grandmother was married. Mr. and Mrs. Simpson's money all went
to his nephew William Mitchell, who, on the death of Miss
Innes of Stow, succeeded to the additional enormous fortune of
£1,500,000; after which, in 1840, he assumed by Royal
licence the name of Mitchell-Innes of Ayton and Whitehall.

Agnes Ingram, the third daughter of the Provost by his first
wife, married Archibald Gilchrist of Dalserf, who was the Provost's own nephew through his sister Mary. Archibald and
Agnes were therefore first cousins; and, though Gilchrist in
name, their numerous children were three-fourths Ingram in
blood. Among these children was my grandmother, Rebecca

Gilchrist. She was born 13 April 1768 at Mountain Hall, Inverisk, Mid Lothian; married in Edinburgh, 26 June 1798, to William Potter, at that time of Whickham near Gateshead; and died at Newcastle upon Tyne 11 March 1855, aged 86. Her father's name is recorded both in the above mentioned Ingram pedigree and also in the Baptismal Register of her daughter, my mother, so that the proof of the connection with the Ingrams is preserved.

The family of Ingram, so far as I know, ended with Charles, the 9th Viscount Irwin; one of whose daughters, Isabella Ann, was married in 1776 to Francis, 2nd Marquis of Hertford; and another, Elizabeth, to Hugo Meynell, Esq., ancestor of the present owner of Temple Newsam.

APPENDIX I.

THE FAMILY OF HEAD.

The connections between the Wrightsons and the Heads, whether through marriages or business, have been so important, that I think it well to make such an extract from their domestic pedigree as may include the names and descents of those who are possessed of a greater or less degree of interest to us.

PEDIGREE.

First Generation

1 :— . . . . HEAD = Alice . . . . . . of Hartest, co. Suffolk; will, dated 1579, proved at Bury St. Edmunds, co. Suffolk.

Second Generation

CHILD OF —— (1)

2 :—JOHN H. of Bury afsd.; youngest son; will proved there 1646 = Grace . . . . . .

Third Generation

CHILD OF JOHN (2)

3 :—JOHN H. of Bury afsd.; eldest son; will proved there 1689 = Esther . . . . . .

Fourth Generation

CHILD OF JOHN (3)

4 :—SAMUEL H. of Bury afsd.; second son; born 1653 = Sarah Jackley; mar. 1684.

Fifth Generation

CHILD OF SAMUEL (4)

5 :—THOMAS H., born at Bury afsd. 1689 ; became a Quaker ; died 1742 = Anne, dau. of John Brewster of Beccles, co. Suffolk, by whom sixteen children.

Sixth Generation

CHILD OF THOMAS (5)

6 :—JOHN H. of Bury afsd. ; eldest surviving son ; born 1731 ; died 1782 = Ann, dau. of John Wheeler of Hitchin, co. Herts ; mar. 1757.

Seventh Generation

CHILDREN OF JOHN (6)

7 :—JOHN H. of Ipswich, co. Suffolk ; born 1759 ; died 1812 = (1st) Mary Seaman ; mar. 1785 ; issue = (2nd) Caroline Bell ; mar. 1794 ; no issue.

8 :—JOSHUA H. of Ipswich, Brewer ; born 1765 ; died 1817 = Isabella, dau. of Edward and Priscilla Wakefield of Tottenham, co. Middlesex ; mar. 12 Sep. 1794 ; died 1841.

Eighth Generation

CHILD OF JOHN (7)

9 :—JEREMIAH H. of Ipswich ; born 1789 ; sometime Mayor of Ipswich ; died 24 Feb. 1866 ; his will proved there 1866 = Mary, dau. of Thomas Howard of St. Paul's Churchyard, London ; mar. 1831.

Children of Joshua (8)

10:—ALFRED H. of the firm of " Charrington, Head and Co.," Mile-end Brewery, London ; born 26 Feb. 1797 ; bap. as adult ; died 15 Feb. 1880 ; his will, dated 2 July 1877, was proved in London 23 Mar. 1880 = Ellen, youngest dau. of Thomas Cooper, solicitor, of Henley on Thames ; born 8 May 1810 ; mar. there 7 May 1839 ; died 12 Feb. 1890 ; her will, dated 5 Nov. 1888, proved in London 13 Mar. 1890.

11:—Caroline H., born 1798 ; died 1861 ; unmar.

12:—JOHN H., born 1800 ; died 1874 = Elizabeth Bailey.

13:—Benjamin H., born 1801 ; died 1878 = Charlotte Paisley, *s.pr.*

14:—Lucy Anne H., born 1803 ; died 1882 = the Rev. Vincent John Stanton, M.A., afterwards Rector of Halesworth, co. Suffolk ; mar. 1843. Their only child, born in 1846, is the Rev. Vincent Henry Stanton, D.D., the Ely Professor of Divinity in the University of Cambridge, and Canon of Ely Cathedral.

Ninth Generation

Children of Jeremiah (9)

15:—JOHN H. of Ipswich, of the firm of " Ransomes, Sims, and Head," Agricultural Engineers ; born 1832 ; died 1881 = Alice Venn ; issue.

16:—THOMAS HOWARD H., born 1833 ; commenced the Engineering Works at Thornaby on Tees, now known as " Head, Wrightson and Co., Ld." ; died 1880 = Eleanor Jane Walker ; issue.

17:—HENRY H. of London ; born 1834 = Hesther Beck ; issue.

18:—JEREMIAH H., M.Inst.C.E., of Coatham, near Redcar, co. York ; born 11 July 1835 ; registered at the Friends' Meeting House, Ipswich. He was President of the Institution of Mechanical Engineers in 1885-6 = Rebecca Ingram Wrightson ; issue. [See Pedigree of Wrightson.]

19 :—GEORGE FREDERICK H., Vicar of Christ Ch., Hampstead, London ; born 1836 = Henrietta Bolton ; issue.

20 :—CHARLES ARTHUR H., J.P., of Hartburn Hall, Stockton on Tees ; born 1838 = Mrs. Justina Green, *née* Long ; issue.

    21 :—Mary H., born 1839 = the Rev. Colin Campbell ; mar. 1863 ; issue.

22 :—ALBERT ALFRED H. of Wimbledon, co. Surrey ; born 1844 = Caroline Hanbury ; issue.

CHILDREN OF ALFRED (10)

    23 :—Priscilla Anne H., born 22 Mar. 1840 = the Rev. W. G. Wrightson ; issue [see Pedigree of Wrightson].

    24 :—Isabella H. of 6 Craven Hill Gardens, Hyde Park ; born 4 Apr. 1841 ; unmar.

    25 :—Caroline Agnes H., born 23 Nov. 1848 = Edward Young Western of 36 Lancaster Gate, Hyde Park, London, solicitor [see Joseph Foster's *Baronetage*] ; mar. at Christ Ch., Lancaster Gate, afsd., 31 Jan. 1871 ; issue living,—Alfred Edward of Trinity College, Cambridge, born 9 July 1873,—Agnes Helen, born 16 July 1874,—Mary Priscilla, born 28 July 1876,—Lucy Caroline, born 7 Dec. 1877,—Frederick James of Marlborough College, born 24 Feb. 1880,— Howard, born 31 Mar. 1882,—Rose Frances, born 12 Dec. 1886,—Oswald, born 28 Feb. 1889.

CHILDREN OF JOHN (12)

26 :—JOHN JOSHUA H., head of H.M. Customs at Newcastle on Tyne ; born 1838 = Charlotte Diaper ; issue.

27 :—BARCLAY VINCENT H., head of the Numismatic Department in the Brit. Museum ; born 1844 = Mary Harley Corkran ; issue.

28 :—Caroline Sarah H., born 1846 ; unmar.

Tenth Generation

CHILDREN OF JEREMIAH (18)

29 :—Mary Ingram H., born 16 Oct. 1862 = Colin Campbell, eldest son of No. 21 ; mar. at Coatham afsd. 29 Aug. 1889 ; issue.

30 :—William Howard H. of London ; born 28 Sep. 1864.

31 :—ARCHIBALD POTTER H. of London ; born 4 Aug. 1866 = Mary Hill ; mar. at the English Church, St. Petersburg, 14 June 1892 ; issue.

32 :—Alfred Wrightson H., born 7 Feb. 1868 ; died 30 May 1872.

33 :—Rebecca Helen Gilchrist H., born 11 June 1870 ; died 17 Oct. 1889.

34 :—Kathleen Campbell H., born 4 July 1872.

35 :—Benjamin Wrightson H., born 12 May 1875.

APPENDIX K.

MRS. PRISCILLA ANNE WRIGHTSON (*NÉE* HEAD).

The connections of Mrs. Priscilla Anne Wrightson (*née* Head), whether in remote or recent times, comprise many interesting names. Not only were both her parents descended from King Edward the Third, but her father was nearly related to many persons distinguished, either for wealth and philanthropy at home, or for daring enterprise in the Colonies.

I. Her descent through her Mother :—

This descent, down to, but not including, her great-grandmother, is constructed from information contained in Brydges' Collins' *Peerage of England*, vol. vi, pp. 516-21, and in Burke's *Extinct Baronetage* under names of Cholmley of Whitby and D'Oyley of Chislehampton.

DESCENTS.

King Edward III.
|
Lionel, Duke of Clarence
|
Philippa Plantagenet
m. Edmund Mortimer, 3rd Earl of March
|
Elizabeth
m. Sir Henry Percy (" Harry Hotspur "), eldest son of the Duke of Northumberland
|

Elizabeth Percy
m. John, 7th Lord de Clifford

|

Thomas, 8th Lord de Clifford

|

John, 9th Lord de Clifford

|

Henry, 10th Lord de Clifford

|

Henry, 11th Lord de Clifford, and 1st Earl of Cumberland

|

Lady Katharine Clifford
m. Sir Richard Cholmley, Knt. of Roxby

|

Sir Henry Chomley, Knt. of Whitby and Roxby

|

Sir Richard Chomley, Knt.
of Whitby, High Sheriff of Yorkshire in 1624, and M.P. for
Scarborough in 1620

|

Sir Richard Chomley, Knight-banneret
of Grosmont, co. York ; a Colonel in the service of Charles I.,
and one of the most gallant Cavaliers of the time. He married
Margaret, dau. of Lord Poulett of Hinton St. John, co.
Somerset.

|

Margaret Chomley
m. Sir John D'Oyley, Bart. of Chislehampton, co. Oxon

|

Sir John D'Oyley, Bart.
of Chislehampton ; mar. 1694 Susanna, dau. of Sir Thomas
Putt, Bart. of Combe, co. Devon

|

Ursula D'Oyley
m. Thomas Young of Newington, co. Oxon

|

Ursula Young
m. 1750 Thomas Cooper of South Weston, co. Oxon

|

Thomas Cooper
of Henley on Thames, co. Oxon, solicitor, born 24 Oct. 1751 ;
mar. 16 Jan. 1787 Mary Bevan of Devizes, co. Wilts

|

Ellen Cooper [1]
m. Alfred Head of London

|

Priscilla Anne Head
m. Rev. W. G. Wrightson

II. Her descent through her Father :—

This descent may be seen, back to John of Gaunt, under the pedigree of Charles Marcus Wakefield, in *Our Noble and Gentle Families of Royal Descent*, by Joseph Foster. Towards the close of the following outline, I introduce various names, which occur under other headings in Mr. Foster's work.

DESCENTS.

King Edward III.

|

John of Gaunt, Duke of Lancaster

|

Sir John Beaufort, Marquis of Dorset and Earl of Somerset

|

---

[1] Of her brothers I may mention John, Samuel, Sir Charles, and Walter. John was the father and grandfather of our good Henley friends John Cooper and his son John Frederick. And Walter was the father of the Rev. Arthur and Messrs. Ernest and Charles Cooper, with whom Harry Wrightson has started to learn business.

Joanna, Queen of Scots
as widow of James I. of Scotland, she mar. Sir James Stewart,
"the black knight of Lorn"

|

Sir John Stewart, Earl of Athole

|

Janet Stewart
m. Alexander, 3rd Earl of Huntley

|

John, Lord Gordon

|

Alexander Gordon
titular Archbishop of Athens in 1547

|

John Gordon
gentleman of the bedchamber to Charles IX., Henry III. and
Henry IV. of France

|

Louisa Gordon
m. 1613 to Sir Robert Gordon, Bart. of Gordonstown

|

Catharine Gordon
m. 1648 to Colonel David Barclay of Urie, co. Kincardine

|

Robert Barclay
of Urie, "The Apologist"; Governor for life of New Jersey

|

David Barclay

|

Catherine Barclay
b. 1727 ; m. 1750 to Daniel Bell of Royston, co. Herts ;
d. 1784

|

Priscilla Bell
b. 31 Jan. 1750-1 ; m. 3 Jan. 1771 to Edward Wakefield of
London ; d. 12 Sep. 1832

|

Isabella Wakefield
b. 3 Mar. 1773; m. 12 Sep. 1794 to Joshua Head of Ipswich ;
d. 17 Oct. 1841

|

Alfred Head
b. 26 Feb. 1797; m. 7 May 1839 Ellen Cooper of Henley on
Thames; d. 15 Feb. 1880

|

Priscilla Anne Head
m. to Rev. W. G. Wrightson

The descendants of the above Catherine Barclay include all the most interesting of Mrs. P. A. Wrightson's connections on her father's side. These are best grouped together in the following pedigree form,—

First Generation

1. CATHERINE BARCLAY, born June 1727; died 19 Oct. 1784 = Daniel Bell; mar. 17 Apr. 1750; died 19 Oct. 1802, aged 76.

Second Generation

CHILDREN OF CATHERINE (1)

2. PRISCILLA BELL, founder of the first Savings Bank and a well-known author of juvenile books, born 20 Jan. 1750-1 ; as a widow she lived with her daughter Isabella at Ipswich, where she died 12 Sep. 1832 = Edward Wakefield of London, merchant, mar. 3 Jan. 1771. [In the family group painted by Gainsborough, apparently about 1775, she is represented sitting, while her husband and sister Katharine stand beside her. This extremely valuable painting passed in succession first to her daughter Isabella, and then to her grandson Alfred Head. His

widow left it by will to her daughter Isabella Head, who in 1890 presented it to her sister Mrs. Priscilla Anne Wrightson, who was already possessed of the shagreen case containing the beautiful old silver tea caddies and sugar basin, made by a Samuel Taylor in 1750, and said to have been presented to Priscilla Wakefield at her wedding in 1771, most probably by the Mr. and Mrs. Bell whose arms are engraved on the silver.]

3. KATHARINE BELL, born 18 Nov. 1754; died 17 Nov. 1792 = John Gurney of Earlham, co. Norfolk; mar. 26 May 1775.

4. JONATHAN BELL, born 1769; died 1855.

Third Generation

Children of Priscilla (2)

5. ISABELLA WAKEFIELD, born 3 Mar. 1773; died 17 Oct. 1841 = Joshua Head of Ipswich; mar. 12 Sep. 1794.

6. EDWARD WAKEFIELD, born 1774; died 1854.

Children of Katharine (3)

7. ELIZABETH GURNEY [Mrs. Fry], the famous philanthropist and reformer of the Prison system; born 1780; died 1845 = Joseph Fry of Plashet, co. Essex; mar. 1800.

SAMUEL GURNEY of Upton, co. Essex, born 1786; died 1856. [He was the founder of the great financial firm of Overend, Gurney and Co., which a generation later, and under other management, shook the whole commercial fabric of the country by its failure 10 May 1866,—a day which in City circles will be remembered for a century as " Black Friday."]

JOSEPH JOHN GURNEY of Earlham, born 1788; died 1847. [He was the zealous and loving companion of Mrs. Fry in her memorable visits to the Prisons of Great Britain and the Continent.]

HANNAH GURNEY = Sir Thomas Fowell Buxton, Bart., M.P. [He was the able supporter of Mrs. Fry in her work among prisons, and the recognized successor of the great Wilberforce in finally achieving the abolition of slavery.]

LOUISA GURNEY = Samuel Hoare of London, banker.

CHILD OF JONATHAN (4)

8. EDWARD MATTHEW BELL.

Fourth Generation

CHILD OF ISABELLA (5)

ALFRED HEAD of London, the father of Mrs. P. A. Wrightson.

CHILDREN OF EDWARD (6)

EDWARD GIBBON WAKEFIELD, chief founder of the colonies of South Australia and New Zealand.

ARTHUR WAKEFIELD, Commander in R.N. ; leader of the first body of colonists to Nelson, New Zealand ; killed in the Wairau massacre 16 June 1843.

WILLIAM HAYWARD WAKEFIELD, Colonel of 1st reg. of lancers in the Brit. auxiliary force in Spain ; leader of the first body of colonists to Wellington, New Zealand ; founder of that city.

FELIX WAKEFIELD, principal superintendent of Army Works Corps in the Crimea ; died in New Zealand. [His sons Salvator and Edward were most kind and helpful to me when I was in South Australia and N.Z. in 1887-8.—W. G. W.]

CHILD OF ELIZABETH (7)

LOUISA FRY = Raymond, second son of Sir John Henry Pelly, Bart. [My old and valued college friend, the Rev.

Raymond Pelly, is their son, and I stayed with them at Plashet House in 1863.—W. G. W.]

Child of Edward (8)

SIR FRANCIS DILLON BELL, C.B., late Agent-general for New Zealand. [At various times my courteous informant on official and family matters.—W. G. W.]

APPENDIX L.

REMARKS AS TO PRESERVING FAMILY RECORDS.

At intervals of two or three generations our pedigree at the College of Arms ought to be brought up to date. The member of the family, who undertakes to see after such a piece of work, should in the first place prepare a careful draft of the additions, taking care to mention where the proof of every statement may be found ; *e.g.*, the dates of births, deaths, marriages, and wills, —the place of a baptism,—where and when a will was proved. In the second place he should show the draft to Somerset, or one of the other Heralds, and arrange the total cost of " entering " the additions. Information would then be given through the Herald, as to how far certificates and other legal evidences of descent were required for actual inspection at the College. If all required evidences were forwarded to the College, I think ten pounds would cover the addition of three or four generations ; but, if the Heralds themselves are left to look up evidences, the cost will be indefinitely large.

Invaluable genealogical material may often be inserted in a will. Thus, besides the descendants of the Testator, the names and addresses of brothers and sisters, etc., may easily be recorded by means of some possibly trifling legacy ; *e.g.*, " to Emily, only child of my late brother John Watts of York, ten pounds." And, if the Testator can associate anything he is leaving with his father, he has the opportunity of mentioning the place and date of the proving of his father's will.

For all members of the family, who have resided in England, the legal proofs of descent are discoverable at the General Register Office in London and at the various Registries of Wills; *e.g.*, in London, York, and Durham. If the searcher knows the approximate date of a birth, death, or marriage, and where a will was proved, the official record can be discovered with very little trouble; but with no trouble at all, if such particulars have been accurately preserved in the family.

In memory of all the labour, time, and money I have lavished on the production of the First Part of these Memorials, I entreat that no one will disfigure it by inserting manuscript additions of any kind. But I urge on every member of our family the institution of such Manuscript books, as I have kept since I was fifteen years of age, for the reception of dates, memoranda, and miscellaneous fragments of domestic information. Assuming that the family survives and is worthy of further notice, such collections of rough material could from time to time be re-edited, or even brought together in a printed form, like my own "Contributions to the Second Part of the Family Memorials."

Of the 120 copies of these Memorials, which are printed exclusively for present and future members of our family, every one bearing our name and attaining full age may ask for and receive one fresh copy, but no more. I am having each copy lightly bound with untrimmed edges, so as to allow one or more blocks of printed "Contributions" to be added in the future, previous to its possessor having it rebound in a style answering to its value. After my time the balance of undistributed copies will remain in the charge, and under the direction, of my eldest son.

CONTRIBUTIONS

BY THE

REV. W. G. WRIGHTSON

TOWARDS THE COMPILATION OF THE

SECOND PART

OF THE

FAMILY MEMORIALS.

1894.

CONTRIBUTIONS.

N.B.—The following contributions are to be regarded simply as raw material supplied for literary treatment. If they err on the side of fullness, it is through the difficulty of foreseeing what may, or may not, have a bearing on after events, or possess interest in the future.

I :—

 THE REV. WILLIAM GARMONS-WAY WRIGHTSON, M.A. Cantab.,[1] was born at Haughton-le-Skerne 24 June 1836. The greater part of my too brief school days were passed at Bramham College near Tadcaster. I then (1 Oct. 1851) became a premium pupil in what was I believe the earliest *Iron* Shipbuilding yard on the Tyne, and was more or less engaged in various Engineering works, including those of Robert Stephenson and Co. at Newcastle-on-Tyne. I was steady and industrious in mastering my special work; but my passionate desire for extended knowledge, and the consciousness of my poor school training, made me fill up almost every leisure hour with study. At length, during a period of disengagement, I became so deeply absorbed in religious work that, with the hearty approval of my dear Father, I resolved to become a clergyman. On 15 Oct. 1860 I went to Caius College, Cambridge. I studied so hard that just before my final examination I became ill and was ordered off for change of air and scene to Italy. I had an enchanting and never-to-be-forgotten trip. Full of historical

[1] My photographic portrait, taken 23 June 1874, was in 1894 admirably etched for this book by Mons. H. Manesse, the well-known Parisian artist.

and antiquarian enthusiasm I visited Rome, Naples, Pompeii, Venice, Genoa, Pisa, Milan, and Paris. I returned to England quite set up again in health; and took my " B.A." degree (26 Nov. 1863), though it was not till long after (3 June 1880) that I took my "M.A." I was ordained Deacon 25 Sep. 1864, and Priest on the 24th of following Sep. by Bishop Baring of Durham, who was always my fatherly friend and adviser. My first curacy was at Bishop-Auckland, co. Durham, under the Rev. G. H. Wilkinson, afterwards the Bishop of Truro, and now of St. Andrews, Scotland. It was a glorious, but wearing life to be with such a man. The strain of work he kept up was severe for five clergy; but after he and one of the curates broke down for many months, leaving the remaining three to carry on a practically undiminished work, it became terrible. After my three years of work there I was never quite the same man again.

Just before my ordination I was visiting my brother-in-law at Stockton, and for the first time (19 Aug. 1864) met my future wife. In 1866 I paid a visit at her father's, Mr. Alfred Head's, lovely country house at Epsom in Surrey, where matters came to a point; and on 4 Dec. 1866 we were married from his town house (13 Craven Hill Gardens, Hyde Park) at Christ Church, Lancaster Gate.

Our residence at Bishop-Auckland was suddenly terminated by a serious accident. I broke (4 July 1867) the semi-lunar cartilage beneath my knee-cap,—was taken to London for surgical treatment,—and did not get rid of my last crutch for two years. During this time Wilkinson accepted a London benefice, and at his request I managed to occupy his pulpit and hold together the congregation, till he himself was able to enter on his charge. I became interested in London work, and commenced regular duty there (7 Aug. 1868) as senior curate at St. John's, Paddington, under my now old and valued friend Sir Emilius Laurie of Maxwelton, Bart.,—but who at that time bore the name of Bayley. As Sir Emilius was always absent during the autumn months, I had the advantage of frequently occupying one of the most important Metropolitan pulpits. It was my delight to do so; and, even at the 'dead season,' I speedily gathered good congregations. Among my most attentive hearers there chanced to be some members of the Cator family, on whose great Beckenham estate a large new church had been commenced. After some hesitation between me and the Rev. Boyd Carpenter, now the eloquent Bishop of Ripon, this new church was presented to me; and on 30 March 1870 we took up our abode at Beckenham, co. Kent. Little had I anticipated the wearing troubles and anxieties that awaited me; but at length, with the help of my ever faithful and attached parishioners, the important work was carried through,—St. Paul's church was finished,—the district and full tithe assigned, —and I was finally inducted (3 June 1872) as the first Vicar. We then bought a good site on the south side of my Church, and built a handsome house, which we named "The Grange," and in which we expected to spend our lives. For a short time it seemed as if no drop of happiness was missing from my cup. I was in the full swing of that work in which above all others I rejoiced, when, after many warnings, my throat gave way. It had been unsuccessfully operated upon by the afterwards famous Sir Morell Mackenzie, and I never really recovered from the injury inflicted by his knife. After a long course of treatment in Paris and at Mont Dore les Bains, I made an abortive effort to resume work, and was then ordered to give my throat rest for two more years, without any assurance of being fit for my pulpit at the end of that time. My kind and sympathizing friend the Archbishop (Tait) of Canterbury gave me authority to go abroad for two years; and then, privately and unofficially, advised me to resign my benefice, if I could afford to do so, and if I could thereby insure my parish being well cared for. I gave the Patron a list of clergy to any one of whom I was willing to resign my benefice. He selected the Rev. Charles Green, one of my old Auckland fellow-curates, who was delighted to receive a living that soon brought him in a thousand a year. I bid my dear people farewell (11 Oct. 1875), and three days later, along with all my family, started for a long residence on the Continent. Our first temporary home was at St. Jean de Luz, a nice little Basque town at the extreme corner of the Bay of Biscay. After leaving this (7 June 1877) we went to Switzerland, where we stayed a year, chiefly at Veytaux Chillon, near Montreux, on the Lake of Geneva. The immediate cause of our return to England (16 May 1878) was complicated business connected with the colliery and landed property left to me by my uncle Archibald Potter. Although we have never again had a foreign home, yet my dear wife and I, occasionally with some of our young people, have travelled much. We have been through Wales and Scotland, and many times upon the Continent: but by far our greatest journey was made in 1887-8, when, along with our two eldest sons, we went through the Suez Canal and Red Sea, visited Ceylon, spent some weeks in Australia, and some months in New Zealand, having by the time we reached home (after nearly eight months' absence) traversed 27,677 miles of ocean.

It was well that I had resigned my living before going abroad, for on my return Sir James Paget, the President of the Royal College of Surgeons, informed me that, though I was suffering from a merely local and mechanical injury, my throat would never again be fit for regular pulpit work. "You must give up," said he, "the idea of ever again taking a church or parish, though you may be able to take occasional work." And so I sank again into private life, except in so far as I have been able gratuitously to assist my brother clergy. I occasionally preach; but of all other work that of conducting Bible classes for educated people is to me the most interesting. From the time that I returned from the Continent to the present, I have at intervals succeeded in carrying on such classes. And at the request of the Editor I embodied my own experience in this particular line of work in the opening article of the *Clergyman's Magazine* for Jan. 1885. My private life became more and more that of a quiet student and literary man. I wrote various papers on Assyrian Inscriptions, on the Basques, on Early English, etc. Those articles which I wrote for the Sunday School Magazine were afterwards published separately under the title of *Condensed Confirmation Addresses.* The most elaborate book I ever wrote is a linguistic one called *Functional Elements of an English Sentence;* and I was much indebted to the Professor of Anglo-Saxon at Cambridge for a careful revisal of the proof sheets, so far as his particular language was concerned. I have also spent much time, money, and labour, in compiling the *Memorials of the Family of Wrightson.* And there is a considerably advanced historical tale called *John Royston,* in which many of our family characters appear, as I conceived them before quite completing my discovery of family documents. If published anonymously, this book would appear under its own name in the catalogues at the British Museum.

It was not for some years after ceasing to be Vicar that I

sold my Beckenham house. After leaving it (22 Mar. 1884) we resided for about three years at Worthing in Sussex, and soon after our return from New Zealand came to Hurworth-on-Tees. On 13 Aug. 1891, having secured a twenty-one years' lease, we entered the Old Hall, which possesses good stabling for our horses; and, since the enlargement of the dining and drawing rooms, has become a really handsome residence. We still continue to go to London for some months each spring, and enjoy seeing much of the Westerns and of my dear and hospitable sister-in-law, Bella Head, whose whole life is spent in doing good. Occasionally we go to the Continent in May and June. At home we seldom give dinner parties; but, especially in summer time, we often have visitors staying in the house. Our lovely grounds, which are about five acres in extent, afford ample room for large gatherings, including many of our young people's friends and numerous cousins. Never were these gatherings more delightful than in the glorious summer of 1893, when our dear son Alfred was at home.

The year after we entered this house, my brother Tom repurchased Neasham Hall. While Member of Parliament for Stockton he can only occasionally reside so near to us; but, when he does, the intercourse between the family groups is most agreeable. His much greater wealth and his political associations give him a social prominence, which we do not possess; but we are far more than content with the peaceful comfort of our home. Like my dear parents, we also live considerably within our means, and have the pleasure of assisting our children in the formation and management of smaller fortunes of their own.

The realization of my father's hope in the recovery of Neasham, and the more than realization of his hopes for the restoration of the family position, serve alike to round-off the domestic story I have told with dramatic completeness: and I trust that the example of my beloved parents may stimulate to a like self-sacrifice those who will assuredly be called upon to face some future cycle of misfortune. Commencing life, as I did, amidst the darkest clouds of debt and difficulty, our present position wakens a sense of solemn gratitude to that God, who, first in my father's time, and then in my own, has removed far from us our old adversities,—"we went through fire and water, and THOU broughtest us out into a wealthy place."

And now, as the shadows of the eventide of life begin to lie across my path, I cast my eyes downward with a sense of unutterable tenderness on the dear companion who, thank God, still walks beside me. No shade of distrust or anger has ever crossed the peaceful loving face, which year by year has met my own ; and year by year that face becomes more dear, as keeping ever in my mind the vast store of tender confidence, accumulated through all the thoughtful, sympathetic, loving past. Like my own dear mother, she ever longs to be doing good. Kept much in-doors, she has mastered the Braille alphabet, and with marvellous skill laboriously copies many valued works, which can then be reproduced a hundredfold by the Blind for themselves. Born at the east-end of London, her heart is full of compassion for the poor there. She and her two noble-minded sisters afford most generous aid to the Rector of Stepney ; and we are always delighted to receive the interesting and even touching letters written by the lady whom my dear wife enables to work in that great east-end parish.

Our daughters, with the exception of Mabel, have now finished their education (Isabel and Lucy at the Ladies' College, Cheltenham), and are at home. My wish that each should have a " hobby " has been met by their enthusiasm in various ways. Ellen is the artist, who, after being under various masters in London, made by far her greatest advance whilst painting almost daily for seven months in the best studio in Dresden. Isabel is the literary student. Lucy, who accompanied Ellen to Dresden, is the musician ; not only playing well on both violin and piano, but also firing Mabel's enthusiasm to do the same. They make home exceeding bright ; and to the Rector of the parish are simply invaluable, whether in the Sunday schools or in visiting among the poor.

------

2 :—My brother, Thomas Wrightson M.P. of Neasham Hall and Norton Hall, was born at Haughton-le-Skerne 31 Mar. 1839, and educated at Bramham College and in Newcastle-on-Tyne. In 1854 he became a premium pupil in the great engineering works of his cousin, afterwards Lord Armstrong, at Elswick near Newcastle : and it was here that he proved himself to be in the profession that beyond all others suited his inclinations and abilities. In July 1862 he went to

London with first-rate introductions from Armstrong, and was at once engaged among some of the most distinguished Civil Engineers of Great George Street, Westminster. During this residence in London he availed himself of some of the educational advantages afforded by the King's College classes. After gaining much experience, especially in connection with the construction of the Metropolitan underground Railway, the desire to prepare the way for the establishment of works in the north brought him nearer home. For a time he accepted a responsible position in works, which had been started some years before at Thornaby-on-Tees by Thomas Howard Head, a brother of his sister's husband. On 1 Oct. 1866 he became a partner in these Works; and, when the firm was reconstituted on the retirement of Howard Head, he along with Arthur, a younger brother of Howard's, carried on, as equal partners, the whole business under the previous name of "Head, Wrightson and Co." The £8,000, with which his father had enabled him to secure half this business, was in ten years turned into £80,000; and from that time the business expanded, until the firm became one of the most important in the north, and was at last turned into a Company with limited liability.

As an accomplished scientific man, he not only made and patented several mechanical inventions, but also devoted very considerable attention to scientific subjects remoter from his special line of work. Thus he went most elaborately into the mechanical aspects of harmony and vibration (being himself an accomplished musician), and made his investigations the subject of his Presidential Address to the Cleveland Institution of Engineers in 1876. Again, his original investigations on the physical properties of metals and their change of volume in passing through high grades of temperature, attracted considerable attention in leading scientific circles, and brought him into communication with Professor Stokes, President of the Royal Society, Sir William Siemens, Professor Chandler Roberts-Austen of the Mint, Sir William Thompson (now Lord Kelvin), and other eminent physicists. The papers describing his numerous experiments are to be found in the *Proceedings of the Physical Society*, and *of the Iron and Steel Institute* from 1879 to 1882; also in the *Philosophical Magazine*, April 1881, and Wiedemann's *Annalen*. The chief interest is to be attached to his demonstration and analysis of the curious property of iron expanding as it passes from the liquid to the solid state (see *Journal of Iron and Steel Institute* 1879 and 1880). Alluding to these experiments Sir William Thompson, in a letter dated Nov. 1884, says to him, "I am glad to see the question of the expansion of Iron in solidifying settled with such thorough investigation."

It was as a bachelor that he went to live at Norton Hall, a residence which he afterwards purchased and has since enlarged and beautified.

On 23 June 1869 he made a most happy marriage with Miss Elizabeth Wise, the eldest daughter of the leading solicitor in Ripon.

From the time of its constitution as a Parliamentary Borough, Stockton-on-Tees had always been represented by a Radical member. In 1880 the Conservative Candidate was in a hopeless minority of 3,559 in a constituency of at that time 8,333 electors, of which only 77 per cent. voted. After this miserable defeat the party invited my brother to come forward as their candidate. During three electoral contests (1885-6-8) he steadily improved their position, until at last on 5 July 1892 he ousted Sir Horace Davey, the Solicitor General of Mr. Gladstone in 1886, with a majority of 311 in a constituency of 10,422 electors, of whom no less than 89 per cent. voted. In this general election my brother was the only Conservative returned in the County of Durham.

Some months before this election Neasham Hall and Estate came into the market. On 7 Dec. 1891 my brother and the head of the Cookson family came to terms, but difficulties were raised by others who had a reversionary interest, so that it was not actually purchased till 30 June 1892, and thus what he described to me as 'two of the ambitions of his life' were attained within a week of each other. The price he gave was £27,000, which with the woods (at a valuation) and needful repairs came to about £30,000. He has stayed at Neasham; but, so long as he is member for Stockton, it seems as if Norton Hall must remain his home. On the nomination of the late Marquess of Londonderry my brother was long since placed on the Bench as a Durham County magistrate. From that time the Londonderry family supported him by their great influence, and have admitted him to very intimate friendship. It was indeed by the present Marquess and Marchioness that he at first, and at a somewhat later date his wife, were presented at Court. Among the many industrial organizations with which my brother is connected, he is a Director in three, viz., in the works of Messrs. Head, Wrightson and Co. Limited,—in those of the North Eastern Steel Co. Limited,—and in the Cramlington Coal Co. Limited. He is indeed a very wealthy and influential man, and is highly respected throughout the north of England.

3:—My brother, Professor John Wrightson, President of the College of Agriculture, Downton, was born at Haughton-le-Skerne, 9 Sep. 1840. His school days were passed chiefly at Newcastle-on-Tyne. From a very early age all around him saw that his mind was intensely alive to everything in the world of Nature ; and John Hancock, at that time the greatest of living ornithologists, loved to have the keen-eyed and intelligent boy as a companion on his expeditions. Agriculture naturally came to be looked at as his destined course of life. On 6 March 1857 he was sent to Dilston as a premium pupil to a leading Tyne-side farmer. Here he remained for more than four years, during which time he won the esteem and friendship of the well-known and venerable John Grey, Commissioner of the Greenwich Hospital estates. After he quitted Dilston he eagerly accepted his father's offer to let him pass an academic year at King's College, London. He went there 1 Oct. 1861, and in the August of the year following to the Royal Agricultural College, Cirencester, where a few months later he passed as first man of his year, securing thereby a £60 scholarship. At his final examination in Dec. 1863 he occupied the same honourable position and received his diploma. For some time he searched in vain for a vacant farm, and then for a few months took in hand his father's farm of Spring House. It was whilst there that he received the offer of the Professorship of Agriculture at Cirencester. He at once accepted it, and for more than twelve years (6 Jan. 1865 to 6 July 1877) he held this post, having from sixty to eighty students under his direction. His name became of course widely known, and he received tempting offers to remove to India or to the United States. But perhaps the highest mark of appreciation was afforded, when in 1873, without any solicitation on his part, he was appointed Commissioner for the Royal Agricultural Society to visit and report upon the agricultural features of the Vienna Exhibition, and on the agriculture of the Austro-Hungarian Empire. He was supplied with the highest introductions, and was made one of the Jurors of the Exhibition. The interesting details of his journey, and the information he collected, were embodied by himself in two Reports, which may be seen in the *Journal of the Royal Agricultural Society* for 1874. It was in these Reports, and subsequently in two letters to the *Times*, that he first brought the idea of Ensilage (*i.e.* the art of pressing green fodder in pits) prominently before the British public. From 1870 to 1877 inclusive he carried out various extensive Series of Agricultural Experiments in connection with the Cirencester Chamber of Agriculture, the results of which were embodied in the Reports annually presented by him before that association. The literary work of his life has been very considerable; and, even before leaving Cirencester, he had made nearly £2,000 by the use of his pen. He is the author of a series of Articles on Farming and Farming Economy in Cassell's *Technical Educator* (1872). He wrote an *Agricultural Text Book* to cover the Syllabus of the Educational Department of South Kensington for this class of subjects; also *Principles of Agricultural Practice* (1888); *Fallow and Fodder Crops* (1889); and edited the Downton Series of Agricultural Text Books (Cassell and Co., London, 1892). The entire list of his works may however be seen in the Catalogue at the British Museum.

On 23 July 1872 he married Maria Isabel Hulton, a young lady who connected him with one of the finest families among the untitled English gentry. A reference to Joseph Foster's *County Families of Lancashire* shows her ancestry through twenty-six generations. Her grandfather, William Hulton of Hulton Park, was High Sheriff of the county in 1809 and Constable of Lancaster Castle. Of his children I will only mention the late William Hulton of Hulton Park,—Charles Norleigh Hulton, Maria's father,—and Amelia Maria, wife of the late Hon. and Right Rev. Montagu Villiers, Lord Bishop of Durham.

After his marriage, the desire for liberty of action, and the fact of his having capital, induced him to resign his position at Cirencester and to take North Charford House. It is a handsome old manor-house, surrounded by a beautiful farm of some

550 acres, on the banks of the Christchurch Avon, near Downton, a village about six miles from Salisbury. He entered this, 11 Oct. 1877, at a bad time, for the next ten years were among the most discouraging on record for agriculturists. A cycle of terrible seasons coincided with a rapid fall in the value of all sorts of produce,—for example, wheat fell from about 56s. to 32s. per quarter. But, in spite of all, my brother made his presence felt in his new sphere. In Dec. 1884 he was one of the promoters of the Wiltshire Agricultural Association, and was elected a Governor and also one of the original Members of its Council. He took a leading position among the breeders of Improved Hampshire-Down sheep, and instituted an annual ram sale, first held in July 1885.

Very soon after establishing himself at Charford, pupils began to collect around him, and it was then that he conceived the leading idea of his life, viz., the founding of that Institution now known as "The College of Agriculture, Downton." The College was started in May 1880, and it has now attained a high position among those technical institutions which have become a feature in the latter half of the nineteenth century. The most severe blow, the College has hitherto experienced, was a terrible fire (13 Jan. 1891), which destroyed almost the whole of what had been erected for the accommodation of the students. The event however led to the rebuilding of the college in a more commodious and handsome style.

In April 1882 he was appointed by the Lord President of the Council of Education to be the first Professor of Agriculture at South Kensington, and soon after was made one of the two Examiners-in-chief for the Science and Art Department in Agriculture. These appointments have of course brought him into very pleasant association with leading scientific men in the Metropolis.

---

4 :—My son, Robert Garmondsway Wrightson, B.A. Cantab., and Barrister-at-Law, was born 6 Apr. 1869. His Public School days (3 May 1883 to 26 July 1886) were passed at Marlborough College. I had made my mind up to let my sons choose their own course in life ; but I was both startled and distressed when Robert asked permission to accompany his brother to New Zealand. In order to prepare them for the colonies I

sent them for a year (8 Oct. 1886 to 19 Aug. 1887) to the College of Agriculture at Downton. Here it was that for the first time Robert showed his abilities, and passed as first man of his year. My wife and I arranged to take our sons out to New Zealand, so as to judge of the country and its prospects. Like myself Robert was disappointed, and I offered, if he would return to England, to let him go through the Science course at Cambridge. This offer he accepted. We left him to complete the circuit of the World by himself,—which he did, going round by Cape Horn. He entered Trinity College, Cambridge, 6 Oct. 1888, and took his B.A. degree 23 June 1891, having obtained a second class in the Natural Science Tripos Part I. He was told by the head examiner that, out of 122 men entered for the Tripos, he was among the highest 20, so that he must have been very near the top of the second class. In the January before taking his degree he commenced keeping terms at the Inner Temple; and, after leaving Cambridge, completed the agricultural course at Downton (18 Sep. 1891 to 17 Aug. 1892), passing easily as head man, and taking both the College Diploma and Certificate. After this he went (26 Sep. 1892) as a premium pupil to the Hon. Cecil Parker, Agent to the Duke of Westminster on the Eaton Estate near Chester. While with Mr. Parker he spent much time studying in London, where he not only passed the examination which made him a Professional Associate of the Surveyors' Institution, but also his final legal examination. On 18 April 1894 he was called to the Bar at the Inner Temple. It had been his wish to practise on the Chancery side. But this wish seems to have been given up on the advice of such a leading London solicitor as his uncle Edward Western, and of such a distinguished legal authority as my old friend Mr. Registrar Brougham, nephew of the late Lord Chancellor Brougham. In view of the extremely overcrowded state of the Bar, both these gentlemen consider that he is much more likely to be a successful man in Land Agency, than practising as a Barrister.

---

5 :—My second son, Alfred Head Wrightson, was born 29 May 1870. While he was at Highgate School near London, I found that his mind was resolutely set on becoming a farmer in New Zealand. In due course he accompanied his eldest brother

for a year to the Downton College of Agriculture. He left England with us on 7 Oct., and first set foot in New Zealand at the Bluff on 11 Dec. 1887. I had many good introductions, and one of these from my friend Sir Emilius Laurie, Bart., led to my staying with such first-rate people as the Hon. J. B. Acland[1] and his brother-in-law Mr. Tripp[1] of Orari Gorge, both of whom were afterwards most kind and valuable friends to my son, bringing him into touch with the very best class of people in both the north and south islands. My wife and I travelled by land or sea the entire length of the two islands and the entire breadth from Wellington to New Plymouth. Over much of this both our sons accompanied us. We finally quitted New Zealand soil 7 March 1888, and for nearly two years Alfred remained at the Lincoln School of Agriculture near Christchurch. While staying with Mr. Tripp, he met and made friends with one of the Cornish Carlyons, who has a noble property in Hawkes-bay. This gentleman invited him to come on to his "run." After a happy and useful year with Mr. Carlyon,[1] he completed his circle of agricultural training for the colonies by going in for a stretch of very hard work on a "bush farm" at Alfredton in Wellington. On his twenty-first birthday he had become entitled to about £700, chiefly from his grandmother Head. A part of this he used in taking up (21 Sep. 1891) half the capital required in starting the new store of McIntyre and Co., under the management of a Mr. Dunderdale; and he has now almost doubled his original capital. His brother Harry had been out for a visit to New Zealand, and we resolved to give Alfred a run home with him. They arrived in England 20 May 1893. We found that Alfred had become a fine powerful young man of over six feet high,— genial, gentlemanly, and universally popular. He visited Mr. Dunderdale's family in Scotland, and a great many friends and relatives in England. During his delightful time at home, he became an excellent photographer. After having shown himself so capable and well-conducted, we have felt it safe to make him an advance of £2,000; which, when added to his previous capital, will enable him to commence farming for himself. We, and all his brothers and sisters, saw him off (2 March) from Tilbury on the Thames, and he again reached Wellington in New Zealand 23 April 1894.

[1] See Burke's *Colonial Gentry*, 1891.

6 :—My third son, Harry Wrightson, was born 29 Sep. 1874. His Public School days were passed at Marlborough (21 Sep. 1888 to 31 Mar. 1892); after which, in consequence of accident and illness, he was sent off for a year's trip (13 May 1892 to 20 May 1893) to his brother in New Zealand. They returned to England together, and on 9 Aug. 1893 he commenced a London business life in the office of his mother's cousin, Mr. Ernest Cooper, with a view to become in time an Underwriter at Lloyd's.

7 :—My nephew, Thomas G. Wrightson (commonly known as "Guy"), was born 21 Aug. 1871. He was educated at Marlborough and Trinity College, Cambridge, at which University he took his B.A. degree in 1892, having passed with Honours in the Natural Science Tripos. On 13 Oct. 1892 he went, as a premium pupil, to the same great Elswick Works, in which his father had commenced his engineering career nearly forty years before.

8 :—My nephew, Charles Wrightson, was born 17 July 1874. In Dec. 1888 he passed as ninth amongst the 45 successful candidates for the Royal Navy. He was a naval cadet on board the "Rodney" off Gibraltar, when in March 1891 the Italian emigrant ship "Utopia" went down on a stormy night, through striking against one of our fleet. On that occasion Charley so distinguished himself by gallant conduct in saving life, that he was specially mentioned in the dispatches; and, at the annual dinner of the Civil Engineers in London soon after, Admiral Sir R. Vesey Hamilton, in referring to the services rendered to the drowning people by our Navy, said, "Mr. Wrightson, naval cadet, considering his age and time of service, behaved with the greatest pluck and coolness throughout the night." It is not to be wondered at that, without any solicitation on the part of his father, Charley was in Oct. 1892 appointed as a midshipman to the "Victoria," flag-ship of Admiral Sir George Tryon, Commander-in-Chief of the Mediterranean Fleet. Soon after this he was seized with fever, and was thrice visited by Sir George in the hospital at

Malta. While there the awful catastrophe of the foundering of the "Victoria" (with the loss of Admiral Tryon and most of the crew) took place. Charley was next a midshipman on board the "Empress of India," flag-ship of Rear-Admiral E. H. Seymour, C.B., second in command of the Channel Squadron. He is now on board the "Calypso" training-ship, studying for his lieutenant's examination.

9:—My nephew, John Frederick Hulton Wrightson, was born 6 Feb. 1875. He was educated at Marlborough College, and in 1892 became a student at the Downton College of Agriculture.

CHISWICK PRESS:—CHARLES WHITTINGHAM AND CO.
TOOKS COURT, CHANCERY LANE, LONDON.